DISHONORABLE
Love

by: Savannah Stewart

Dishonorable Love Copyright © 2015 by Savannah Stewart

All rights reserved. No part of this book may be reproduced or transmitted in any form without written permission, except by a reviewer who may quote passages for review purposes only. This book is a work of fiction and any resemblance to any person, living or dead, any place, events or occurrences, is purely coincidental. The characters and story lines are created fictitiously.

Cover Design: Savannah Stewart
Photography: Dollar Photo Club

Books by Savannah Stewart:

Moments of Reckoning (standalone)

Behind the Words Series
(Can be read as standalones)
Arianna
Jayde
Poppy

Graceful Scars (standalone)

Dishonorable Love (standalone)

Find the author at:

http://www.authorsavannahstewart.com/
http://www.facebook.com/AuthorSavannahS
http://www.goodreads.comAuthorSavannahS
http://www.twitter.com/Savvy2287
http://www.tsu.co/SavannahStewart

"Your soulmate is not someone that comes into your life peacefully. It is who comes to make you question things, who changes your reality, somebody that marks a before and after in your life. It is not the human being everyone has idealized, but an ordinary person, who manages to revolutionize your world in a second..."

-Anonymous

Prologue

I clutched the folded flag in my arms as the first notes of "Taps" began. Twenty-one gun shots rang out throughout the cemetery as the sounds of people crying for the loss of Sergeant Thomas Cole echoed through the warm breezy air. I wasn't crying for Sergeant Thomas Cole, I was crying for the loss of my other half, my best friend, my *husband*.

I cleared my throat as the overwhelming smell of his cologne filled my nostrils. I frantically looked around, thinking it was all some sick joke and that Thomas was standing off in the distance waiting for the precise moment to surprise me with his arrival and beg for my forgiveness for playing such a cruel and heartbreaking joke. I'm not sure how long I sat there scanning the cemetery for a glimpse of Thomas when a man's voice pulled me back to reality.

"MacKenzie Cole?" I turned my head towards his voice and sucked in a breath from the close proximity of the man sitting beside me. I hadn't been this close to another man's face since the last time I was near my husband, the day he left for his last tour of duty.

"Yeah?" I sat back in my chair, putting a little more distance between me and the stranger. He was dressed in the same uniform Thomas was buried in.

"I'm so sorry for your loss…" He choked back his own emotions and extended a hand for me to shake. His sandy brown eyes were glistening from unshed tears. "Sergeant Julian Cooper."

As soon as his name left his lips I knew exactly who he was. He was Thomas' right hand man during the last tour of duty. Every time I talked to Thomas he spoke about Julian and how good of a man and soldier he was. I slid my trembling hand into his.

"Nice to meet you, Julian." A sad smile pulled my lips up just enough to look friendly instead of completely broken.

"Thomas and I were on the same mission when…" Julian trailed off.

"It's okay," I placed a hand on his shoulder, still clutching the flag with my other arm. "I know what happened that day." My voice sounded stronger than I actually was.

Julian's eyes were full of sorrow and understanding. "He was a helluva Marine." The strength and honor was laced thickly in his voice as he spoke of Thomas.

"That he was." I smiled again at the memory of how much Thomas loved fighting for our country. He was brave, loving, and always believed in the mission of keeping our country safe from harm. I loved that about him.

The wind blew in my face and the smell of Thomas' cologne hit me hard once again. I coughed a couple times as tears pricked my eyes. "Are you okay?" Julian asked, concerned from my small coughing spell.

"I'm—I'm okay," I lied as I realized the cologne was coming from Julian. I closed my eyes and took in the familiar smell that reminded me so much of my husband. It was almost too much to bear.

"I know you have a lot on your plate, and I don't want to keep you." I opened my eyes to find Julian standing. "It was nice to finally meet you, MacKenzie." He smiled sadly. "I'm sorry it was under these circumstances."

I stood and placed the flag under my left arm. "Thank you for being a good friend of Thomas', and thank you for coming today." A set of tears rolled down my face and I quickly wiped them away.

He nodded. "You don't have to thank me, ma'am. Thomas saved me on numerous occasions; I just wish I could have done the same for him."

The thickness of my emotions was closing off my throat. A large sob ripped through my body as I took in the truth of the day. Thomas was gone, his brothers-in-arms couldn't save him, and I was officially all alone again. The trembling in my legs was so severe that I thought I could collapse at any moment; my arm reached for the wooden chair as I slowly lowered myself back into it.

"I didn't mean to upset you." He leaned forward and took one of my hands in his.

"It's not you," I managed to say through my heartache. "I just don't know where to go from here," I admitted.

Julian took a seat beside me again and allowed the silence to fill the air. He knew there was nothing he could say that would make me feel better; I just wished that there was a way to bring back Thomas. My life was changing and there wasn't a damn thing I could do about it except move forward.

As my tears dried up I watched the leaves hanging from a tree a few yards away swaying in the light wind. Julian was still sitting beside me, taking in the silence just as I was. I shook myself out of my trance and turned away from the tree to look at him. "What are your plans while you're in town?"

"I don't have any." He turned his attention to my face. "As soon as the hospital released me, I came straight here."

"You were in the hospital?"

"I was hurt during the raid." Julian diverted his eyes to the area where Thomas lay.

"I—I didn't know." Tears stung my eyes once again.

"I'll be okay." His grin didn't touch his eyes. "It's a pretty deep flesh wound, but it'll heal."

As awful as it sounded, I had never thought about the others that were injured that day. Was it selfish of me?

I wasn't sure. I was still learning how to cope with the news that Thomas wouldn't be coming home ever again. Guilt twisted in my gut at hearing that Julian had been injured during the same raid that ended Thomas' life. I wondered how many others were hurt, but I was too afraid to ask.

The sound of a phone buzzing caught both of our attention. Julian dug in his front left pocket and pulled out his cell phone. "I apologize." He typed away on the screen before placing it back in the same pocket. "I have to go." His eyes met mine for a second before standing.

I stood as well and wrapped my arms around him tightly. "Thank you for sitting with me."

Julian hesitated before hugging me back. "You don't have to thank me. I would have done anything for Thomas." He took a step back, and I picked the flag up from the chair I had been sitting in. "I'll be in town for a few days, if you need anything." Julian pulled a pen from his pocket and scribbled his phone number on the inside of my free hand.

"Okay, thanks," I smiled. We said our goodbyes and I watched as the only person who was as close to my husband as I was disappeared over the hill.

Chapter One

I pulled the covers over my head and tried to force myself back to sleep. I hadn't had a good night's rest in a long time because dreams of Thomas being killed overseas filled my head every time it hit the pillow. The sound of his screams, bullets flying, and blood…lots of blood. I knew he had died in an explosion, not from being shot, but either way it was haunting me. Even though I wasn't there when it happened, I was living my own form of the nightmare. It had been three weeks since the funeral and every single night I woke up around four in the morning, clutching the covers and covered in sweat as I screamed for dear life.

A few Army wives had reached out to me a couple days after the funeral, telling me that if I needed anything, or simply just to talk, that they were there for me. It was nice of them, but who wanted to talk to complete strangers about losing your husband during war when they had no connection to you or him? I certainly didn't.

Giving up on sleep yet again, I threw the covers back and padded into the bathroom directly across the hall from the spare bedroom. I flipped on the light and took in my reflection in the mirror hanging above the sink. My eyes were puffy from crying, their usual vibrant mossy-green color was dim, and my dark brown hair was ratty and flat against my head. I let out a long breath and dropped my attention to the tube of toothpaste and my toothbrush. I was officially done looking at myself in the mirror. I opened the medicine cabinet and pulled out the two prescriptions my doctor had given me to deal with the loss of Thomas. Usually I wouldn't drown myself out with pills, but sometimes you can't help taking something that actually helps you deal with the hard parts of life. I tossed two pills into the back of my throat and leaned forward to drink some water from the running faucet.

Finishing my morning routines, I walked into the kitchen and poured myself a glass of apple juice. I wasn't a coffee kind of girl, even though I'd tried it on many occasions; it was like drinking dirt to me. Why would anyone find that appealing? Bracing my forearms against the counter I took a another drink of the juice as I stared at a lone piece of paper sitting on the counter a couple inches away from me with Julian's name and phone number written on it. The first thing I had done when I walked through the garage door after Thomas' funeral was jot Julian's number down, the second thing was take a long, hot shower.

The silence in our house was deafening. It's funny how I never realized how quiet it was until he was gone from this world. I'd spent most of our relationship alone in whatever home we owned at the time, with him overseas. But yet, the silence never got to me before. I finished my glass of apple juice and set the empty glass in the sink. As I had for the past three mornings, I made my way into the living room and found the remote that controlled any and every device in the house. I pushed the button designated for the in-home surround sound and cranked it two-thirds of the way up. A few button pushes later and the smooth sounds of Creedence Clearwater Revival's "Fortunate Son" were blaring throughout the entire house. I closed my eyes and allowed the beat of the song to take over my body. Before long I was bouncing around the living room, singing ever single word as loud as I could. My chest was heaving as the song came to close. I flopped back on the couch with my face towards the ceiling and started laughing wildly. Just like every other morning, my laughs soon turned to uncontrollable sobs that wracked my body until it was hard to catch a breath.

"That was your favorite song, Thomas," I whispered through the tears, hoping like hell that he could hear me wherever he was. "God, I miss you." A round of fat ugly tears rolled out of my eyelids and raced down my cheeks, falling off my neck and onto the couch beneath me.

Eventually my body calmed but I continued to lie there, staring up at the white and grey coffered ceiling design above me. I remember the day we sat in our small one bedroom apartment, which was more like a Cracker Jack box, and planned out exactly what we wanted in our first official home. It was one of the happiest days of our lives together. We had been married for six months when Thomas received a promotion in the Marines. Our dream of becoming home owners was quickly becoming a reality and as the house plans came together, they broke ground on the land we would soon call home. Thomas wasn't in the states on the day I moved in, but I was able to video chat with him and show him around. It was one of those bittersweet moments about being a military wife; I was beyond happy about our home but unbelievably sad that he couldn't share the first night sleeping under its roof with me.

Another round of tears threatened to spill over my lids, but I wasn't allowing them. "Dammit, Kenzie, pull yourself together." I thought saying it out loud would make it sink in better, and for a moment it did.

I rolled over until my feet touched the floor and forced myself to stand. I hadn't left the house since the funeral. The groceries were becoming scarce and my body was in need of some vitamin D from the sun but I was trying to avoid people that knew what happened. Small towns were the worst during heart-breaking times. Everybody knew one another and they wouldn't just let someone mourn the loss of their loved one, it had to be the main topic of conversation.

I pulled my long, dark-brown hair around and quickly braided it, leaving it lying across the front of my shoulder, grabbed my grey fedora from the hat rack in the laundry room and slid it on my head. Thomas always loved when I wore it. He claimed it made me look like an artist, and I always laughed. I'm not sure why he thought that because I was the complete opposite of being artsy. The most I could do was throw some paint at a canvas and call it something special. I laughed at the memory as I slipped my feet into a pair of navy blue flats and tossed the strap of my purse onto my shoulder. A deep breath left my lungs as I headed out for the day.

After finally finding a parking spot at the local grocery store and slamming my door shut, the sound of my alarm beeping blended in with the sounds of people chatting, vehicles passing by, and a young girl laughing hysterically, making me wish I knew what was so funny because I longed to laugh like she was doing. I smiled at the blonde-haired, blue-eyed beauty as we passed. After testing three carts, I finally found one that didn't seem like a piece of shit and headed into the store. It didn't take long before the front right wheel started squeaking on the damn thing and I was cursing its existence. It really should be a law that stores retire carts once they get to the point of causing so much annoyance that someone might end up going on a murder spree because of it. Maybe it was just me, but I could see it happening at one point or another.

    I tossed random things into the cart as I moved up and down each aisle: a turkey breast, some string cheese, and some chocolate cereal that stated it was the best there was, because who doesn't like chocolate cereal? "I really should have made a list…" I placed a couple of frozen pizzas in the cart.

    "I hope you aren't living off of that stuff." A familiar voice made me giggle.

    "Julian," I smiled. "I'm surprised you're still in town." I tilted my fedora back a bit so that I could see him better. His chocolate brown hair was longer than the last time I had seen him and his sandy-brown eyes seemed a little brighter. He was wearing a pair of khaki pants and a white V-neck T-shirt stretched across his broad chest and was tucked into his khakis with a thick black belt holding them in place. I hadn't really taken him in before; he was a *very* nice looking man.

"Do you want to know a secret?" He nervously smiled and leaned in closer to me, bracing himself on the side of my cart. "I really don't know what to do with myself since I'm out of the military." A humorless laugh escaped him as his eyes caught mine.

"You're out?" I asked. "Like for good?"

"Yeah, *like* for good." He laughed, this time, his mouth curving up into a beautiful smile. "I was honorably discharged after the raid. Once they transferred me to a hospital in Virginia I was informed of the discharge. It's weird when you don't have any family and all of your friends are still over there fighting…or gone." He trailed off. I knew exactly what he meant, well, sort of. Thomas and I hadn't had many friends, mainly because he was hardly ever home and we had moved to Shallotte, North Carolina out of the blue after our engagement. It's a little under an hour away from Wilmington and less than two hours away from the Camp Lejeune Marine Corps base, so it was the ideal spot for us.

Julian and I carried on with our light-hearted conversation and laughter as we walked around the store. Obviously the sound of a squeaky cart bugged him just as much as it bugged me because he tried everything to get it to stop while I watched him and laughed. I was surprised to find out that he had rented a house a couple miles from me. He didn't give much information as to why he decided to, except that the town was nice and not too far from Camp Lejeune–the same reasons Thomas had wanted to live in Shallotte. As we approached the checkout lanes I started to feel anxious. I couldn't pinpoint why, but it was almost too overwhelming.

"It was good to see you again, MacKenzie," Julian smiled and entered the lane next to the one I was standing in.

"You too, Julian."

"I hope to see you around," he replied as everyone around us zoned in on our conversation. I wanted to reply, but I didn't. I simply nodded my head in acknowledgement and started placing my items on the conveyor belt for the cashier to ring up. Julian waved as he left the grocery store, and I smiled politely in return.

The sound of my cart squeaking as I pushed it towards my car made me laugh. I hit the trunk button on the fob and loaded the groceries. I wasn't paying much attention to anything going on around me; it had become my way of living it seemed. I closed out my surroundings and only paid attention to what I was doing, which wasn't very safe but it was the only way I seemed to get out of bed in the mornings.

I bent over into the trunk to put some stray cans back in their bags. "Want some help?" I jumped just enough to slam the back of my head against the trunk lid above me.

"Gah!" I cried out as I leaned back, finding Julian standing beside me with an apologetic look across his face as I grimaced in pain. My hand pulled the fedora off of my head and dropped it into the trunk.

"Are you okay?" He took a step towards me. "Let me see your head."

"I'm fine. It's just a bump." I rubbed the now sore spot.

"Let me see it, you might be bleeding," he demanded, so I let him take a look. His fingers gently moved across the top of my scalp. "Looks like it's going to bruise, but there's no cut or blood thankfully." Julian ran his hand down my braid, letting it drop back against my shoulder.

I sucked in a sharp breath and placed my fedora back on. I watched his throat as he swallowed and shoved his hands into the front pockets of his khakis. "Next time don't scare a girl," I joked, pushing his shoulder back just lightly.

Julian laughed and held his hands up in surrender. "Hey, that wasn't my intention."

I shook my head from side-to-side as I started loading the remainder of my groceries in the trunk. Julian walked around to my other side and grabbed some bags from the cart.

"You really don't have to help me." I glanced at him as we continued loading groceries.

"I know I don't *have* to, I *want* to."

"Okay," I gave in. I wasn't used to people helping me with things. Thomas was gone more than he was home so I had learned to be independent. To do everything I needed done on my own, unless of course it required a professional to do it, but even then I at least attempted it.

Julian took the cart to the designated area for it while I closed the trunk. I turned around and leaned back against my car, crossing my arms over my chest as I watched him walk back towards me. Our eyes were locked on one another's, neither of us shying away from looking at the other. Usually it would have felt odd, but it didn't with him.

"What are your plans for the day?" Julian asked as soon as he was close enough for me to hear him.

"Well," I thought about what I had planned, which wasn't much of anything besides laying my ass on the couch and going through some sappy-ass movies, most likely crying and eating something completely fattening. I couldn't quite tell him that though, could I? "I have zero plans for the day."

"You don't work anywhere?"

"I do. I just," I paused for a second. "I took about a month off from work. I finished my last client I had on the books before I found out about Thomas, so I didn't take on any more for a while," I admitted. I was a freelance graphic designer; I did a lot of off the wall designing jobs for clients that ranged from small companies, to self- published authors, to large grocery store chains. It was the only thing I had in my life, besides Thomas, that I felt completely passionate about.

"What do you do?"

"Graphic design."

"Really?" Julian arched an eyebrow in surprise.

"Yes, really."

"I would have pegged you for a banker or someone that owns a little boutique."

"Those are night and day from one another," I laughed.

"Yeah." He laughed. "They are, aren't they?" His laugh was like music to my ears, pulling my own from me.

It felt good to smile and laugh again.

"So, back to your planless day. Would you like to grab lunch?" Julian asked.

Searing pain hit my gut as if a prized fighter had sucker punched me. I wanted to go to lunch, but it was too soon to be seen out with another man, even it was one hundred percent innocent. I could be friends with a man, especially someone who had a connection to my deceased husband, Thomas, couldn't I?

"I don't know…" I scrunched my nose up and frowned as I thought it over some more. "Maybe another time?"

Julian's smile slowly faded, "Sure." He grinned, "You know, lunch is only lunch, right?"

My head jerked back like someone had slapped me. "Yeah, I know it's just lunch." My cheeks redden from the embarrassment of what was happening. "I—I didn't think it was anything more," I stuttered.

"Shit," Julian muttered. "I didn't mean for what I said to come across as me thinking that you thought I wanted more than just lunch. I meant that it's okay to have lunch with someone else. You don't have to coop yourself up in that house." He ran a hand down the back of his neck. "I suck at explaining things." A nervous grin tugged the corner of his lips up.

I sighed, "Sorry, I'm not usually this awkward. My mind is in a jumble from everything right now. How about a rain check on lunch? I'll text you my number since I have yours and maybe we can get together later in the week."

"That'll work." Julian's pearly whites were making yet another appearance. "Have a good day, MacKenzie."

"You too, Julian." I stayed leaning against the back of my car until he got into his vehicle and drove away.

"MacKenzie Cole? Is that you?" A familiar woman's voice grabbed my attention. I turned in the direction of the store and found Olivia Jones walking towards me. She lived in the same neighborhood as me, but we rarely crossed paths—mainly because she was drama to the T; always in the middle of everyone else's business.

"Olivia…" I tried to sound as nice as possible, but failed miserably.

She didn't waste any time rambling off about everything I had going on in my life. "I'm so sorry to hear about Thomas' passing. I know it must be hard for you!" She pulled me into a hug that I didn't reciprocate. "Although it probably doesn't seem that different since he was gone most of the time." My blood boiled from her statement. "Are you seeing a therapist, or talking to some of the other Army wives?"

My hands trembled and my heart beat against my chest, I was so pissed. "Honestly, Olivia…It's none of your business." Her mouth dropped open in shock. "So, you have a nice day." I turned and opened my car door.

"MacKenzie, you really should talk to someone." She started running her mouth again. "All of that anger you are throwing around needs to be taken care of or someone might think you're losing yourself."

I slammed my car door shut and started towards her when I felt arms embrace my waist. Before I realized what was happening I was being turned around the opposite way from Olivia.

"I'll take care of her," Julian's stern voice froze me in my spot.

"*Well*, who are you?" Olivia's tone of voice changed to a much sweeter tone as Julian stepped closer to her.

"Julian," He stopped about a foot away from her. "I think it's best if you leave Kenzie alone. She's already dealing with a lot; she doesn't need other people sticking their noses in her business, now does she?" The way Julian spoke was stern but nice, and I could tell that it was affecting Olivia by the way her face morphed from nice back to bitchy.

"I—I was just trying to help her out." She stood up a little straighter.

"You might want to learn how to *help* people out then." Julian crossed his well-defined arms over his chest as he looked down at her.

Olivia huffed, "Have a nice day, Julian." She waved as she turned and walked away without acknowledging me again.

"What a bitch." He shook his head as he walked back over to me as I re-opened my car door.

"That's putting it mildly."

"Why did she come at you like that? I only caught part of the conversation but I knew it wasn't going anywhere but downhill." He placed a hand on the top of my door.

"I thought you had left. How did you see Olivia coming at me?"

He pointed to where his car was parked at the gas pumps not too far away from where I was parked. "I had to get gas."

"Got ya. Olivia is the type who has to be in everybody's business, whether it's good or bad. Mostly she sticks her nose in the bad…hence her making a point to talk—I mean harass—me about Thomas." I dropped my eyes to the ground below me as I kicked some stray gravel.

"Sounds like she needs to get a life." He placed a hand on my arm, causing me to look up at him.

"That she does." I kicked another rock. "Sorry that it seems like I always need saving," I blurted out without thinking through what I was saying.

Julian dropped his hand from my arm. "You don't always need saving." That was not what I had expected him to say; I looked up at him. "Would it be weird to say I feel a little protective of you?" He laughed. "Yeah, that even sounded weird saying it out loud."

I was smiling wider than I had in a while. "It's not weird. I understand what you mean. You feel like you should protect me since Thomas isn't here to do so anymore, kind of like you were his right hand man, you protected him, so you want to protect me."

"Julian's demeanor changed from happy to sad. "Something like that."

I knew his change in demeanor had to do with the fact that Thomas had died while they were doing a raid together. The thought of him not protecting Thomas was rearing its ugly head. "Hey," I grabbed one of his hands. "You did all you could do that day, don't beat yourself up because Thomas died. It wasn't your fault; those terrorists killed him, not you."

"You are one strong woman, MacKenzie."

I wanted to tell him that I was far from strong, that I just knew how to hide my emotions well. But I couldn't. Then it dawned on me…Julian had called me Kenzie during his interaction with Olivia. "Did you call me Kenzie earlier?"

"I did."

"How did you know my nickname from back home?" I arched an eyebrow at him in curiosity.

"I didn't." He tucked his hands into the front pockets of his khakis.

"You didn't?" I found that hard to believe. But the odd thing was that Thomas didn't even know my nickname from when I was younger because no one around us called me that. I only called myself that on occasions.

"I just wanted to call you that."

"Interesting…" I looked past him at the cars driving along the main road. Either he knew somehow or it was a very odd coincidence.

"You know," Julian's voice broke my trance and I brought my attention back to him. "As long as we have been standing out here, we could have grabbed lunch," he stated matter-of-factly.

"Shit! Our groceries are probably thawed out by now," I exclaimed.

"I'd say if they aren't, they are close."

"How about you come by my place after you put your groceries away," I pulled my phone out. "I'll text you the address and we can have lunch there, sound good?" I couldn't believe that I was inviting Julian to come to my house for lunch when the only person who had been in that house since the funeral was me.

"Are you sure?" His brows furrowed deeply between his eyes as he gauged my response.

I smiled widely, "Yes, I'm sure." I took a seat in my car, turned it on, and rolled the window down before shutting the door.

"Okay then." His face was beaming with a bright smile as he slid his sunglasses over his eyes.

"See you in a little bit," I waved.

"Don't forget to send me your address!" He replied as I backed out of my parking spot and started to drive off. I gave him the thumbs up as I passed him, still standing in the same spot and smiling.

Chapter Two

I sat my phone down on the arm of the couch and took off down the hallway to make sure everything was straightened up throughout the house. The worst thing ever is walking into someone's home for the first time and finding it a catastrophic mess. The sound of my text notification going off had me running back into the living room.

Julian: See you in twenty.

"Shit!" I huffed and took off into the kitchen. I had no idea what I was going to fix; hopefully Julian had something up his sleeve or at least some suggestions. Yeah, I had bought some stuff at the grocery, but most of it wasn't anything you would offer someone who was coming over for lunch.

After I finished tidying up, I flopped down on the couch for a breather, which was short-lived as the sound of the doorbell rang out throughout the house. I hopped up from the couch and walked over to the door. Every time the doorbell rang I made it a habit to check the peephole, mainly because I didn't want to deal with any news people coming by asking about Thomas, that pesky group of Army wives that wanted to pull me into their shenanigans, or anyone else I didn't want to be bothered with. This time all I found was Julian standing on the other side of the door holding a couple of bags and looking off to the right as he waited.

Unlocking the deadbolt and doorknob lock I pulled the large wooden door open. "Hey!" I spoke to a smiling Julian.

"We live pretty close," he replied.

"Yeah, a couple miles or so."

"At least I know if I need to borrow some milk, I can come to you." He joked.

"Ditto." I moved so he could walk inside, and shut the door behind him.

Julian was looking around the living room as he walked further into my home, clutching both of the bags in one of his hands. "You have a beautiful place."

My throat tighten from the emotions that were trying to rear their ugly head as Julian stood before my mantel, which was decorated with photos of Thomas and me together. "Thank you."

Julian turned around at the quaver in my voice. "Are you okay?" His eyes seemed to soften as he awaited my reply.

"I'm fine," I waved a hand at him. "It's still so fresh…" I walked over and stopped directly beside him. "I'm not sure I can continue to live here, though. There are too many memories that break my heart to think of them."

Julian smoothed his free hand across my back as we both stood there staring at the photos, one from the day Thomas had left for his first tour of duty, with others from throughout the years we'd been together. "That's understandable, but maybe with time it'll get easier and you won't want to let go of the memories that this house holds."

"I hope you're right," I forced a smile and quickly changed the subject. "What's in the bags?" I motioned towards them, still hanging in his hand.

"Ah!" He headed towards the large open doorway that led into the kitchen. "I brought some food." He chuckled. "I had a feeling you only had random stuff in your house after I saw the options you had in your grocery cart earlier."

I laughed, "You seem to know me so well already."

He placed the bags on the counter and pulled out two boxes. "I stopped by Grant's Deli."

Julian opened the two boxes and turned them towards me. "Turkey club or ham and cheese?"

"Turkey club."

He pushed the box holding the sandwich towards me before reaching into the bag again. "I also have potato salad and homemade chips." He sat the containers of each on the counter.

"Can we share?" I arched an eyebrow at him.

Dishonorable Love | 23

"Of course," He smiled.

I walked over to the dark cabinets lining the wall above my stove and pulled out two plates, before grabbing two forks from the drawer below.

"I hope you don't think I didn't want to eat any of your food. I just thought bringing lunch over would be easier than either of us cooking something." The unsure tone of his voice made me stop what I was doing and look at him. It was easy to read Julian's emotions because he so easily displayed them across his chiseled face. It made me wonder how that worked when he was in the Marines.

"I don't think that at all." A genuine smile tipped my lips upwards as I handed Julian a plate and fork. "I actually was scrambling around trying to figure out just what in the hell I was going to fix and totally gave up. So you actually saved us from having overly hungry stomachs by bringing this food from the deli."

As I put a second scoop of potato salad on my plate I realized we didn't have drinks. "What would you like to drink? I have bottled water, soda, beer, and some white wine."

"Whichever is fine, he shrugged. *Typical man.*

I grabbed two beers from the refrigerator, popped the tops, and tossed them in the trashcan before taking a seat back at the table. I watched Julian take a pull from his beer before doing so myself.

"You know…I used to hate beer. I couldn't stand the taste of it one bit. The only time you caught me drinking it was if I was already three sheets to the wind and there was nothing else around." I chuckled at the thought as I inspected the outside of the bottle in my hand.

"What made you start drinking it?" Julian sat his beer back down on the table and waited for my answer.

"Honestly, I'm not really sure. Thomas always loved it with pizza or while watching football on Sundays when he was home." My smiled started to fade at the heartache of Thomas being gone. "I guess I learned how to like it over time." I shrugged my shoulders and dropped my eyes to my plate. I didn't want our lunch to be awkward or sad, but I had picked at the gaping wound of my heart by talking about Thomas again.

Julian cleared his throat after a few awkward silent moments of neither of us eating. "Go ahead, take a bite. Let me know just how good that damn turkey club is." I couldn't help the giggle that escaped me.

"You wanted the turkey club, didn't you?" I held the sandwich close to my mouth.

"Hell yes, I did."

As soon as his response left his mouth I bit down on that turkey club, closing my eyes and allowing the flavors to flood my taste buds. I moaned in pleasure from its deliciousness and swallowed the bite I had taken. I opened my eyes and instantly took in Julian sitting back in the kitchen chair with his mouth slack. I couldn't help the large smile that spread across my face. "It's delicious!" I boasted.

"You're unbelievably mean, Kenzie." There was that nickname again.

"You're the one who gave me an option of which sandwich I could have, so hush." I swatted my hand at him and went back to devouring *my* turkey club.

Spending lunch with Julian turned into a full afternoon thing. The last time I had looked at the clock it was well after four and we had moved from the kitchen to the living room where we lounged on two separate sofas chatting about our favorite bands while drinking the last two beers from the twelve-pack I had picked up while at the grocery.

"No way!" I scoffed. "Journey blows Bon Jovi out of the water any day." I slouched back against the couch cushions and shook my head.

"I don't know if we can be friends after that comment," Julian shook his head in disbelief and took the last swig of his beer, emptying the bottle completely.

A loud laugh escaped me as I shot up from my slouching position. I pointed an index finger at him, "You have lost your mind if you seriously think Bon Jovi is better than Journey." I slid forward until I was sitting on the edge of the cushion beneath me. "For one, Journey has like, a bajillion songs that almost everyone knows the lyrics to." I counted off each song on my fingertips. "'Don't Stop Believing,' 'Faithfully,' 'Separate Ways,' and that's just naming a few!"

Julian slid to the edge of the couch he was on, getting ready to argue with me. "And Bon Jovi doesn't?" He held his hand up and started counting off songs on his fingers like I had done. "'Wanted Dead or Alive,' 'You Give Love a Bad Name,' 'Bed of Roses,' *and* 'Livin' on a Prayer.' To name a few."

"Did you just try to one-up me?"

"I think I just did," Julian's shoulders shook as he silently laughed at me.

"Well," I laughed, "I guess we will just have to agree to disagree." I crossed my arms over my chest.

"You're cute when you stand your ground." My heart picked up its pace as his words sunk in. Was Julian flirting with me? I didn't know what to say to that, or how I felt. I lost track of how long we were sitting there in silence until he pulled me from my inner battle. "MacKenzie?" I refocused my eyes on his face. His eyebrows were pulled down deep in the center, making a defined wrinkle between them.

"I'm fine," I offered a small smile to hopefully reassure him that I was fine, even if I wasn't.

"Well," Julian nervously ran a hand down the back of his neck. "I guess I need to head home." I followed his eyes over to the two-foot-tall version of a Big Ben clock sitting on the mantel.

"Okay," I stood from the sofa and started cleaning up the beer bottles on the table between us.

"Here," Julian jumped up and grabbed a few of the bottles I hadn't yet, "let me help you."

"You don't have to," I interjected as I walked into the kitchen to throw away the bottles.

"I helped make the mess, didn't I?" I turned and found him standing directly behind me, waiting to drop the bottles he was holding into the trashcan.

"Yeah, you kind of did," I smiled playfully at him before taking a couple steps to the right so that he could get to the trashcan. "Are you sure you can drive?" I eyed him warily as he picked his keys up from the counter.

"I'm good, I promise."

"I'll feel bad if something happens to you, since you drank my beers and all."

"I'm only right down the road." He placed a hand on my arm. "And I promise I'll let you know when I get there."

"I'm holding you to that promise." I arched an eyebrow at him. "Don't make me send out the watch dogs."

As he stepped out onto the porch, I grabbed hold of the door. "Thanks for having me over, Kenzie. It was a good time." He smiled.

"It was nice to actually enjoy the day for once," I replied honestly with a happy smile dancing across my lips.

"Have a good night," Julian replied, and I stood there watching him until his car was no longer in my line of vision.

Closing the door I went back into the kitchen to finish cleaning up. There wasn't a whole lot left to do except start the dishwasher and take the trash out. I didn't want my house smelling like a stale brewery from all of those beer bottles in the trashcan. I hadn't drunk that much in a long time, and surprisingly I felt fine, just a slight buzz that kept my happiness afloat.

    I pushed the start button on the dishwasher and pulled the trash bag from the can. Just as I got it to the top of the can the bag caught on something within it and tore open, causing the beer bottles to fall through the bottom and shatter into shards. "You have *got* to be kidding me!"

    Once I had everything cleaned up I went back into the living room and plopped down on the sofa and absently stared at the seat where Julian's large body sat earlier. Instead of feeling a sense of loss and sadness, like I did most days since Thomas' passing, I felt calm. I hadn't felt like that in a very long time and before I knew it my eyelids were becoming heavy and a peaceful sleep swept over me.

Chapter Three

I rubbed my eyes and blinked several times, trying to figure out where I was; whatever I was lying on didn't feel like the bed in the spare bedroom. When the sofa across from me came into view, I realized that I had fallen asleep in the living room and it was well into the wee hours of the morning. My body felt stiff so I stood and stretched, trying to bring back the feeling in my right arm after lying on it for hours. I couldn't believe that I had slept so long without waking up from a nightmare. That was a first.

Once I gained full movement in my extremities I checked my cell phone. I had fallen asleep before I heard anything from Julian about making it home, so I was a little worried about whether or not he had.

No messages. I hit Julian's contact and nervously waited for him to answer. It rang three times before a ruffling noise came from the other end. "Hello?" Julian's sleep-filled voice rang through my ear.

"I'm so sorry to wake you."

"MacKenzie?" Julian cleared his throat. "Is everything okay?" His voice was almost back to normal by that point.

"Yeah, everything's fine. I woke up from an unexpected nap and didn't have any messages from you so I wanted to make sure you made it home okay earlier," I rambled.

"You didn't get my message?"

"Let me double-check." I pushed the message icon and quickly looked for a message from Julian, but nothing was there. "Nope."

A few silent beats later and Julian's voice filled my ear again. "I'm sorry. It shows that it didn't send. That's my bad."

"It's fine. I just wanted to make sure you made it home all right."

"I did." I could hear the smile in his voice.

"Good." An awkward silence settled in for a split second before I spoke up. "I'll let you go back to sleep. Talk to you soon."

"Talk to you tomorrow, Kenzie."

With that I sat my phone down on the coffee table and went into the kitchen to fix a late night snack.

After munching down a tomato and cheese sandwich on slices of cucumber, I found myself lying wide awake in the spare bedroom, staring up at the white speckled ceiling My eyes adjusted to the darkness which made me capable of seeing the ceiling, not fully, but just enough to let my mind wander.

I wasn't far into my thoughts of what I was going to do with my life when the sound of my cell phone vibrating pulled me back to reality. I rolled onto my side and stretched to grab my phone from the nightstand beside the bed.

Nothing. No messages, no calls, nothing.

"How odd." I set it back down and rolled onto my back to continue staring at the ceiling when it happened again. "I know I'm not losing my damn mind." I hopped out of the bed and stood beside the nightstand to see if it would do it again.

At least two minutes had passed and I was about to give up and put my happy ass back into bed when I heard it again. It wasn't coming from my phone, it was coming from inside the drawer of the nightstand. Pulling the drawer open, my eyes landed on the one thing I had forgotten about: Thomas' cell phone.

My heart drop at the sight of it plugged into the power strip that he had hooked into the back of the drawer. It was a little piece of him that I had tossed into the drawer the day before his funeral. How had I forgotten about it? The screen lit up as it vibrated again, reminding me exactly why I was staring at it so I picked it up and hit the side button to bring the screen back up.

There were numerous notifications from his social media pages that hadn't been taken down. I couldn't do that just yet, and I wasn't about to read all of those posts that would break my heart all over again. As I clicked on his text message icon my heart felt like it fell from my chest at the first message that was staring me in the face.

The burning from the onslaught of tears pushing my fists deep into my eyes to try and force them away. I took a breath and reopened my eyes, confirming that it wasn't a dream. The messages were real. I sat back on the bed and started scrolling through each one. With every word another chunk of my broken heart shattered on the hardwood floor beneath me.

A loud sob ripped up my throat as I read the last message Thomas had sent.

Thomas: The distance between us doesn't change how I feel for you. I love you more than words can express. Don't ever think otherwise. Give our baby in your belly a rub for me. See the two of you soon.

I wasn't sure which hurt worse…the fact that the baby Thomas was talking about would have been born already by the time stamp on the message, or the fact that he was cheating on me with some woman named Sara.

The phone slipped from my hand and crashed onto the floor as an animalistic scream ripped from my lungs. The grip I hand on the comforter turned my knuckles white as I buried my face deep into the thick material and continued to wail loudly. As time passed my throat and eyes burned from over exertion, and when I thought I couldn't produce anymore tears, another round flooded over my eyelids and fell relentlessly.

    The minutes ticked by at a slow agonizing pace as I laid in that bed going through the stages of loss. Denial was the first to rear its ugly head. I thought maybe the messages I had read weren't from Thomas to that woman; they were from a friend of his that didn't have a phone. That's always a possibility, right? When anger took over I screamed and cried to the heavens, hoping he could hear what he had done to me. I was broken from his death, but I was even more gutted from his infidelity. Bargaining was the one instance of loss that I passed over easily. I had nothing to bargain for so I went head first into depression. The heavy weight of Thomas' actions was pushing me further and further into the black hole that I called my life. I guess you could say I was stuck on depression, mainly because there was no way in hell I could accept what I had read in those messages. There was no way that Thomas had a second life that I knew nothing about. I had to of missed the signs, right?

    My mind was a whirlwind of all of the memories from our time together, like I was trying to fit together a puzzle that I didn't have all the right pieces for and the ones I did have were broken. Second-guessing every little thing about what I had thought we had was exhausting. From the looks of those messages, my marriage was the biggest lie I had ever been a part of.

    The throbbing of my head from crying was becoming so overbearing that I forced myself to get out of the bed and go take something. I headed to the kitchen but stopped dead in my tracks in the living room when the eight-by-ten photo of Thomas and me from our wedding day came into view. I walked closer and stopped about half a foot away from it. My bottom lip was quivering as I took in the image of him in his dress blues with his head turned towards me and the biggest smile adorning his lips. I was smiling happily at the photographer while we were wrapped in one another's arms. I wanted to feel sad about the photo before me, but instead I was angry. My hands started to shake as I reached up and yanked the picture frame from the wall, screaming with anger and tossing it with all of my might towards the floor. The frame shattered into pieces and the mess below me didn't make me feel any better. I sighed heavily and stepped around the remnants of our wedding photo.

By the time I reached the kitchen I was in hysterics. My limbs felt heavy, but like jelly, as I stepped up to the refrigerator and jerked the doors open. I pulled a bottle of Vitamin Water from the shelf and held it against my forehead as I rummaged through the cabinet beside the refrigerator for some migraine medicine. Once I found it I tapped the bottle until two pills fell into my palm and placed the bottle back into the cabinet. I tossed the pills to the back of my throat and chugged down half of the Vitamin Water without taking a breath. My arms were braced on the counter as my head hung freely. My mind, body, and soul were worn out and all I wanted to do was go back to sleep in hopes that I would wake up to find that the nightmare I had been thrown into wasn't real.

My legs wobbled as I tried to hold back the millionth round of tears from falling and failed miserably. A moment later my legs gave out and I collapsed into a heaping mess on the tiled floor and curled up into a ball to console myself. I needed to figure out a way to find out exactly who Sara was and where she lived. Some form of proof was the only thing that would help me put to rest the thoughts of whether or not Thomas was involved with her. But I had no inkling of where to start.

Chapter Four

The sound of my cell phone ringing for the twelfth time wasn't going to get me out of the bed. After I finally pulled myself up from the kitchen floor, I forced my body to move back to the spare bedroom and into the bed. Thomas' phone was lost somewhere within the blankets, and I honestly didn't care if I looked at it ever again. Why couldn't I have gone on without the knowledge of Thomas' infidelity? It would have made things a helluva lot easier, but life was a bitch and she wasn't going to let me off that easily.

Loud pounding coming from the front door had my head aching right along with each knock. I groaned as I slid from the bed and padded into the living room to see who was at the damn door. If it was one of the Army wives, I was going to officially flip my shit. Without peeking through the peephole, I swung the door open and found Julian standing before me. I instantly felt insecure, knowing I hadn't brushed my hair or teeth, and I was still wearing my pajamas.

"Everything okay?" Julian's worried voice almost made me smile. Almost.

"I'm fine," I replied dryly.

"Not being rude or anything, but you don't look fine." Julian took a step forward, forcing me to move aside so he could come in.

"Thanks," I huffed.

"Kenzie…" My name came off like a question so I turned to find Julian standing near the shattered wedding photo I had left on the floor.

"Oh, that." I tucked my arms over my chest after shutting the front door and locking it back. "It's nothing." I walked past Julian and the mess in the floor to take a seat on one of the sofas.

Julian took a seat beside me. His forearms were resting against his thighs and he was leaning forward just slightly. I didn't want to look at him because I was afraid I would break down.

"You know you can talk to me, don't you?" Julian kept his eyes fixated on his linked hands. "I know you haven't known me long, and it's hard to talk about losing someone you love, but I want you to know that I'm here to listen when you need someone to. Thomas was a good man—"

A boisterous laugh escaped me before I realized it, stopping Julian midsentence. I quickly slapped a hand over my mouth as my heart thumped heavily within my chest. After a few seconds I slowly dropped my hand.

"Sorry," I whispered, and that's when I noticed he was looking at me like I had lost my mind. "Don't look at me like that." My head moved from side-to-side as I got up from the sofa.

"Something's off with you, MacKenzie." Julian's eyebrows were raised, causing small wrinkles to form across his forehead.

His words stopped me in my tracks. My back was to him and my arms were tucked tightly across my chest as my lip quivered. I knew I needed to get it off of my chest, and sadly Julian was the only person I felt like I could to talk to about it; which was insane because we hardly knew one another.

As the first tear slid down my cheek I let the truth slip from my mouth, "Thomas was having an affair."

My body shook as I silently cried. Julian's hands gently wrapped around my shoulders and turned me toward him, pulling me into his embrace. I buried my face into his light blue polo and sobbed.

"Are you sure?" Julian asked softly and I nodded in confirmation. "That doesn't seem like the Thomas I knew, Kenzie."

I sniffled, "It doesn't seem like the Thomas I knew either, Julian, but the truth is the truth. And that's not even the worst part." Julian took a step back and looked down at me, waiting for the next ball to drop. "He would have been a father if he was still alive." I bit down on my lower lip to stop it from trembling.

Julian dropped his arms and began pacing back and forth. I watched as he rubbed his jaw, it looked as if the wheels in his head kept turning with every step he took until he stopped. "You mean to tell me, Thomas not only had a mistress on the side, but they were expecting a child?" He sounded just as dumbfounded as I felt when I found the messages.

"Yes." I left Julian standing with his mouth slack as I headed to retrieve Thomas' cell phone. When I returned he was still standing in the same spot with the same expression on his face. I brought the phone to life and pushed Sara's name in his messages and handed it over to Julian.

My mind was on the brink of crashing and burning. I needed to get out of the house as soon as possible so I snatched my sunglasses off of the coffee table and made my way out onto the back deck before Julian had enough time to read the first message in Thomas' phone. The weight of the sliding glass door almost overpowered me as I pushed it closed. My feet quickly carried me to a swing that was hanging from the giant oak tree in the middle of the large backyard. I'd always loved that tree, it was the best part about the backyard.

My back was facing the house as I swung slowly in the wooden single-person seat. The light breeze felt nice as it danced across my face. When I looked down at my legs I caught sight of my pajama pants. I'd completely forgotten to change when Julian had shown up. A small staccato laugh left me as the faint sound of crunching grass echoed behind me. That familiar cologne danced around with the breeze, filling my nostrils and causing tears to prick my eyes from the memory of Thomas wearing that same damn cologne.

"We have to find out who Sara is," Julian's serious tone made me look over my shoulder at him.

"We?"

Julian walked around the swing and took the ropes in his hands, stopping all movement. He leaned down so that his face was close to mine; I could see the fury swimming in his eyes from what he had read. "Do you really think I would let you investigate this on your own?"

I shook my head no. "I don't even know where to start, Julian." My already fragile voice wavered on the end.

"First, I want you to know that this is not going to be a walk in the park. So you need to prepare yourself for whatever we find."

I looked past his muscular shoulder to the field behind him. "I know." Did I? I wasn't so sure about that, but I couldn't ignore the atomic bomb waiting to ignite and act like life was peachy keen either.

Julian stood up straight and slid a hand into one of his front pockets. My eyes were fixated on his hand slowly pulling Thomas' cell phone from it. "I found a couple things you should see."

My heart dropped into my stomach from those simple words because I knew there was more in that phone that would shatter me.

Julian tapped the screen a few times before turning it towards me, revealing a photo of a beautiful dark-haired woman smiling widely back at me. She was lying in a bed, wearing nothing but a pale pink bra. Thankfully the photo only showed her from the waist up, but that was more than enough for me. "I take it that's Sara." My voice was rough and filled thickly with annoyance.

"I'm assuming so." Julian closed the photo and ran a hand down the back of his neck. "Does she look familiar at all?"

I extended my hand towards him, "Give me the phone." Julian laid the phone into my palm and I quickly went back to the photo section to pull the picture back up on the screen.

Everything about the woman in the photo was gorgeous: her smile, her teeth, the faint dimples in her cheeks, the perfect arch of her eyebrows, her dark hazel-green eyes, and the flat stomach. I squeezed my eyes shut tightly and took a deep breath before looking at the photo again. That's when the nightstand beside the bed came into view, along with a welcome packet that read 'Sunset Inn Bed and Breakfast.' My internal temperature spiked when I realized the woman's photo was taken at the same bed and breakfast Thomas and I had gone to right after we moved to Shallotte.

Clearing my throat I looked up at Julian, "I know where this was taken." I got up from the swing and started back towards the house as Julian called after me, asking where the photo was taken.

Ignoring him completely, I stepped into the house and went straight for my bedroom to change, leaving the sliding glass doors open for Julian. I knew exactly when he reached the house because his yelling for me to stop and talk to him became louder, no longer muffled from him being outside. I ignored him. The latch of the door to my bedroom clicked shut and I turned the lock so that he couldn't get in while I was changing, but it didn't stop him from finding where I had gone.

Julian pounded on the bedroom door. "Dammit, MacKenzie! Open the door. We can't work together if you are going to shut me out like this!" His baritone voice vibrated through the thick wood.

I tossed my pajamas into the hamper near the bathroom door and quickly slid into a pair of black yoga pants with a long cross-back neon orange tank top. Opening the door so Julian didn't beat the thing off of its hinges, "Calm your tits, I was simply changing," I huffed.

Julian's brows furrowed. "Did you just tell me to calm my tits?" A full blown smile spread across his lips as I nodded yes and shrugged my shoulders. "You are definitely not the norm, Kenzie." Whatever he meant by that I ignored and slipped my socked feet into a pair of my Nikes.

"Here's the plan." My attention stayed on the mirror that was connected to the dresser before me as I twisted my hair up into a messy knot atop my head and swiped some deodorant under my arms. "Sara's your sister and you are looking for her."

"Come again?"

My statement definitely threw him off so I picked up the phone from its resting spot on the dresser and showed him the welcome packet for the bed and breakfast they were staying at when the photo was taken. "I've been to this bed and breakfast before, with Thomas, as a matter of fact. They are super friendly people, so if you go in there acting like you haven't heard from your sister since she stayed there maybe they will recognize her and give you a time frame of when they were there."

"That's not going to work."

"And why not?" I crossed my arms over my chest, tucking the phone under my arm.

"Wouldn't I know my own sister's last name?" He had a point.

"Shit! That didn't even cross my mind." I sat down on the edge of the bed to think. "I've got nothing else."

Julian grabbed my hand and pulled me up from the bed. "Come on." He kept hold of my hand as he pulled me out of the bedroom and back into the living room.

"Where are we going?" I asked as I frantically tried to keep up with his longer stride.

Julian stopped walking and I ran smack dab into the back of him. "Sunset Inn Bed and Breakfast."

"Oh." I adjusted my tank top a little better. "Let me grab my purse and a jacket."

The seats in Julian's fancy-smancy car were the most comfortable leather seats I had ever sat in. My body was molded into the material as my right elbow rested against the door, cradling my chin in my hand as I watched the scenery we passed by. Never would I have thought that I would be riding in Julian's vehicle to the bed and breakfast my deceased husband took me to right after we moved into our home in an attempt to track down the woman that he was having an affair with, that he also fathered her child. My mind was blown.

"You all right over there?" Julian's voice pulled me from my thoughts.

"I guess," I replied without moving my attention from the window.

"I can't imagine what you're going through, MacKenzie." He sighed. "Thomas was my best friend in the Marines. We had each other's back through thick and thin, day and night. But never once did he mention Sara or that he was going to be a father. I'm still not convinced that this has to do with him, and I don't want to lie to you about why I'm going through with finding her with you. No, I don't want you going off and doing this on your own, but I need to know almost as much as you do whether or not all of this is true. If it is, everything I thought I knew about Thomas would be a lie."

His words bounced around in my head for a little bit before I responded. "As much as I hate to say this…I can feel it deep down in my bones that it's the truth. And Julian…," I turned away from the window to look at him in the driver's seat, "you don't have to justify to me why you are helping me. There's no need. But I am grateful for it." A feeble smile turned up the corners of my lips before fading away as the bed and breakfast came into view.

The car slightly bounced around from the change of terrain. The bed and breakfast was down a gravel drive, far off the main road, but the lack of trees surrounding the inn made it visible from the distance. There was a medium-size lake to the left of the building where the people staying could fish, relax on one of the docks, or have a nice little picnic. I'd experienced all three the time Thomas and I had visited. My palms broke out in a cold sweat simply from the sight of the place, so I knew my nerves were going to get worse as the journey progressed.

"Hey," Julian placed a hand on my shoulder as we came to a stop in the parking lot designated for the bed and breakfast. "I know this is stressful. But don't let it get the best of you." I turned to face him. "You're strong as hell and you've made it this far, you can't stop now. For one thing I won't let you." The right corner of his lips tipped up in a heartfelt grin as his eyes softened.

I sighed and sucked my bottom lip into my mouth before responding. "This…is just terrifying." My attention quickly went back to the passenger's door as I opened it and slid out of the vehicle before he would say anything else. My feet hit the pebbled driveway as I walked toward the entrance.

"MacKenzie!" Julian called after me so I stopped at the bottom of the rock steps that led up to the front door of the place. When Julian caught up to me he stepped in front of me so that we were looking eye to eye, minus the height difference of course. "If we can get one thing clear between us, please stop running off from me. I'm not the bad guy here, and I sure as hell don't enjoy feeling like one."

I nodded as I slipped my purse strap higher on my shoulder and diverted my eyes to the steps behind him. "Well, let's do this." I followed an aggravated Julian up the steps and into the Sunset Inn Bed and Breakfast.

Everything looked exactly how I remembered it. The large stone home had dark wood floors throughout with a front desk painted white but still had some of the original wood peeking through. The staircase stood directly beside the desk and took you up to the guestrooms. A large open doorway to the right led to a dining area, while the one to the left opened into a playroom for children and out into the backyard area that housed the lake along with an in-ground pool.

Julian rang the bell at the desk since no one was present behind it as I looked around at the many photos of recent guests on the wall behind the desk. They always loved taking pictures for their display wall; it showed just how happy everyone that came to Sunset Inn Bed and Breakfast was in that moment. A sigh of relief left me as I finished scanning the photos and realized none contained images of Thomas and Sara.

"Well, hello there!" A peppy female's voice to our left grabbed mine and Julian's attention. The woman was average height, with long blonde hair pulled around in a loose ponytail with a straw hat resting atop her head. She smiled widely as she took in the two of us and stepped around the counter. "I'm Darla!" She extended her hand to each of us.

"I'm MacKenzie." I worked to keep the nervous stutter from my voice.

"Yes, and I'm Julian," Julian followed with more confidence.

"Nice to meet the both of you." She smiled again. "Did you have a reservation or are you wanting to book a room for the night?" She looked down at the book before her to search for our names.

"Actually-" Julian cleared his throat before digging in his pocket for Thomas' phone. He had cropped the photo of Sara so the revealing parts of her couldn't be seen. "We are looking for a friend of ours that stayed here not too long ago. We met her and a man in town when they were staying here and lost touch with them. I was wondering if you could tell us if they have been back or plan on coming back anytime soon."

The woman's face scrunched up with worry as she grabbed for a pair of silver-rimmed glasses that were hanging around her neck. She slid them up her nose and stared at the photo Julian was showing her of Sara. After a few seconds she looked over the rims of the glasses at Julian and smiled yet again. "I'm sorry, but I haven't seen this woman before." Her eyebrows dipped low as a tremor ran across her bottom lip, along with the nervous shake in her voice informed us that she in fact knew Sara, but for some reason she was boldface lying to us. So I took things into my own hands.

"Are you sure, Darla? Sara was telling us about her upcoming baby shower and I lost the invitation, so I was really hoping to be able to see her again soon to give her the gift we bought her and her husband."

"Oh, I don't think they were married," Darla blurted out before she could stop herself.

"Why is that?" Instead of calling her out about her previous lie I continued on with my questioning, hoping she would answer.

"I really shouldn't be telling you this..." Darla looked around to make sure no one was listening to us. "The last night they were staying here about half a year ago, I heard Sara crying out by the pool while I was cleaning up the playroom just inside the doors. The man she was with, I can't remember his name for the life of me, was frantic. I'm not sure why to be exact, but all I remember hearing Sara say was that he needed to tell his wife the truth. That she deserved to know."

My throat tightened as I took in what Darla was telling us. Sara knew about me. She knew Thomas was married and still slept with him, still carried his baby, and never took the time out to find me and let me know. Black dots filled my vision and I knew I was about to pass out so I grabbed hold of Julian's arm. "I need to sit down," The words left my lips as a whisper.

"Are you okay?" Julian helped me over to one of the waiting chairs against the wall behind us as I shook my head no.

Darla came around the counter, "Is there anything I can do?" she frantically asked.

"Could you get her some water, please?" As soon as Darla was out of earshot Julian kneeled in front of me and rested his hands on my thighs. "Are you sure you're okay?" His sandy brown eyes were full of concern.

"I'm fine." I tried to convince him. "All of that was a little much to hear, is all."

"Here's you some water, dear." Darla handed me a glass of ice water and I smiled sweetly back at her.

"Thank you." The coolness of the water sliding down my throat felt nice. It was easing the spike in temperature my body had from the information Darla had willingly given us. "I'm really not sure what happened, it's like I overheated for a second there." I attempted to explain why I had almost passed out without actually divulging our true intent.

"Oh, honey," Darla waved a hand at me like she understood. "Happens to me quite a bit. It's the changing of the weather from Spring to Summer. Never fails."

Julian kept quiet as the two of us conversed. "Do you mind if we take a look around? Neither of us have been here before; the place is absolutely beautiful," I gushed.

"Well of course!" Darla beamed with pride. "Take as much time as you want. Rooms three, eight, and suite twelve are all vacant if you would like to have a look in them."

"Wonderful." Julian helped me to my feet as I finished the ice water and handed Darla the glass. "Thank you again for the water."

"Don't mention it." Darla watched us walk up the staircase with a smile plastered on her face.

Once we reached the top of the stairs Julian took my hand and pulled me to a stop. "Any time this gets to be too much for you, tell me." If he thought I was going to back down at any point before we found the truth, he was out of his mind.

"I will." Little white lies weren't as bad as the big ones, right?

Chapter Five

Julian pushed open the door to the last available room Darla told us about, suite twelve. As soon as my feet crossed the threshold I knew it was the room where the infamous photo had been taken. Everything was the same as in the photo—the nightstand, the tall, cherry four-pillar bed, the painting of the setting sun over an open field. Stepping forward, I pulled the door shut behind me. "This is the room."

Julian turned to face me, "How do you know?" He pulled the phone from his pocket and pulled up the original, un-cropped photo.

"Look at the painting above the bed, the nightstand, the bed itself…" I trailed off as I watched Julian match up each item I had mentioned.

"If you're thinking we're going to find something in this room, Kenzie, that's highly unlikely. They clean the rooms after every person that stays in here, and they haven't been here in a while."

Without saying a thing, I bent down and opened the bottom drawer of the nightstand. Just as I remembered from our stay, a memory album along with a black sharpie was staring back at me. I pulled the album from the drawer and held it up to show Julian. "I remember this when we stayed here. They like when the guests leave a photo of themselves and/or write a little something in these books they leave in each room." I flipped through the pages of the book, searching for and entry by Sara and Thomas. "Hopefully this is the same book that was here during their stay, and they actual left an entry."

"Maybe we'll get lucky."

As my fingers flew through the pages, I stopped at the second to last one when Thomas' handwriting jumped out at me.

February 15th

Our stay here has been the best to date. My beautiful Sara has made my life more than it has ever been, and I want to thank this establishment for being part of our wonderful getaway from the real world. Love is blooming through all of the darkness.

The burn of bile rising up my throat caused me to choke.

"MacKenzie?" Julian started patting me on the back, thinking I was choking, as the book slipped from my hands and crashed to the floor.

The force of my coughing helped me choke the bile back down. "There's something written by Thomas." My finger shook as I pointed towards the book on the floor. "Second to the last page." The strain of my voice hurt as I stammered out each sentence.

Julian bent down and retrieved the memory album from the floor and quickly flipped to the page that held Thomas' words.

"That ending statement was what he always would write to me in his letters while overseas. He always said I made love bloom in the darkness."

I watched as his eyes scanned the page before pulling his cell phone out of his back jeans pocket and snapping a photo. "I'm so sorry. This Thomas didn't deserve someone like you."

"Why'd you do that?"

"Do what?"

"Take a picture of the page."

"So we have a copy of it without messing up the book."

How did I not think of that?

"Good thinking."

Julian put the book back in the bottom drawer of the nightstand. "Are you ready to get out of here?"

"Where do we go from here?"

"To find food, I'm starving."

Julian's reply pulled a laugh from deep within my belly. "Well, I'd hate to see you starve."

Julian patted his nonexistent stomach and said, "Since I'm so close to it."

A small, unexpected smile escaped me as I rolled my eyes. "Come on." I waved for him to follow me out. He had a way of lightening my mood, making me laugh even when I was on the brink of a meltdown from heartache. Saying I was thankful to have Julian help me through it all was an understatement.

"I haven't had one of these in so long," Julian mumbled through a mouth full of a double cheeseburger from Jake's Burger Shack. My giggling didn't go unnoticed. "What?"

"You're demolishing that burger like no other." I shoved fries in my mouth to hide my continuous laughter.

"Being in the Marines makes it hard to get stuff like this." He held up the remainder of his burger to emphasize his statement. "Sure, we can grill burgers every so often, but you can't beat Jake's Burger Shack."

I took a big swig of my vanilla milkshake and groaned from its deliciousness. When I looked up, Julian's eyes were wide as he held the remainder of his burger in mid-air to his mouth. "What?"

"Is that milkshake that good?" He laughed.

My cheeks heated from my embarrassment and I laughed, "My groans do not give it justice." I turned my attention to the fries in front of me when Julian reached across the table, grabbed my milkshake, and took a big draw from my straw.

"What the…"

"Damn!" Julian interrupted me. "That is one helluva milkshake."

I shook my head and laughed, "I told you."

Silence filled the air as we finished our food and drinks. I hadn't been eating very well since Thomas' death, so Jake's hit the spot. We were sitting in the front of the place against the large glass windows that faced the street. Jake's was a good thirty minutes from the bed and breakfast and about forty-five minutes in the opposite direction from where each of us lived, but Julian suggested it and I wasn't about to say no.

A couple holding hands at the crosswalk caught my attention as the blonde tipped her head up and the dark-haired man leaned over and softly kissed her lips. It made me wonder if Thomas and Sara had looked like that; happy beyond measure, like I thought he had been with me.

The warmth of Julian's hand covering mine pulled my attention away from the couple and to him. He wasn't looking at me, he was watching the same couple. "Life is strange, isn't it?" I wasn't sure where he was going with his comment so I remained silent. "Thomas seems to have been living a completely separate life that no one knew about; it took his death to throw it out in the open and hurt you. I will never understand why he would do something like this. Hell, we used to spend many nights on watch, talking about the future; I was hoping to be able to find someone that would put up with my ass for the long haul and he simply wanted to start a family with you and get out of the military after his next tour. I just don't get it…"

    I slipped my hand from beneath his and sat back against the plump red cushion behind me. "One thing that I can't seem to wrap my head around is that I wanted to get pregnant. I was ready to have a baby at any moment, but every time I brought up the subject Thomas would say that he wasn't ready. That he wanted to be out of the military before we had a baby and it would be a while before that could happen. He never mentioned when he would get out, or if it was an option anytime in the near future. I guess when he spoke about me to you; he was actually talking about his life with Sara." My heart was like a heavy weight in the center of my chest, pushing down on my lungs and making it hard to breathe.

    My hands trembled in my lap. "Excuse me. I need to use the restroom." I slid from the booth and made a beeline for the bathroom before Julian had a chance to respond. The bathroom had a single toilet; I had never been more thankful for that in my life as I locked the door and slouched back against it. Thomas' phone felt like it was burning a hole in my jacket pocket so I jerked the thing out and held it in my shaky hands. A few deep breaths passed my lips as I stared at the dark screen, contemplating if I really wanted to dig further into it. Before I realized what I was doing, the screen was lit up and I was scrolling through the contacts list. Most of the people listed were military friends or family, but one caught my attention. It was saved in the second speed dial slot, higher than anything else besides his voicemail. Sara's name and number stared back at me as I quickly found my phone and dialed her digits after the short code to block my caller identity. I had been too afraid to make the call, but nothing was stopping me as the line rang.

My heart amped with every shrill ring until I thought it would explode. After four long, excruciating rings, the voicemail picked up. *Sorry I couldn't get to your call right now, leave a message and I will get back with you as soon as possible.* The sweet, southern voice of who I assumed to be Sara echoed through my ears. Both phones slid from my grasp as I hurried over to the toilet just feet away and lost every bit of the food I had previously eaten. My knees were aching from slamming against the tile floor, and I had a death grip on the toilet seat, even though the thought of the germs on that thing made me cringe.

"I need a damn bleach bath after this." I pushed myself up and wiped my mouth on the back of my hand before turning the faucet on to the hottest setting I could stand and dousing my hands with antibacterial soap. I scrubbed and scrubbed before rinsing them and my mouth out with the warm water.

When I turned to leave I noticed the two phones still lying on the floor. Neither were busted apart, which was one good thing, so I picked them up one at a time and made sure they worked before putting them back in my jacket pockets. Julian was still seated in the booth I had left him in. His eyes were fixated on something outside those large windows so he didn't see me approaching.

"Are you ready?" I asked as I stepped up to the table, without taking a seat.

"Yeah, if you are." He looked up at me. "Everything all right?" His brows furrowed as he took me in.

"Just peachy." I took a step to the right so he could get out of the booth.

"You really need to learn to lie better." He tapped me on the end of my nose with his finger and I scoffed.

"Thomas would've been a damn good person to learn from," I mumbled before turning towards the door to leave, but not before I caught the sadness swimming in Julian's sandy brown eyes.

The car ride home was a quiet one. I offered to drive since Julian had driven all day, so the soft snores coming from the passenger's seat had me trying to control my laughter. His head was tilted back against the headrest with his muscular arms crossed tightly over his chest and his mouth slack. His lashes seemed longer than normal as they rested against his cheeks and the line between his eyebrows was a little more defined than usual from frowning in his sleep. A car horn blaring behind me made me jump and look ahead again. The light had turned green while I was gawking at Julian's sleeping self.

The leather of the seat groaned as Julian stirred awake. "I didn't mean to fall asleep." His tired baritone voice made me smile.

"It's fine, apparently you needed it." I turned left into my neighborhood and slowly drove until I reached my driveway. I hit the ignition button to kill the engine on the car. "Thanks for helping me out today. I really appreciate it. I probably wouldn't have gone through with it if it wasn't for you."

Julian sat up in his seat and turned to face me. "Even though the circumstances suck, today was a productive day. Don't you think?"

"Yeah, it was." I opened the driver door and got out; Julian did the same on the passenger's side. "It's getting pretty late; I think I'm going to crash for the night." I extended my hand holding his car fob towards him.

He took a step towards me and pulled me into a nice firm hug. "Get some rest, Kenzie. I know you must be exhausted and today wasn't an easy day."

I squeezed him tightly before taking a step back. "I will. Talk to you tomorrow, Julian."

"Night," he replied as I walked to my front door, unlocked it, and headed straight for the bed I hadn't slept in since before the news of Thomas's death.

Chapter Six

My body felt refreshed as I stepped out of the fogged-up sliding glass doors of the shower in my master bedroom. The night had passed without any crazy dreams fogging my mind. I had indeed dreamt, but the only thing that stood out was it being about the time Thomas and I had spent together at that damn bed and breakfast. Instead of being angry or upset when I awoke, I was surprisingly calm.

Some say when a calming sensation comes over you regarding a horrible situation in your life, one of two things are about to happen: you're either about to finally flip your shit over it all or you are coming to a close on the grieving process. There was no way I was coming to a close on the grieving process so I prepared myself for the storm that was to come.

The master bathroom was my favorite part of my house. It had a large glass-enclosed shower with brown and tan tiles, a large his and her vanity, and a spot between the two sinks for me to sit and apply my makeup. The bathroom led into a large closet and then into the bedroom. The layout made it a lot easier to step out of the shower and into the room—yes, I call it a room because it's almost the size of one—which has all of your clothes in it.

    I flipped my head over and wrapped a towel around my damp hair and then walked into my closet. I thumbed through the row of clothes lining the walls, sliding each hanger across the rod as I searched for an outfit. It was one of those days where you have nothing planned but don't feel like being cooped up in the house all day by yourself; I had a feeling I was going to have a lot of those days for a while. Settling on a pair of charcoal grey boyfriend capris along with a simple cobalt tank top, I flipped on the television to check the weather. The weather man on the news proclaimed it was going to be close to eighty with sunshine all day, so why would I waste such a beautiful day stuck inside?

    Instead of messing with my hair, I towel dried it and pulled it into my usual over-the-shoulder braid. Makeup for the day was a minimum: light foundation and pale eye shadow with a couple swipes of mascara so I didn't look like someone from the land of the dead. The silence in the house was getting to the point of annoyance so I hit one of my playlists in my phone and connected it to the speaker system throughout the house. Music had always been my go-to when it came to any situation, good or bad. A few moments later and the smooth voice of Sam Smith filled the house as I finished getting ready.

    The day was going to be one that didn't burden me with heartache, regret, or any other form of sadness or pain. At least that's the mindset I was in. Thomas' cell phone was tucked in the drawer beside our bed, instead of in the spare bedroom. I wanted it to be out of sight, hoping that would make it a little easier to ignore all of the drama swimming around him. Ever since I had discovered Thomas' deception I felt like I was bleeding out in the ocean with sharks surrounding me, but my time of being prey was over; I wanted to be a damn shark.

After grabbing a quick bagel for breakfast, I snatched my keys off of the counter and tossed my purse across my body before heading out the door. The warmth of the sun on my face had me smiling as I walked down the driveway to my car and started the engine. My fingers drummed against the steering wheel to the beat of the song on the radio as I contemplated where to start my day. The park was the first place that came to mind. The shoes I wore definitely weren't walking shoes, but I could sit on a park bench and enjoy the day with any one of the books that were on my tablet waiting for me to read them.

Traffic was at a minimum as I maneuvered to the other side of town toward the park. The shade trees hung over the outer parking spots and I always liked to snag one of them so my car didn't feel like hell itself once I got back inside. Luckily, there were two empty spots in the shade because the rest of the parking lot was full. "Looks like everyone had the same idea that I had," I mumbled to myself as I gathered my purse from the passenger's seat and headed towards the crowded area.

The sound of children's laughter and screams as they jumped on the playscape and rode their bikes and scooters filled the air. My mood hadn't been so great in months; hopefully it would stay that way for at least the day. A lone bench caught my eye on the opposite side of the park from where I entered, so I quickly crossed the field, pulled my tablet from my purse and made myself comfortable on the bench. I sat under the protective canopy of a large shade tree, giving me just enough shade to be comfortable instead of sweltering hot from the sun.

    It didn't take me long to be sucked into the book I had started reading weeks prior. A love story with a dark twist that I hadn't read yet, but from the reviews I was terrified of the ending. Seemed like people had mixed emotions about the main male character and a lot of hearts were broken. I loved books that weren't the norm: insta-love that was far from reality for most of the world's population. Yeah, I'm sure it happened to a very limited few…but in all it was a myth in real-life love stories. Especially mine. As the current chapter I was reading came to a close, I took a short break from the drama of the story and watched the various people interact within the park. A couple was having a picnic while a group of girls were power walking around the path that circled the entire park; many children were running and playing with one another while people like me sat back and watched. A tiny gasp escaped my mouth when my eyes locked on the unusual couple walking across from me. Julian was side-by-side with none other than Olivia Jones.

    My instinct told me to run, to get the hell out of the park before they had the chance to see me, but the second I stood up to collect my things, Olivia's fucking hand went flying in the air as she began waving like a lunatic at me. "MacKenzie! Hey!" Her annoying-as-hell voice echoed across the park. Julian's eyes landed on mine as I stopped putting my Kindle into my bag and sighed in defeat. There was no running away from her, no matter how badly I wanted to.

Olivia Jones was a thorn in my side that would never go away, and it seemed like she was striking again in the nosey department by being with Julian. As they approached, I knew she was going to make it a point to stop and chat.

"Olivia, so nice to see you." My voice was anything but happy. "Julian." I nodded at him and directed my attention back to Olivia.

"I'm surprised to see you here, MacKenzie." The smugness in her tone made me want to punch her in the face. She was all about passing judgment and assuming any form of bullshit she wanted to assume.

"Why is that?" My smile was tight, but I kept it on display for her.

She dismissively waved a hand around. "Oh, I just assumed you would be at home still mourning the loss of Thomas. We hadn't seen you at any of the Army wives socials, so I assumed you were still having a very hard time."

Funny thing about her mentioning the Army wives socials was that she wasn't an Army wife anymore. Apparently three divorces from soldiers gave her the right to be the head of the gatherings; just one reason why I wouldn't be caught dead at one of those things.

"Those silly little gatherings are just not my cup of tea, Olivia." By the look on her face I had hit a nerve, which was exactly what I wanted. I hoped that pissing her off would end with her storming away and keeping her mouth shut for a little while, but it seemed to only fuel the fire.

"Silly little gatherings?" She chuckled a humorless laugh and took a step closer to Julian. "I'm sure the soldiers don't think they are silly! It's a way for their women to spend time together and deal with them being gone for long periods of time." She turned her attention to him. "Isn't that right, Julian?"

My eyes found Julian's and I raised a brow, letting him know I was awaiting his response just like Olivia was. "I wouldn't know. I'm not married and never have been, so I don't think I'm a good person to ask that." He pushed his hands into the pockets of his running shorts, which I hadn't noticed until then.

"Oh, I figured someone would have scooped you up already." Olivia laid a hand over her heart and touched Julian's bicep. The bitch was flirting right in front of me. Even though I had zero claim to Julian or what he could do, it still pissed me off and made me want to gag.

Julian's eyes locked with mine as he replied, "No, I haven't been lucky enough yet." His choice of words was interesting to me. Julian was a very attractive man; it wouldn't be hard for him to find someone to share his time with.

"Here's my card," Olivia handed him one of her Army wives club cards that had her number on them. "If you want someone to hang out with, I'll be around." Her wide seductive smile made me want to vomit.

"I'm currently having a great time hanging out with Kenzie." The right side of his lips tipped up in a snarky grin. He knew what he was doing, baiting Olivia to start some gossip revolving around me and Julian. If I didn't think it was just the slightest bit hilarious, due to

Olivia's eyes narrowing in my direction and her lips being puckered into a sourpuss grimace, I would have pummeled his ass for it.

"Well," Olivia huffed. "I had no idea you were so quickly back on the market, *Mac*Kenzie. I'm sure Thomas is rolling over in his grave." She made sure to pronounce my name correctly instead of using the nickname Julian had used.

"You bitch…" I went at her and Julian grabbed me around the waist to stop me, just like he had the first time.

"I think it's time to go, Olivia."

"I agree." A slow, victorious smile stretched across Olivia's lips before it was quickly smacked down by Julian's next remarks. Her arm looped through Julian's and he pulled away.

"Kenzie and I have some things to catch up on. I'll see you around." He shot her down nicely.

"Oh." She looked like she had been backhanded across her sickening pretty face. "All right then." And with that, Olivia Jones walked towards the parking lot without another hideous word leaving her annoying mouth.

"Well, that was fun." Julian was smiling from ear-to-ear. I narrowed my eyes and slugged him in the arm. "What was that for?" His bewildered look made me laugh.

"Why in the hell were you with Olivia Jones in the first place?"

Dishonorable Love | 67

"First off, I wasn't *with* her, and second, someone seems a little rattled by the fact that *she* made it a point to catch *my* attention and screw up my morning run."

The strap on my purse started to slip off of my shoulder so I readjusted it and crossed my arms tightly over my chest. "I'm not rattled." The lie slipped from my lips before I could stop it.

"Right…" Julian was laughing at that point as we started walking on the blacktopped path.

"Shut up." My eye roll was almost audible.

He laughed. "I'm just saying. I thought the two of you were about to throw down there for a second."

"'Cause she's a major bitch."

"She's not that bad…"

The look I gave him could have leveled an entire town from its deadliness. "I really hope you're joking."

"Completely joking, there is no way I could spend long periods of time with that woman."

"She is *not* a woman," I countered.

"You crack me up." He lazily tossed his arm over my shoulder and pulled me into his side.

"I speak the truth, and you realize the gossip you just stirred up, right?"

"Yeah, sorry about that." He dropped his arm from my shoulder and scratched the back of his neck. "I wasn't thinking about everything when I said that. She'll probably attempt to make your life a living hell with rumors."

A loud laugh escaped me, "She's been doing that for a long-ass time." The smile on my face had Julian's frown morphing into a full-blown smile of his own. "Although it will be kind of funny if she starts rumors about me and then it comes out that Thomas was the cheating piece of shit in the relationship."

Julian fell silent beside me. Turning to look at him I noticed the unsure look on his face which was most likely caused by my previous comment. What I had said was humorous to me, even if he didn't think so. Silence hung in the air as we walked to the parking lot where I had parked earlier and apparently Julian had as well.

"Where are you headed from here?" Julian leaned against the trunk of my car once we reached it.

"Not sure. Today was supposed to be a me day without anything bringing me down and any thoughts of the bullshit going on with my deceased husband's memory." I tilted my head towards the sky and closed my eyes, allowing the heat of the sun to consume my face. "So far that hasn't been accomplished."

"Sorry."

My eyes opened and my chin dropped down so that I was looking directly at Julian, "What are you sorry for?" His apology had confused me.

"For being the reason your day went to shit."

My head tilted to the side and my eyebrows furrowed. "You didn't turn my day to shit, Olivia did."

"I was an accomplice in the matter," he argued.

"You're silly." I smiled. It seemed I only did that in his presence anymore. "If you're hell bent on being the reason my day went from fantastic to shitty, then so be it."

"Now what can I do to turn it around for ya?" His ankles were crossed as he made himself more comfortable, leaning against the trunk of my car.

"Umm…" I sucked my bottom lip into my mouth to think over what exactly he could do to change my day around, but nothing came to mind. Julian was a constant reminder of Thomas because of their history in the Marines together, which in turn made me think about all of the bullshit Thomas had been doing behind my back.

"I've got an idea." Julian brought my attention back to our conversation.

"What might that be?" I leaned my hip against the trunk next to him.

"Go home and change into your swimsuit and meet me at my place once you're done."

Swimsuit? Why in the hell would that be something I need to change into?

"This girl is *not* comfortable in a swimsuit. In fact, I haven't put one on in quite some time."

Julian's eyes roamed down my body and back up before landing on mine. The intensity in them caught me off guard and I squirmed just a bit. "If you aren't going to wear a swimsuit, at least wear something you won't mind getting wet."

Okay, then.

My skin heated from his words and I wasn't sure what was happening to me. I cleared my throat, walked away, and opened the driver's side door to leave. "See you in a little bit," I managed to say without glancing back at Julian.

"Okay," he replied. My car gently rocked as he pushed off of it, and the sound of his shoes hitting the blacktop echoed as he made his way to his own vehicle.

Finding something to wear that would be suitable in the water was becoming a pain in my ass. If Julian had given me more of an idea of what he had up his sleeve, my closet wouldn't look like a tornado had gone through it. My body was surrounded by mounds of clothes as I sat in the center of the floor of the closet, looking around at the hellacious mess I had created.

My eyes landed on Thomas' side of the closet.

Fury.

My internal temperature spiked from the anger that was pulsing through my veins. I pushed myself up from the floor, grabbed arms full of his clothes, hangers and all, stomped through the house to the sliding glass doors. I stepped out onto the deck and tossed them into the open trashcan on the concrete slab beside the deck. A loud growling sound vibrated up my chest as I went back for the second round of clothing.

    Once Thomas' side of the closet was empty and officially housed within the two trashcans out back, I cleaned up the mess I had made of my own clothes and hung them throughout the newly opened space.

    The pile of clothes had diminished quite a bit when the doorbell rang. "If that's Olivia…" That threatening sentence went unfinished as I stomped through the house to the front door and peeked through the peephole.

    Julian.

    In swim shorts and a cut off shirt.

    "Oh, shit!"

    Swinging the door open I plastered on a smile to greet him. "What in the hell is taking you so long?" He pushed past me.

    "Well, hello to you, too," I countered, shutting the door. "I've been…uh…a little busy." The inside of my cheek burned as I nervously chewed on it.

    "Doing what?" Julian followed me into my bedroom, looking around at everything as we went. But I didn't stop, I went directly into the closet and he followed. "Ugh…"

    Embarrassment and amusement were dancing around on my face as I broke into a fit of laughs at Julian's reaction to the craziness that was my closet. I flopped down into the open spot where I had been previously sitting as my psycho sounding cackles morphed into hysterical tears. They wracked through my body as I went from humor to complete and utter sadness in the blink of an eye.

"Kenzie?" Julian dropped to his knees beside me and pushed the clothes out of his way. My sobs ripped through my body as I crumpled against my folded legs until Julian pulled my body up and into his lap.

I fisted his shirt and my hands buried deep into the material for leverage as my tears soaked through to his skin. "I'm—I'm sorry." I managed to choke out as I sat up, still resting in his lap with his strong arms wrapped around me like a vice grip.

Julian rubbed one of his hands up and down my back, trying to soothe me. "Do you want to talk about it?"

My chin was tilted down and my eyes were fixated on some faded design of his cut-off shirt so I wouldn't have to look him in the eyes. But instead of ignoring the elephant in the room, I dove right into why I was so upset. "I don't know what came over me, but as I was digging through my clothes looking for something to wear, I kept finding myself staring at Thomas' side of the closet. Seeing his clothes hanging there pissed me off." My voice was shaking as I admitted what I had done and how it made me feel. "Next thing I knew I was running back and forth through the house with arms full of clothes and tossing them in the trashcans beside the deck."

"You're hurt. Yeah, nobody but me knows what is fully going on, but no one expects you to go about your day like everything is fine." He tipped my chin up so that I was staring into his warm, concerned eyes. "Letting out your pain will help you heal. Whether that means crying, screaming, throwing out clothes, or locking yourself away for days, you can't hide from the shitty parts of life."

Another onset of tears blurred my vision and threatened to spill over my lids. I was touched by Julian's understanding for what I was going through. My arms wrapped tightly around his neck as I pulled his body into mine. I had no words for what he had said, so I was hoping a hug would say enough.

Once I released my arms from his neck, I stood from his lap and began putting away the remainder of my clothes that were scattered across the closet floor. Julian moved to the doorway that led into my bedroom; his shoulder pressed into the frame to hold him up as he watched me without saying a thing.

I hung the last shirt back up and turned to find the doorway empty, so I took advantage of him not standing there to slip into a pair of running shorts. Keeping my back to the door, I slipped my shirt off and replaced it with a racer back tank. Workout clothes were what I had settled on because a swimsuit just wasn't happening. I never felt comfortable in one, but most women didn't, right?

The sound of Julian clearing his voice made me spin around as the material fell the remainder of the way down to cover my stomach. "You scared the crap out of me!" My hand instinctively went over my heart in an attempt to calm its erratic pace.

"I just wanted to make sure you didn't strip any more clothes off without knowing that I was standing here again." A sensual smirk was dancing around his lips. My internal temperature spiked as a blush warmed my cheeks from him seeing my naked back, but thankfully it hadn't been more than that.

"Sorry." I diverted my eyes to the floor.

"No need to apologize." Julian's smirk had grown to a full-blown smile.

Still holding the shirt I had taken off, I threw it at his face. "You perv!" We both fell into a fit of laughter.

"I'm a man, sweetheart. That's all I can say." He shrugged his shoulders while laughing and tossed the shirt into the hamper beside the door like he knew that's where I would put it. "Put some shoes on and let's go." He motioned towards the part of the closet that housed my many pairs of shoes, boots, sandals, and heels.

"It would help if you told me exactly what we would be doing…"

"Yeah, that's not going to happen so pick a pair." He motioned towards the shoes again.

"How much walking will we be doing?"

"Not much."

"Can I wear flip-flops?" I arched a brow at him.

"Sure."

"You're really not going to budge on telling me, are you?"

"Not one single bit." He crossed his arms over his broad chest and smiled.

"Butthead," I mumbled and slipped my feet into a pair of black flip-flops.

A boisterous laugh rumbled through Julian's chest, I wasn't sure why. "Did you just call me a butthead?"

"Shut up and come on." Shaking my head with amusement, I pushed past Julian and headed for his car in the driveway.

As soon as Julian turned onto US 17 I had a good idea of where we were going. My bare feet rested against the dash as my toes danced along to the beat of the song playing through the speakers of the car. It was an upbeat tune, one I hadn't heard yet. Julian always seemed to have new music that I had never heard before—just one of the qualities I liked about him.

"I know where we're going!" The confession left my lips as we passed the sign that announced Wilmington was ten miles ahead.

Julian glanced at me out of the corner of his eye with a sly grin, "Where might that be?"

"Wilmington."

"You think you're smart, don't ya?" he teased.

"I don't think…I know." My head fell back against the headrest as I grinned like a Cheshire cat. The sun was blaring so I pulled my shades down from their resting spot on top of my head to shield my eyes and continued dancing with my feet on the dash to the new song playing across his speakers.

Twenty minutes and numerous kick-ass songs later we were pulling into a gravel drive that led back into a lightly wooded area. The tall trees blocked the view on our sides, but I knew we hadn't reached Wilmington yet.

A small beach house came into view as we took a sharp right turn, and the most gorgeous array of flowers decorated the porch in hanging baskets, vines, and pots. I was in awe as the car came to a stop and Julian asked me if I was going to either get out of the car or open-mouth stare all day.

Smart ass.

Pushing myself out of the car, I walked along the gravel drive that had turned into more sand than gravel, towards the porch. The closer I got, the flowers became even more beautiful...hell, the entire beach house was breathtaking: a soft blue with white shutters and railing that had been worn from the sand and rain to make them distressed. It was a place I could see myself staying for all eternity, tucked away from the world in a little oasis of peace and quiet.

"Who owns this place?" My eyes scanned what I thought to be a porch but actually wrapped around to the back, making it a large deck.

"I do," Julian replied as he unlocked the front door and stepped inside.

I paused. "I thought you said you just moved here?"

"I did."

"Then how do you own this place?"

"I bought it." He sounded like the question I had asked was a silly one.

"When?"

"Yesterday." He dropped the keys in a bowl on a small wooden table just inside the door. "I had my eye on it when I was scouting the area for a place and I finally closed on it yesterday."

"So let me get this straight…" I dug my fingers into my scalp as I talked. "You have a place a couple miles from me, *and* this beach house?"

Julian rested against the kitchen island as he nodded, confirming that I was correct. "Like I said, I've had my eye on this place." That damn smile of his was making its appearance yet again. "You can look around if you'd like."

I nodded and walked to the opposite side of the house. Everything was beach themed, but not in the tacky, large fish and bright-as-hell-colored way. It was relaxed with lots of tans, whites, silvers, and pale blues; soothing. The ceiling in the living room and adjoining kitchen was vaulted with distressed white beams.

The sound of an outside door shutting caught my attention while I looked around the guest bedroom; the beach house only had two bedrooms and the other one was on the opposite side. Pulling back the white lace curtain that covered the window, I took in Julian walking down the steps that led to the beach. He grabbed the back of his cut-off shirt at the neck and yanked it over his head. The muscles in his back rolled and stretched with each movement he made and his tan skin glistened in the bright summer sun. I watched as he turned to the left where an open shower hung. He pushed a pedal on the concrete slab below his bare feet and stepped under the fall of water. The droplets raced down his skin as he tilted his face towards the showerhead, and something deep in my belly called out to me. That unfamiliar ache made me realize I was developing feelings for Julian, feelings that I wasn't so sure would be reciprocated or even if they *should* be reciprocated.

The curtain slipped from my hand and I leaned back against the wall. "What are you doing, MacKenzie…" The words came out as a whispered plea, begging myself not to dig a new hole deeper than I already had in my life.

Chapter Seven

Julian was deep in the water by the time I reached the beach, so I fanned out my towel, followed by his, in the sand. I wished I had known we were going to be on the beach, I *might* have considered wearing a swimsuit. Who was I kidding? MacKenzie Cole never flaunted her body easily in a swimsuit. Most likely I would have still ended up in the attire I had chosen. I hiked my shorts up as far as they would go and situated my tank top so I wouldn't have those wicked strap lines as I basked in the sun. The warmth of the sun's rays warmed my skin. I closed my eyes behind my sunglasses and listened to the small waves crash against the shore. The entire scene was so soothing that before I knew it, I was falling in and out of sleep.

"You're gonna' get burned if you don't put some sunscreen on," Julian's deep voice pulled me awake.

"Mmmm…I don't wanna move," I whined.

"I don't want to hear you complain when it happens, then." The teasing in his voice made me smile. I pushed up and braced my hands against the towel behind me to hold myself up.

"You should have told me we were coming to the beach." I watched Julian over my shoulder.

"Why? Would you have worn a bikini then?" He wagged his eyebrows up and down teasing me.

Leaning over, I playfully pushed his shoulder. "No...well, I don't know. Maybe." I always fumbled with my words when my nerves took over, and for some reason Julian was making me nervous.

"Damn. Maybe I should have told you we were coming here, then." My head whipped back around in his direction, with what I'm sure was a shocked expression on my face, and a blush crept across my cheeks as he winked.

"You're crazy," I laughed.

He leaned over closer to my ear and whispered, "All the best people are...or so I hear." His warm breath moved across the shell of my ear as his deep voice vibrated deep to my core.

Holy hell.

My throat went dry all of a sudden so I stood from the towel I was lying on and dusted myself off, even though I knew I had no sand on me. "I'm going to head inside for a bit. Feeling a little toasty and I need something to drink." Word vomit, that's what I had, and I couldn't seem to stop it.

"Told you that you would burn out here." Julian was grinning with that I-told-you-so look proudly plastered on his face.

"Yeah, yeah." I waved my hand dismissively at him and tossed my towel over my shoulder as I made my way towards the beach house.

Shutting the door behind me, I went straight to the bathroom. After stepping out of the sun, I could feel my skin was dry, and a little sting crawled across my flesh. If I wasn't sunburnt, my luck would be at an all-time high. As soon as I saw my reflection in the floor-length mirror on the back of the bathroom door I gasped. The pink flesh was angry. I had completely forgotten that I'd turned my tank top into a tube top.

"Lovely…" I groaned as I searched the cabinet behind me for any kind of cream to apply to ease the ache from my overly sun-kissed skin.

After coming up empty-handed I headed to the other side of the house toward the master bedroom. A photograph sitting on a small table beside the bed caught my attention. It didn't look dusty or like it had been left behind from the previous owners of the beach house. I got close enough to see the man that had his arms wrapped around a petite redhead and my heart sank.

Julian.

Did he have a wife somewhere? Was he like Thomas? No, we hadn't stepped over any lines, but he had been overly flirty recently. Could I believe him when he said that he hadn't known about Thomas cheating on me, since he had concealed the existence of this woman?

My mind was spiraling out of control when I realized I couldn't leave the beach house even if I wanted to. Julian had brought us in his car; I had no idea if a cab could even find the place. My fight or flight instinct was on high.

Giving up on escaping without Julian knowing, I went into the en suite bathroom and rummaged through the cabinets and drawers. Thankfully I found some burn cream. "Thank god!" I took a seat on the closed toilet seat and applied it to my shoulders, arms, and chest. The coolness of the cream soothed the sting of the pain. Julian was right, I had burnt myself up to the point of resembling a lobster.

Great job, Kenzie...

Why the sun made people tired, I would never understand but once the cream from heaven above was applied to my angry skin I padded into the living room and planted myself on the couch. Curling up against a couple throw pillows, I closed my eyes and took in the silence of the beach house. It wasn't alarming or putting me on edge to find something to fill the noiseless void; it actually made me feel even sleepier than the sun had.

"MacKenzie!!!" Thomas yelled from across the large sandy plain. "Don't come any closer, baby! They'll kill you." His sincerity had tears pooling in my eyes. I wanted to touch him, needed to get him out of this hell that he called his career.

A heavy gust of wind picked up the sand and swirled it thickly around in the air, momentarily hiding Thomas from my line of vision until the wind died down. I frantically searched the area where Thomas had been standing through the remnants of the sandy wind when I saw them...Thomas was planted in the same spot with one arm wrapped tightly around Sara's waist while his other hand was buried deep into her dark locks as they made love to one another with their mouths.

"You son of a bitch!" My voice broke as I pushed my legs, to the point of my muscles burning as I raced across the fire zone.

"Kenzie! NO!" Julian shouted when the shot of a gun echoed a few seconds before pain radiated through my chest and darkness consumed me.

"Kenzie!" Julian's frantic voice jarred me awake.

I was gasping for air as I rose from the couch, slamming my forehead into Julian's before collapsing back against the cushions in agony. "Shit!" My hand covered the throbbing spot on my head as my eyes fluttered open to take in Julian's similar state.

"Remind me not to wake you when you're sleeping again," he groaned as he sat fully up and rubbed his red forehead.

"Sorry." Embarrassment rolled through my body.

"It's okay." He rubbed his head again. "You were thrashing and whimpering when I came in. The moment I touched your arm to wake you, you screamed bloody murder…and well, you know the rest."

"It was a nightmare…" I sat up and crisscrossed my legs in front of me.

"Do you have those often?"

"I did right after they informed me of Thomas' death, but they hadn't been happening recently...and this one was *different*." I shook my head, trying to rid myself of the image from my dream.

"Different how?" Julian scooted a little closer to me, not enough for it to be obvious, but enough that I noticed.

"We were in a sandstorm in Iraq, I think, just like every other time, except this time when the sand died down I saw him and Sara lip-locked. I ran as fast as I could across the fire zone when you started yelling for me to stop. That's when a bullet hit me in the chest." My eyes dropped to my shorts and I picked at the hem to avoid eye contact with Julian. "Usually it's just me and Thomas, and I'm trying my damnedest to get to him before it fades to black, but the addition of you and Sara, as well as the bullet hitting me, was new."

"You're stressed." Julian turned away from me, sitting correctly on the couch with his head resting back against the cushion behind him. "I used to have these dreams...well, nightmares, when we actually got to sleep. One particular one used to play on repeat. I'd get the call to shoot a target and it would be a little boy. As soon as I decided not to shoot the kid, because I thought he was safe, he would blow up a group of Marines that I could have saved. I would jolt awake, sweating my ass off from the thought of being the reason all of those men died. Knowing it was a dream made it a little easier to swallow, but that could easily have been real life for me." Julian turned his head to look at me. His eyes were full of pain. "After Thomas died in the explosion during the raid I found myself wondering if that dream was a sign of things to come...you know?"

I pushed up onto my knees, closing the distance between us. "We need to stop blaming ourselves for things that happen that are out of our hands. You were responsible for Thomas' death just about as much as I was responsible for his cheating. We still have the chance to live life to its fullest, and we need to start doing just that." The pain in Julian's eyes morphed into an expression I didn't recognize. Before I could dwell on it, one of his massive hands smoothed across my face and pulled my mouth down to his.

Our lips touched against one another for a few brief seconds before Julian abruptly stood and walked away, leaving me in a breathless heap of confusion. The back door slammed close, the echo of his departure ringing through the beach house.

The gravel crunched beneath my feet as I quickly walked to the end of the drive that led out to the main road from the beach house. If I remembered correctly, there was a small store just down the road. My brain was on overload from Julian's kiss so I did the only thing I could think of doing without a car: I ran.

I couldn't understand why Julian kissed me, except being caught up in the intensity of the moment we were sharing. Flashing back to his nightmares, while I spilled every ounce of feelings regarding how my own nightmares were affecting me, had both of our emotions on high. I shook away the thoughts as I pushed open the glass door to the store. It was wore from years of weather abuse, like an old shack, but the inside didn't look like it was going to fall down anytime soon like one would have suspected from the outside. Instead, it was filled with everything you would need for daily essentials and beach happenings. A stack of grocery baskets sat just inside the door, since the place wasn't big enough for numerous people to maneuver around with carts, so I grabbed one and placed the rubber covered handle of it in the crook of my arm.

    Julian hadn't informed me how long we would stay at the beach house, but from the looks of the place it needed a lot of essentials either way. Hell, I needed clothes for even one night. As I moseyed around the store I filled the basket with soap, detergent, tooth paste, tooth brushes, burn cream, lotion, and enough other basic household items. The forty-something year old man behind the counter was friendly, smiling from ear-to-ear as he asked where I was from and how I liked the area. Genuinely nice people were hard to find in society anymore, but he was one of those rare people. When he slid three paper sacks towards me on the counter, I almost cringed because I hadn't thought about how I was going to carry all of the stuff back to the beach house. After sliding the change from my purchase into a front pocket, I managed to situate all three sacks into my arms as someone coming into the store held the door for me to walk out.

    "Smart move, Kenzie," I grumbled to myself as I started the trek back to the beach house.

The sun beat down on me, its brutal rays causing sweat to bead where my tank top was lying on my back. I moved my shoulders around so the material would soak it up instead of it running down my spine, paying way too much attention to my sweat than walking when a rock stuck into the front of my flip flop and almost made me tumble to the ground. Flipping my shoe, the rock went flying, along with one of the paper sacks. "No!" I yelled. The bag crashed to the ground, ripping the sack down the middle. I watched helplessly as the contents spilled all over the sandy grass before me.

As I sat the other two sacks carefully on the ground, the sound of a car stopping in the gravel just off of the road had me hoping that whoever it was would simply ignore my situation. I turned my head towards the vehicle and saw Julian coming around the car to help me.

"Are you okay?" His usual question when it came to me rolled off of his tongue. He ignored the mess of items strung out in the grass and jogged directly to me.

"I'm fine." I waved him off before he could help me up. "Just trying to pick all of this shit up." I motioned to the mess before us.

"Why didn't you tell me you were heading up here? I would have given you the keys or driven you myself. Walking on the side of the road isn't safe." Concern rolled off his tongue with each word he spoke. I did feel bad for not at least leaving him a note, but I wasn't thinking clearly when I jetted out of the beach house in the first place.

"I'm sorry, I wasn't thinking."

We picked up the items that had spilled from the busted bag in silence. The odd thing was, it wasn't an awkward silence like I had thought it would be after that kiss. Was it bad that I didn't feel guilty about the kiss either? Hell, if he hadn't pulled away like he did I probably would have continued on. Guilt was not registering with me for our actions, but in reality…what would I have to feel guilty about? Thomas was gone, and after finding out he cheated on me, I no longer held any loyalty to his memory. Julian wasn't tied to anyone, and neither was I anymore. The one thing that made it hard for me to swallow was how kissing another man felt right to me, guilt wasn't even remotely around to rear its head. What had I become?

Chapter Eight
Julian

MacKenzie was tucked under a throw blanket in the beach chair on the other side of the small plastic table between us. The moonlight illuminated the sky just enough for me to see that she was out cold. Man, MacKenzie Cole was the most beautiful woman that I had laid eyes on in quite some time. The way her emotions played across her face, showing the world just how she felt without a filter, captivated me. The photos Thomas used to carry of her never grabbed my attention like the day I saw her at his funeral. How fucking terrible could I be? Thomas had been my best friend for years, and I was constantly having to fight my feelings for his wife since meeting her at *his* funeral the day we laid to my brother-in-arms to rest. The only reason I didn't feel like a complete asshole regarding it all was because he was living a double life, taking advantage of Kenzie while having a life with this Sara chick that he had knocked up. How can you spend twenty-four hours a day with someone and never know they are living two separate lives? He had everyone fooled.

I chugged down the last little bit of beer in my bottle and picked up the mess we'd made from cooking out on the small grill beside the deck. Kenzie praised me on how good the chicken and shrimp tasted, but little did she know I used to cook whenever I had the chance overseas. It never failed, the guys would vote me as chef almost every time.

My favorite time of day at the beach was at night. The sound of the waves crashing against the bank and the salty breeze that kept it from being too sticky hot was relaxing. In a way it reminded me of Iraq—although I much preferred the sound of the waves crashing to the sound of bullets flying through the air. I propped the door open so I could carry Kenzie into the beach house more easily. As I tucked my arms under her legs she rolled into my chest, snuggling deep into me. She fit perfectly in my arms; I would be a lying bastard if I claimed I didn't enjoy it…it seemed I was enjoying everything about her.

I nudged the door with my foot to get it to close on its own as I carried her towards the master bedroom. The few times I'd crashed I'd slept in that bed, but she deserved a good night's rest after everything she'd been going through. I wasn't about to put her in the guestroom with the smaller bed. With my free hand, I pulled the blankets back and gently lowered her into the center of the bed before covering her up. Her skin was angry from the sun, but she still looked unbelievably beautiful. I shook my head back and forth, trying to shake the images of MacKenzie's body on the beach floating through my mind. I knew the thoughts weren't right, like I knew I shouldn't have kissed her earlier in the day. That moment on the couch, something pulled me to her, an unknown force that beckoned me as close as possible to her, and when she positioned herself towards me as we talked about the heartache we had both been going through, I couldn't help myself. I had to taste her lips against mine.

Quietly clearing my throat, I took one last look at the sleeping beauty in the center of the bed and turned the lamp out before crossing the beach house to the guest bedroom. I dropped my shorts beside the bed and climbed under the thin cotton blanket. With Kenzie being across the house, I didn't want to risk sleeping in the nude like I usually did. The last thing we would need is that elephant in the room.

Sleep escaped me. My mind was jam packed with the memory of the way Kenzie's lips felt moving against my own and how her body melted into my arms. I was losing my fucking mind over her. My body was craving more, but I couldn't be that kind of guy…I couldn't take that step so soon after Thomas' death. It wouldn't be right. A low growl of annoyance left me as I rolled onto my back with my face turned towards the opened door of the guestroom.

I had been tossing and turning for going on four hours when I finally got my ass out of the bed and went into the kitchen for a glass of water. As I stood in front of the fridge, filling the glass from the dispenser on the door, I heard a whimper coming from the master bedroom. MacKenzie was having another nightmare. My heart ached for her because I knew exactly how nightmares could haunt you; I'd had plenty of those myself. Over time they had slowed, only coming around every so often, but when they did they were hellacious. As I chugged down the water Kenzie let out a long sob that echoed through the small beach house. I couldn't just go back to bed and ignore her pain. So instead of doing what I probably should have done, I rounded the corner into the bedroom and flipped on the lamp sitting on the dresser. The covers were bunched down around her waist and her face was contorted into a heartbreaking frown as tears seeped out of the corners of her closed eyes. Her body jerked towards me as she sobbed again so I did the only thing I could think of doing, I slid beneath the covers beside her and pulled her small body into mine.

    She turned towards me while still sleeping and wrapped an arm over my chest. The frown that had been dramatically present subsided as a deep exhale deflated her chest. Her eyelashes fluttered against her cheek as I moved some of her unruly hair from her face. I had planned to leave once her breathing evened out, but her limbs were tangled around me, making it difficult for me to move without waking her. I slid my body down just enough to rest my head against the other pillow so my neck wouldn't end up killing me and closed my eyes. The warmth of her skin against mine was soothing, pushing me closer and closer to sleep as each moment of the time we had spent together played behind my eyelids. The last thing I saw before drifting off to sleep was MacKenzie's beautiful smile as we talked in the parking lot of the grocery store.

Chapter Nine
MacKenzie

My body felt like it was in an inferno as I stirred awake. My hand glided down smooth, defined skin and I snapped my eyes open to see why. The warmth wasn't from the temperature of the room, but from Julian's sleeping body entwined with mine in the bed. My heart raced as I realized that I had no memory of how I ended up in the bed. I gently peeked beneath the covers to make sure he was clothed and I found him in nothing but a pair of boxer briefs, while a certain part of his anatomy was standing tall for the world to see. I quickly dropped the covers and closed my eyes.

Please tell me nothing happened with Julian…

Please tell me nothing happened with Julian…

"You awake?" His deep, sleep-filled voice made the heat from my blushing cheeks go straight to my core. My eyes fluttered open and his lazy smiling face came into view. Stubble had grown overnight across his jawline and his beautiful brown eyes were a bit glassy from waking up, but he looked breathtakingly handsome.

"Yeah." The word came out small as I smiled involuntarily back at him. He made me do things before I could truly think about them, like smiling at him when we woke up in the same bed the night after I didn't even remember going to bed.

I was mentally smacking myself when he reached beneath the covers and adjusted his man parts. "I didn't mean to sleep in here." His admission made the situation even more awkward.

"How…" I started to ask but lost my train of thought.

Julian turned away from me, placed his feet on the floor and stood up. He turned to the side, giving me yet another angle of the bulge he was rocking. Like a moth to a flame, my eyes went directly to it before snapping back up to his. Confusion briefly washed across his face before turning into acknowledgement. "Ugh, sorry." He awkwardly adjusted himself and left the room.

I flopped back onto the pillow and whipped the cover up over my head and groaned, "Way to be awkward as hell, Kenzie." I huffed, pushing the covers off myself and getting out of the bed.

My skin was taut and aching from the over exposure to the sun, not to mention I was still wearing the clothes from the previous day; why I hadn't returned home was beyond me...well, I actually knew why, but I didn't want to fully admit that to myself. A certain man that I had woken up beside had a lot to do with it.

I went about my morning rituals the best I could without my stuff from home--brushed my teeth, washed my face, threw my hair up in a messy bird's nest atop my head, but I didn't have anything to change into. When I came out of the bathroom adjoining the bedroom I had slept in, I found a pair of men's basketball shorts and a cut-off shirt lying on the bed. Julian's thoughtfulness didn't surprise me. I couldn't help the smile that took flight across my lips as I grabbed the clothes and headed back into the bathroom to shower. The warmth of the water burned my burnt skin, but it felt good nonetheless. I wasn't about to complain about the water pressure, or lack thereof, because a shower in general felt amazing.

Washing and scrubbing every crevasse of my body set my skin on fire. The burn of the soap against my sunburnt flesh was horrible. I hadn't been sunburnt in a long ass time, and I didn't plan on getting toasted by the sun again if I had anything to do with it. As I rinsed my hair clean I thought about the kiss Julian and I had exchanged. Was it wrong? Probably. But it felt so right. You can't deny the feelings you have, can you? I surely didn't want to, but my mind kept telling me that he made a mistake, that's why he left me sitting there so abruptly. Life was confusing enough without any added stress from something transpiring between Julian and me. But what can you do when the heart is dead set on something…and I think mine was becoming dead set on him.

I scrubbed my hands up and down my face as I groaned out in annoyance. The battles between your heart and mind were not only tricky, they were a complete bitch! My mind was telling me to keep it clean…a friendship only, but my heart was telling me that I had never felt such a deep connection with anyone as I had with Julian...not even Thomas. Sadness washed over me from being able to develop feelings for another man so easily after losing my husband, who I had been with for many years. But the loss of Thomas was quickly replaced by the betrayal of his infidelity. My parents raised me to believe in marriage, to believe that the vows you take on your wedding day bond you together for eternity. Cheating wasn't even an option. It was a sin. So finding out that Thomas did just that, not only gutted me, but it made me realize that not everybody had the same values as myself. How could he go about his days knowing how he was doing me? Even if Sara knew about his life with me, how could he be okay with that? How could she? I couldn't even remotely grasp the concept of being such a cold hearted person like that to someone. How big of a fool was I for never ever thinking he could shatter me the way he had? Maybe my feelings that had been awoken for Julian were simply from the want and need to feel something for someone again? Maybe I was reaching for straws. Taking a step back, a deep breath was needed to clear my head, but I was unsure how Julian would react to the news of me wanting to take a breather.

 I was unsure about my entire life.

 After my morning counseling session with myself, otherwise known as a shower, I felt like I had made things even more awkward between Julian and myself. I diverted my eyes anytime he looked at me, instead of making eye contact. The tension in the way he carried himself around the kitchen made my heart clench in my chest because it was most likely from my unusual behavior. I grabbed my plate from breakfast and put it in the sink when I bumped into Julian and started sputtering off apologizes like the world was about to end.

"Catch a breath, it's fine." His hands were latched onto my hips so I wouldn't fall. It felt like his fingertips were piercing my skin, not from his strength, but from how hyperaware my body was any time he touched me.

Exhaling a shaky breath I stepped back so that his hands fell from my hips. "Could you take me home?"

Julian's eyebrows rose, "Ugh, yeah…sure…just give me a minute to grab my things." He fumbled with his response as I walked out of the kitchen and into the guest bedroom to collect the few items I had brought with me. Covering my face with my palm I whispered a few select curse words for reacting to Julian the way I had since I'd showered.

"MacKenzie?" Julian called out, snapping me out of my self-pity moment.

"I'm coming!"

Julian was standing with a hand on the knob of the front door, waiting for me so we could head back to Shallotte. My chest ached at the sight of the solemn look on his face where his usual smile was. I was the cause for that, but I couldn't find the strength to tell him why I was having my own internal freak out. It wasn't his fault, it was my own self-doubt, questioning whether I was actually having feelings for Julian or if I was simply trying to fill a void. Julian was too good of a man to just be someone who filled a void.

The car ride home was silent, completely silent, not even the radio was on to help drown out the tension swimming thickly in the air. You know when you think you hear a faint noise because the silence is so loud? That was exactly what was happening in the car. My eyes were firmly planted on the scenery passing by as Julian maneuvered the car down the highway towards home. I wanted so badly to say something, I really did, but I couldn't form a sentence in my head that made enough sense to say out loud. What if he thought I was a complete idiot for thinking he had feelings for me? He hadn't brought up that kiss, so why should I? Distance was the only way to decide my true emotions regarding Julian.

As we pulled into my driveway, I silently let out the nervous breath I had been holding since we had turned onto my road. The car jolted as Julian shoved the gear shift into park. I placed my hand on the door handle and pulled it back to open the door. As I positioned my legs outside of the car to stand up, Julian stopped me with a hand on my arm. "Wait."

My head snapped around towards him as I awaited what he was about to say next. "If I did something wrong, I want to apologize. I never meant to over step any boundaries and me being in bed with you this morning wasn't what you are probably thinking. I heard you whimpering and sobbing in your sleep, so I did the only thing I knew how to do to comfort someone. I held you."

My throat closed off from the emotions bubbling inside of me. I must've had another nightmare and Julian was trying to console me in my sleep. I covered his hand with my own. "Everything's fine." A sad smile barely tipped the corners of my lips as I rubbed his hand, got out of the car, and shut the door behind me. The feeling of Julian's eyes on me as I walked up the front steps to my porch and inside the house was burning a hole through my back. As I shut the door I peeked through the shades on the window beside it. Julian still sat in the driveway with his head resting against the hand he had clenched around the steering wheel. Our relationship was officially complicated.

Trying to keep my mind off of Julian was becoming an insurmountable task. I had cleaned the entire house from top to bottom, leaving myself in a heap of sweatiness lying on my bed. My stomach was howling from hunger like a wolf on the prowl at nighttime. I hadn't eaten since breakfast, and it was well into the afternoon. I knew I needed to eat something or I would find myself sick as hell. Any time I slacked on eating, I usually paid for it with a massive headache, and that wasn't something I wanted to go through.

An unknown melody echoed through my silent house. "What in the world..." I pushed myself off the bed and searched for my phone. Then it hit me. Thomas' cell phone was ringing. I ran towards my bedroom as fast as my tired legs would carry me, dropping to my knees in front of the nightstand beside the bed. Thomas' phone had been tucked away in the top drawer for days; I'd almost forgotten about it. By the time I picked up the phone it had stopped ringing. But the missed call notification was beckoning me to see who had called. I was a glutton for punishment, so I did just that. My hands shook as I pushed the view button, my heart dropped at the words before me: *Missed Call from Sara.*

I pushed myself up from the floor with the cell phone in my hand and those words staring back at me as I searched for my own phone. My heart hammered so hard within my chest that I was sure it would burst through my ribcage at any moment, so I did the only thing I could think of to do, I called Julian.

"Hey…" His soothing voice came through the line.

"Sara called."

"What?"

"Sara called Thomas' cell phone. I don't know what to do!" My voice screeched at the end.

"Did you answer it?" Julian was just about as frantic as I was.

"No!"

"Then why are you freaking out right now?" His voice was calmer than before.

"Hell! I don't know!" I took a couple deep breaths before continuing. "Why would she be calling him?" The voicemail notification popped up on the screen as the phone vibrated in my hand. "She left a voicemail…" My voice was barely above a whisper.

"Put your phone on speaker and check the voicemail." Julian walked me through the steps because it was obvious that I was on the edge of a breakdown.

I did as he instructed and watched the screen of Thomas' phone as the voicemail code automatically dialed into the line. The numbers he used weren't ones I knew, or would have guessed. Then *her* voice came across the line.

"Hey babe, it's me...I'm assuming you're on a mission that doesn't have good reception, but we are missing you like crazy. I need to hear your voice—not just this voicemail message. Thomas Junior is starting to say Dada a little better, hopefully he will be able to fully say it the next time we see you."

Silence hung in the air for a brief moment before Sara continued.

"I know our worlds have been turned upside down from everything, and I hate that you have the worst part to do once you get back to the states. But just think about the future our little family will have here soon. I love you, Thomas Cole. Stay safe and we will see you soon."

The little bit I had eaten for breakfast was about to make a reappearance. Pushing up from the floor, I ran to the bathroom just in time to save myself a mess to clean up. Once my stomach stopped assaulting me, I sat back on the floor and rested my back against the wall directly in front of the toilet. They had named their *son* Thomas Junior...

I pulled my knees up to my chest and buried my head into my hands as I lost the little bit of sanity I was holding onto. Tears streamed down my face as I sobbed until I couldn't catch a breath. Thomas Cole was not the man I had loved, or spent years of my life with. No, Thomas Cole was an evil man who manipulated people's lives—or at least mine—and went about his days with another woman that created the family he apparently always had wanted. MacKenzie Cole was the least important character in the plot of the story he had been writing.

"MacKenzie!"

My name being shouted throughout the house didn't even register to me until I realized that *I* was the only person that was supposed to be in the house. I pulled my head up from my lap and turned towards the door just before Julian stepped into the doorway. His eyes fell on me and they softened; there was no hiding how badly I was shattered. He dropped to his knees before me and pulled me into his strong body. His embrace was warm, comforting. I didn't want to be anywhere else. "You left me on the phone…I wasn't sure what happened so I came. I'm sorry if that's too much, but I couldn't let you deal with what we heard on your own."

I shook my head back and forth before looking up from his chest to his compassionate eyes. "I'm sorry I left you hanging on the phone. I just—I couldn't—"

"Shhh…." Julian rubbed my back soothingly and kissed my forehead. "You don't have to explain, I'm pretty sure I know." His sad eyes were locked with mine as I nodded.

Gathering my emotions the best I could, I stood from Julian's embrace and he followed. Suddenly the bathroom seemed extremely small with the two of us almost chest to chest standing in the center of it. The stream of tears down my cheeks started to subside as the tension between us thickened the air of the room. So instead of tucking and running, I broke the ice.

"Why did you kiss me, Julian?" My voice was breathless, my words just above a whisper, but I knew he was close enough to hear it.

Julian took a step closer until our chests touched, then dropped his forehead to mine. "Because..." he brushed his index finger down my lips, causing them to part. "I had to have a taste of you, even if it was only once." My breathing became erratic as I chewed on my bottom lip. His eyes connected with mine and I did the one thing I never thought I would, I moved forward just enough to press my lips against Julian's.

He cupped my face and moved his lips against mine, flicking the seam with his tongue as he begged for entrance, which I granted. The nerve endings in my entire body burst in full force as our mouths, tongues, and bodies moved together in a passionate rhythm that wiped away all my reservations.

Julian walked us backwards until I felt my body hit the walk-in shower. I groaned from the sudden movement, giving him even more room to devour my mouth. The height difference between us was starting to make things awkward; Julian must've had the same thought because he hoisted me up into his arms so that my legs could wrap easily around his narrow waist, making us the same height. His pelvis ground into my core and I moaned into his mouth. He swallowed it along with his own groans. The situation was getting out of hand, but my body was screaming for me to let it unfold however it was going to while my mind was trying to send up the red flags.

My mind won the battle.

"Julian…" I moaned his name but he didn't respond. "Julian." This time it came out a little firmer instead of sexy. He stopped kissing me and focused his lust-filled eyes on mine. "We need to stop." My labored breaths made it hard to get the words out, but I could tell that he understood where I was going as he closed his eyelids.

"We do," he whispered across my lips, but neither of us moved. Our eyes stayed locked, as well as my legs around his waist. Both of us were waiting for the other to make the first move, but it wasn't happening. We both wanted it…wanted more…but were too afraid to take the leap and go with it. I wanted so damn badly to take that leap.

But instead, I went with a subject change. "How did you get in here anyway?" The question had been hovering in the back of my mind since I saw him step into the doorway of the bathroom.

"Well, when I found the front door locked I jumped the fence to the backyard and shimmed the door open with my credit card. You really need to lock the deadbolt on that door." My legs unraveled themselves from his waist and he took a step back, giving me room to breathe without him filling my lungs.

The awkwardness was back. We were standing in the shower, neither of us knowing what to do next, so I made the first move and walked around him to get out of the bathroom. I could feel him behind me as I went straight into the kitchen and poured myself a glass of water. My throat was as dry as the Sierra desert thanks to our heated moment. My back was to Julian as I heard him open the refrigerator and pull something out. I assumed it was something to drink as well, but I couldn't muster up the nerve to turn around and face him just yet.

"MacKenzie?" My name fell from his lips in a concerned sigh.

"Yeah?" I kept my back to him as I chugged down more water.

"What are we doing?" His question caught me off guard. I hadn't expected him to ask something like that...mainly because I had no idea just what in the hell we were actually doing myself.

Placing the empty glass on the counter, I braced my arms on the edge of it and dropped my head forward while I thought about his questions. I took a deep, lung-burning breath and exhaled as I turned to face him. Julian held a bottle of juice with his hip leaning against the refrigerator a couple feet from where I stood near the sink. The look in his eyes was a nervous one, much like how I was feeling myself. We were walking a line that most people wouldn't agree with, but you couldn't help what your heart tells you to do, could you?

Maybe it was more me being afraid of what others would think. But why should I care? Nothing tied me to Shallotte anymore; I could easily sell the house, pack my things, and move away. "MacKenzie?" Julian's voice broke my inner struggle. I was so caught up in my own internal battle that I had forgotten to reply to him.

"Sorry..." I nervously dropped my eyes to the tile floor and swooped a piece of hair behind my ear before looking back up at him. "I really don't want things to be complicated between us, Julian. I didn't expect for any of this to happen, actually. With Thomas' death, you showing up at his funeral, Sara coming into the mix, and now my growing feelings for you—" The last part slipped from my mouth before I could stop it from happening.

"So you do have feelings for me?" Julian sat the bottle of juice he was drinking on the counter and stalked toward me. I threw a hand up to stop him before he got close enough to throw off my train of thought.

"Of course I do! But is it the right thing right now? It's so wrong. Even if my husband was cheating on me, I still feel like I am betraying him in some weird way. I have so much on my plate that having a good night's sleep is a task I can't even fully accomplish. Thomas hasn't been buried long enough for me to move on, even after all of the bullshit I've found out regarding him and Sara. Hell, for all I know there could be more than just one 'Sara' in his life." My rant was getting the best of me as I fought back the tears that were threatening to overtake my eyes.

Julian's sandy brown eyes were full of regret. What he was regretting I wasn't sure, but I hated seeing that in them. "I didn't mean for any of this to happen either. I hope you understand that." He ran his hands up his face, into his hair and back down again. "If I knew I would feel this way about you, I would have never come here. Not because I don't want to feel this way, but because I would never want to make you feel like you are doing something wrong. That has never been my intention."

My bottom lip noticeably quivered as I worked to control it before Julian saw. Breaking down in front of him for the millionth time was not an option. I couldn't do it. I wouldn't do it. "Neither of us intended for these feelings to happen, Julian. But I think it would be best if we kept our distance for a little while." Julian started to speak but I put my hand up again to stop him. "I'm not saying we can't talk at all, I'm just saying we need to pull the reins in a bit and focus on the other things that are going on, especially me with the Thomas situation. I have to be able to put that chapter to rest before I can move on from it. Otherwise it will feel like I am short handing my future."

"I completely understand." When Julian tried to step closer I didn't stop him, and when his hand cupped my face and his lips pressed against my forehead, my breath caught in my throat. With his face mere inches from mine and his eyes boring into my own he offered one last thing before leaving me breathless, "If you need anything, you know where to find me."

Chapter Ten

Time crawled at a snail's pace. Not that I was wishing my life away, but I needed something to take up the time I was wasting sitting on my ass eating cookies that were making my waist hate me. Sara had called Thomas' phone three other times, leaving one other voicemail, but I couldn't find the strength to listen to the damn thing. If I asked Julian to do it, it would mean us being in the same room after all of the shit from the other night.

Four long as hell days had passed since everything between Julian and I blew up. I found myself staring at Julian's contact in my phone with my finger hovering over the call button, but just before I pushed it, I stopped myself. I hadn't heard much from him, either. A few text messages telling me to have a good day were the extent of it. But I couldn't blame anyone but myself. So after getting my ass out of the bed, into the shower, and clothed in something other than yoga pants, I decided to call a girl I had met during one of the parties on base before the guys had left for tour. Loren and I kept in contact here and there, mainly a random phone call to say hello or a text saying the same. I felt bad for being such a distant friend when we got along great, but I wasn't one to hang out much with anyone. A homebody, I guess you could say. So the moment I pressed Loren's name in my contacts and the line rang, I knew there was no turning back.

"Hello?" Loren answered on the second ring.

"Hey, it's MacKenzie."

"Oh my gosh! I've been meaning to come by and see you. I'm so sorry to hear about Thomas' passing. I can't imagine what you are going through right now." Loren was rambling about the one thing I wanted to avoid talking about. How did I not realize that it would be the topic of discussion?

"I'm doing okay…" The line fell silent for a moment. "Would you want to grab lunch? I need to get out of the house."

"Sure. Where were you thinking?"

"Grant's."

"I love that place! Sounds good to me."

"Okay, then. See you in about half an hour?"

"Can't wait."

The call ended and I instantly started second-guessing the lunch outing. As long as I could steer clear of the Thomas topic everything would be fine. Loren wasn't one to try and pry answers out of you, so hopefully it wouldn't even be brought up after that initial apology for being absent after his death. I wasn't the type to hold judgment against others that didn't acknowledge when life altering moments happened to someone. No one enjoys funerals or death in general for that matter. It makes conversation awkward and sad. I'd rather avoid it myself at all costs so I didn't have any hard feelings for her unintentional disregard after Thomas' death. There were plenty of military personnel stopping by to show their condolences, along with mounds of casseroles being put in the refrigerator, or trashcan depending on who had made it, so another person to add to the pile wasn't that big of a deal.

There wasn't a cloud in the sky as I drove across town to Grant's Deli. I had the sunroof wide open and the windows cracked so the humid breeze could flow in; the smell of the ocean drifting through the air seemed to put me at ease. My hair was pulled back into a messy French braid; it was the easiest hairdo I could go with besides a messy bun, which I had been rocking on way too many occasions. Makeup was yet again at a minimum, which had become the norm for me. That is, *if* I put it on. But going out in public without makeup and crazy hair would give Olivia Jones the ammunition she would need to make the town believe that I had officially boarded the Crazy Train.

As I pulled into the parking lot in front of Grant's Deli, I instantly spotted Loren sitting at a table under a large green-and-white umbrella on the front deck. It was the perfect day to sit outside and catch up, so I was happy that she had picked a patio table. I slid from the front seat, shut the door to my car, and touched the handle to lock it when she spotted me. We both waved as I headed inside the building. You could only reach the deck seating by walking into the Deli and out the side door, but it hadn't always been like that. Apparently customers used to take off without paying for their meals so they took care of that problem in the easiest way by shutting the deck off to outside people.

The noise of laughter and conversation filled my ears as I pushed the door open to make my way through the Deli and out to the deck. The place was always jam-packed full of the regulars, along with tourists that fumbled into the area from Wilmington and other surrounding key spots people visited on vacation. I couldn't help the smile that spread across my face as the guy behind the counter, Grayson, called out to me and waved hello. His grandfather was the one who had founded Grant's Deli, and thirty years later it was still going strong.

"Hey, Grayson!" I waved as I rounded the hostess station towards the door that led out to the deck.

"It's good to see you, MacKenzie. I hope life is treating you well." Grayson's dimples creased his cheeks as he smiled sincerely at me.

"Life has been…interesting, I guess you could say." It was the best way I could sum up the past month. "I'll talk to ya later, Grayson. I'm here to meet a friend."

"Enjoy," he called back as I turned towards the door.

My eyes stopped on the long driftwood bar in the back of the place where they served any type of alcohol one could dream of. Julian was perched on the center stool, chatting away with an older man who was wearing a hat that was decorated in Veteran buttons. I stood for I don't know how long, watching the two of them interact when a brunette walked over to the older man and extended her hand to Julian. He smiled that same gorgeous smile, that he usually gave me, back at her and she took a seat beside the older man. I felt like an intruder watching them interact so I forced myself to look away and walk my happy little ass out to the deck where Loren was probably impatiently waiting for me.

I picked the chair directly across from Loren and pulled my shades down from my head to fully keep the sun out of my eyes. "Sorry, I didn't realize half of the county would stop me to talk." *Way to lie, Kenzie.*

"No problem at all. It's a beautiful day to sit out here and enjoy." Loren's optimism was always shining bright no matter the situation. I guess you could say she was one of those 'glass half full' people. I envied her for that.

Flipping the menu open, I settled as comfortably as possible into the metal chair. It was the only downside about sitting on the deck. Your ass would end up being numb from the lack of cushion before you had your meal eaten. "I am starving." I scanned the plastic covered pages for something that wouldn't make me feel sick as hell after eating.

Turkey Club.

Of course, the turkey club would be the one sandwich my stomach yearned for and my heart ached over. Flashes of the day Julian and I had lunch at my house made me grin and turn my attention to the windows that gave me the perfect view of Julian and the brunette sitting at the bar…

Wait, what?

The old man was missing from the scenario and the song *Hey Jealousy* was blaring in the back of my mind like the soundtrack of the moment. Most people would find it annoying, but I actually found it kind of hilarious. A few light chuckles erupted from my lips; Loren was looking at me with a raised brow, wondering just what in the hell I was laughing at, I'm sure.

"Sorry," I replied and covered my mouth with my hand. "Something inside made me chuckle." Brushing off the reason for my laughter was the easiest way to keep from diving into the subject that was Julian Cooper.

Loren waved me off. "That happens to me all the time." Her singsong laugh made me smile. I needed more people like Loren in my life, especially with all of the Debbie Downer mess that was going on. She seemed to be a breath of fresh air, one that I desperately needed.

"So what's new with you?" I asked as the waitress set our drinks down. Then it dawned on me that I hadn't ordered anything to drink yet.

Loren must've caught the confused look I was giving the glass before me, "I hope you don't mind. The waitress came by while you were inside so I got you a sweet tea."

She's even nicer than I remembered. "Thank you! It's what I was actually going to order." I smiled reassuringly at her.

We fell into easy conversation. Her husband was coming home in less than a month, around the same time Thomas would have been coming home. She didn't linger very long on that topic, probably because she thought it would bring up the pain from the loss of my husband.

Yes, the pain was in fact there...but a different kind of pain was mixed in with it. Like two separate cans of paint swirled together to form a completely new color, but each hue still visible if you looked closely.

    I caught myself looking through the window of the Deli to see if Julian and the brunette were still at the bar, and every time, they were. When the waitress brought our food out, the chatter between Loren and I died off a bit as I focused on my turkey club, but I continued to sneak glances at Julian. He had embedded himself into my life in such a short amount of time. Getting him out of my system to the point of strictly friendship was going to be a task from hell, but Rome wasn't built overnight.

    Movement on the other side of the window caught my attention. Julian and the brunette were both leaving. My heart was racing as I watched them like a creeper. She tilted her head back laughing as Julian smiled widely back at her. They seemed friendly, a little friendlier than I had hoped. When her eyes connected with mine I averted mine towards the sandwich I had ordered. I was pretty sure she had noticed that I was blatantly staring at the two of them. Hopefully she didn't point that out to Julian.

    The chime of the door opening could be heard from where we sat on the deck. My instinct was to look up to see who was leaving, but I had a good feeling I already knew who was walking out that door. I took a huge bite of the club to keep my attention on it and not them when the girl erupted with laughter. *Even her damn laugh is attractive.* Loren could probably hear my eyes rolling on the opposite side of the table.

    "Kenzie?" The sound of Julian saying my name had me setting the Club back on the plate.

Quickly swallowing down the remainder of the large bite I had in my mouth, I turned to face Julian. Not only was he standing there staring at me, but the brunette was right by his side.

"Hey!" A wide smile spread across my face as I gave them a small wave.

"How are you?" Julian wasn't one for small talk, so when he asked a question I knew it was because he honestly cared.

"I'm okay." My smile faltered just a tiny bit, but I knew he saw it from the sadness that washed over his bright brown eyes.

"I hate to interrupt the two of you, but I really have to go." The brunette spoke up, pulling our attention to her. She was rummaging through her bag before pulling out a pen and a small piece of ripped paper, scribbling what I assumed was her phone number on it, and then handing it to Julian. "Give me a call some time." She smiled at him and walked away. Julian's gaze never left mine, seemingly unaware of the girl's departure as she sashayed away. My heart fluttered wildly in my chest.

"It's good to see you." My words came out stronger than I assumed they would be by the rapid beating of my heart and tightening of my throat.

"Aren't you going to introduce me to Mr. Sexy-on-a-stick?" Loren tried to whisper so only I heard, but she failed miserably. I closed my eyes and shook my head in disbelief before I introduced the two of them.

"Julian, this is my friend Loren. Loren, this is Julian, he was Thomas' close friend in the Marines."

Loren nodded in understanding before waving at Julian. "It's nice to meet you, Julian."

"Nice to meet you too, ma'am." Julian's manners were shining through by calling Loren ma'am. He had her swooning like a goofy-ass schoolgirl, but I couldn't blame her.

"I should be going." Julian hooked his thumb back towards where his car was parked as he took a few steps backwards, keeping his eyes locked on me.

I was fumbling with what to say, so I went with the line everyone says when they run into someone they usually didn't want to see, "It was good to see you." Yeah, I felt like the awkward fair-weather friend.

"You too." He smiled and dropped his eyes to the dark brown boots he was wearing and headed for his car.

"Who is Julian and why I am just now seeing him?" Loren all but drooled as she watched him walk away.

"I told you." The annoyance in my voice was more prominent than I had meant for it to be.

"My bad…" she countered.

"Sorry. I didn't mean to sound so…bitchy."

"You're fine," she mumbled between bites of her burger. "But please do tell me who Julian is." She was being relentless, and I had no choice but to tell her a little more than him simply being Thomas' best friend in the Marines.

"Well, Julian and Thomas were in the Marines together for years, but I hadn't ever met him until the funeral. We've been talking a lot and have hung out on a few occasions…nothing big. He's a good guy who apparently doesn't have much, if any, family, because he moved here after being discharged."

Loren leaned forward with her head resting in her hand as she listened to me talk about Julian. "Why was he discharged?"

"He was injured during the raid that Thomas died in."

She let out a gasp I almost didn't hear. "That poor man." Tears began pooling in her eyes so I looked away towards the passing traffic.

"Yeah…" I managed to choke out as I willed back my own tears.

Silence settled in around us. "It's good that you have one another, though. You both lost someone close to you, finding solace in each another will help you heal." I heard what she was saying loud and clear. It made sense, it really did. But if she knew the extent of how our friendship had been unfolding, I wondered if she would have told me the same thing.

We finished our food, paid our bills, and said our goodbyes. She promised to call me more often and I agreed to do the same. Having a friendship with Loren would be nice. Maybe it wouldn't be as close of a friendship as I would like since the secrets and lies in my life wouldn't allow it, but it would still be a good change for me.

Lying on the couch watching a Nicholas Sparks film while going through a second box of Kleenexes wasn't how I had intended to spend the night, but in reality I hadn't intended to spend my night in any certain fashion. As the credits rolled I wiped away the last round of tears that were pouring down my face and gathered all of the used tissues to throw away when the sound of Thomas' phone ringing stopped me dead in my tracks.

Sara was most likely the one calling, since she was the only person who had called his phone since the funeral, so it didn't surprise me when I found her name flashing on the screen once I reached it. What I did next wasn't planned, but I hit the green icon that indicated you wanted to answer the call and held it up to my ear.

"Thomas? Oh, God, Thomas…please be you!" One at a time her emotionally packed words hit me, making my stomach churn with nausea.

I didn't reply.

"Thomas, if this is you and you can hear me...I love you. I hope you're okay. I'm sure service is *horrible* where you are, but I hope you can at least hear what I'm saying."

I couldn't handle hearing her voice; it seemed too intimate, mainly because she was saying those words in that actual moment instead of a past recording of them, but I had heard more than enough for the night. My finger swiped over the end button disconnecting the call, and I

Dishonorable Love

sunk back against the wall behind me to try and steady my erratic breathing. What did I think I would get out of answering that call? Who the hell knows…but something pushed me to do it and as bad as I was regretting it, I knew the time would come that I would end up being face-to-face with that woman so I couldn't let hearing her talk affect me as badly as it was.

I padded into the bathroom and splashed my face with ice cold water from the faucet. After the third round and a soaked shirt, I turned the faucet off and wiped my face dry. I had gone from heartbroken to angry in matter of a few minutes, so when I stomped back into the bedroom and hit her name in the contacts to call her back I had no idea what I was about to do.

"Thomas? Can you hear me?" The hope in her voice infuriated me even more than I had already been.

I was seething as I finally spoke back to the woman who had forever changed my life. "He can't hear you because he is dead." My words dripped with venom as I spat them out at her through gritted teeth and hung the phone up afterwards.

Childish, probably, but I wanted to hurt her. I wanted her to feel the pain I had felt the day I found out Thomas would never be coming home again, and the pain I felt when I found out that he was living a double life with a woman who apparently knew about me. Heartache was a word that didn't even remotely touch the pain ripping apart my heart, splitting my soul, and shattering my bones.

The phone came to life in my hand, showing her name flashing once again. "You're fucking kidding me…" I growled. Quickly answering and holding it to my ear, I was hit with heavy sobs from the other end.

"P—please tell me ho—ow he died."

"You cannot be serious right now!" Her calling back to ask me that question had me blown away. "Answer me this…how did you sleep at night knowing that Thomas' wife was at home in their bed without an inkling that the two of you were screwing behind her back?"

Sara's sobbing became even harder as she mumbled off words I couldn't make sense of until she finally pulled herself together with a long, deep breath. "I know I'm the bad guy to you, but you honestly don't know what Thomas and I had. We have a son! A little boy whose father is no longer living, the least you could do is tell me how he died so I can tell him how we lost his father when he gets older."

My heart stung from the proverbial beating she had given it with her words. Who the hell did she think she was by asking me to feel sorry for her? My nails dug into the flesh of my palm, turning my knuckles white while pulling blood to the surface. Yes, I felt horrible for the boy because he didn't ask to be in a situation like the one his father had put him in, but my heart didn't bleed anything for Sara's feelings. She made a choice by sleeping with a married man and having his child. How could she ask anyone to feel sorry for her?

"Don't you *ever* try to make me feel sorry for you. You knew about me! You took my life and turned it upside down. How could you? If you want to know what happened to Thomas, figure it out your damn self because

I don't owe you a thing." As tears sped down my face I launched Thomas' phone across the room and crumbled onto the floor in a heaping mess of emotions. The sound of it smashing against the floor or wall or whatever the hell it hit hardly registered as I finally allowed myself to grieve, surrendering to the heartache that had threatened to swallow me for so long.

    MacKenzie Cole was no longer the strong woman who wore her heart on her sleeve for those that she loved. She had been torn to shreds on more than one occasion, leaving a shell of the person that she used to be. In her wake was someone that was done taking the punches that life kept dishing out. It was time to break in her own set of gloves and start to fight for her life.

Chapter Eleven

What you do out of anger is never a good thing, there are almost always repercussions. Thomas' phone wouldn't turn back on after I launched it across the room. Not to mention the moment I started to come down from the angry adrenaline pumping through my veins, I felt a tiny bit bad for going off on Sara to the extent I'd done; even if the bitch did try to put a guilt trip on me by dangling their son in my face. My mind was a giant cluster fuck; one minute I was furious, and the next I was fighting back a sea of tears from my heartache. How in the hell was someone supposed to heal after all of the madness that I had been through? My gut was telling me that it wasn't close to being over, even after Sara found out about Thomas' untimely death the way she had. Most people wouldn't have called right back, or at least I didn't think I would have, but she did. It was only a matter of time before I heard from her again, I was sure of that.

Mounds of boxes were taking up my home as I started to go through the items that were Thomas' or reminded me of him. I had come to the point of needing to part ways with it all so that I wouldn't be constantly reminded of the life that I had loved and found out to be a lie. Some might say I was going overboard too soon, but everyone deals with life's traumas in different ways. Getting rid of his stuff was one step in stitching up the gaping hole in my soul.

It dawned on me as I shifted through the safe in our bedroom closet that Thomas kept important and private documents in his study above the garage. I hadn't been up there since he had left for his last tour of duty, except to clean. Every single thing that was housed in that room was Thomas', and I had no idea what kind of secrets could possibly be hiding in there.

We kept the key to the study in a small bronze box on the mantel in the living room, and as I stared at it sitting dead center in the bottom of the mostly empty box, I started to question my resolve. *Am I ready for this?* There would never be a time that I would be one hundred percent ready to unravel my husband's secret life, but I had to start somewhere. There was never a better time than the present to take the first step.

A staircase just inside the garage, next to the door to the house led up to the study. I unlocked the door and pushed it open. Swallowing the lump in my throat I flipped on the light, illuminating all the things that were Thomas Cole. A large, wooden frame that housed his medals and a small American flag hung above the desk with two large cherry wood bookshelves on each side. The shelves were full of framed photos of him with his Marine buddies, family photos, and other memorabilia from each of his tours. He was good about bringing home a couple items from wherever he was stationed so that he would never forget the time he spent there, and so he could share it with me in a way that wasn't just words. A sharp pain radiated through my heart as I moved around the study, taking in all of the memories of Thomas that he not only loved, but I did as well. The little bit of my heart that hadn't crumbled was beginning to.

    I took a seat at his desk and opened the laptop that sat neatly before me. It was dead. I leaned over the top of it and found the cord sitting a couple inches away from the plug-in. I connected the two and waited a couple seconds before hitting the power button again. This time it powered to life.

    I blew out a heavy breath as I chewed the remainder of my index fingernail. You would think I wouldn't have been nervous about what I could possibly find, especially after finding out about Sara. Was there really anything worse than discovering that your husband was a cheating bastard after being hit with his death not even a month before? I shook my hands and fingers out as the password screen sprang to life.

    Shit.

    Hovering the mouse over the question mark so that it would give me a hint, the word *forever* popped up. "Well that helped me a lot…" I chewed on my bottom lip as I wracked my brain on what word could possibly be associated in Thomas' mind with the word forever. It sure as hell couldn't be marriage, but my comical side typed the word in anyway.

    Denied.

    "Go figure." I rolled my eyes.

Cradling my head in my hand I tapped my finger tips against the side of my face as I stared at the password screen. "What did you make as your password, Thomas?" My eyes scanned all of the articles around his desk, the décor of the room, along with the photos on the bookshelves when it hit me.

Honor.

Thomas always preached about honor and how much it meant to the military. How did I not think of it sooner? I quickly typed the word and pushed the enter button on the keyboard as I held my breath. What was only a couple seconds seemed like an eternity as the screen morphed from the password lock screen to the desktop.

"Yes!" I smiled widely to myself as I sat up straighter and pulled the chair closer to the desk so that it was easier to type.

The desktop was decorated with the Marine emblem and slogan. Thomas lived and breathed his career as a Marine and I was proud of him for it. Even if I didn't know the person he truly was, I knew he loved his country and would do anything to try and keep the people of it safe. Except he hadn't kept me safe…he had been the one enemy to infiltrate my heart, burying a grenade deep into my soul and watched it detonate, shattering me into a million pieces, leaving behind the shell of a woman.

Nothing on the laptop caught my attention so I closed it and sat back in the comfy dark leather computer chair. "What am I doing?" I rose from the chair and headed back down into the house, grabbed some empty boxes, and stomped back up the staircase to the study. It was time to box away all of the remnants of Sergeant Thomas Cole.

    The bookshelves were my first victims. I packed all of the items, even the photos of the two of us, into two large boxes before moving on to the filing cabinet that was tucked away against the far right wall. I pulled a smaller box over and sat crisscrossed on the floor. Since the filing cabinet was only two drawers high, I started with the top one. Yet again, nothing stood out as I rummaged through old copies of bills we had paid and receipts of purchases Thomas had made. It wasn't until I reached the bottom drawer that my suspicion was piqued. A small slip of paper had the combination to something scribbled on it in Thomas' handwriting with an address directly below it. The address wasn't one I knew off the top of my head, so I quickly jumped back onto the lap top and searched exactly where it was.

    It took me a while to pinpoint what was at the address on the slip of paper because the building had recently been sold. It had been vacant since it was built three years prior, but it was currently a gym that offered storage lockers to the people who had memberships there. Thomas had never mentioned having a membership at that gym, let alone a storage locker. I left the information pulled up on the laptop and went back to rummaging through the filing cabinet to see what else I could find, but came up empty-handed. It looked like visiting the gym was the next item on my to-do list.

    After loading my car down with a few boxes of Thomas' things to drop off at a local donation center, I typed the gym's address into my GPS as a stop on my way back home. The sun was shining through my opened sunroof as I maneuvered down the empty roads of Shallotte. Between two and three were the best times to drive around town without hitting much traffic, thanks to most people being at work. Not that Shallotte had lots of traffic in the first place.

    A large sign that read Iron Gym in black and red adorned the front of the building. It was hard to miss it. The parking lot was fuller than I had anticipated for two-thirty on a Thursday, but I pulled in and parked anyway. The slip of paper was pushed deep into a front pocket of my jean shorts and it felt like it was burning a hole through them. My nerves were beginning to get the best of me with each step I took towards the front door; the moment I pulled it open and was hit with the noise of weights and loud music I almost turned around and ran back to my car, but the sound of a man calling my name stopped me from doing so.

    "Hey, MacKenzie!" I turned my head to the left as I stepped into the building and found Grayson standing behind the front desk with a huge smile spread across his face, the same Grayson who worked at Grant's Deli for his grandfather.

    "Grayson!" I smiled back as I stepped up to the desk. "I had no idea that you worked here as well as the deli."

    "Yeah, the deli doesn't pay me as much as I need, so I got this as a second job while I'm finishing up college." He leaned his broad arms onto the counter. I hadn't realized just how fit he was, mainly because he stood behind a tall counter at the deli with a baggy polo on. "Here to join the gym?"

"No..." I drew in a deep breath to calm my racing heart, trying to keep my fumbling words at bay. I wasn't sure dealing with someone that knew Thomas and myself was a great idea, but pretty much everyone in the town knew who we were, especially after his death. "I'm actually here because Thomas had a storage locker that I need to clean out."

The happy expression on Grayson's face faltered, revealing a smidge of sadness intertwined. "Let me check the system to make sure they haven't already boxed his stuff up for mailing." He started typing on the keyboard with his eyes fixated on the screen. I looked around at the mixture of people using various machines and weights. "It hasn't been cleaned out yet. I can show you where it is if you want to go through it."

I nodded. "Thank you."

Grayson rounded the desk. "Right this way." He walked and I followed.

We passed through the first set of doors that led into what looked like a waiting area with four doors in front of it that were labeled for different tanning beds. He took a right and we passed through another door that went directly into a large room that had numerous storage lockers. Some were small while others were taller than me. I followed in silence as Grayson guided me to the locker numbered two fifty-eight. "Here's the locker." He pointed towards it and grinned sadly at me. It was a medium-sized one, about the same height as the ones kids had in high school.

"Thank you, Grayson."

"If you need anything, let me know, okay? I mean it." He touched my shoulder with his hand and smiled sadly.

"I appreciate that." Grayson nodded and walked away, leaving me with the dreadful storage locker.

I pulled the piece of paper that had the combination to the lock on it from my pocket and fumbled with it. The first two tries were a failure. I had no idea how the damn thing worked, but when they say the third time's the charm it was indeed, as the combination worked and the lock gave way.

The lock clicked loudly in the room as I removed it from the locker and took a deep breath. "Why do I feel like I'm about to open Pandora's Box?" I mumbled to myself as I pulled the tab up on the locker and opened the door. There wasn't much inside: a large duffle bag, some tape for his hands, bandages, a set of boxing gloves, and a zippered leather binder. A small crate was leaning against the wall so I grabbed it and placed the bandages, wrapping tape, and gloves in it. Grayson would be getting those since I had no need for them.

I wrapped my hands around the handles of the duffle bag to pull it out and was surprised by the weight of the thing. The way the outer shell concaved made it look to be light, not heavy. I jerked back once, twice, and a third good time before it flew out of the locker and I went crashing to the floor on my ass. "Son of a…" the sting of my butt hitting the concrete so hard stung like a hammer hitting your thumb. I took a moment before getting up. The duffle bag was on its side as I tipped it back over.

Big mistake.

The zipper had come open and the contents had spilled partially out onto the floor. I gasped as stared at what had been stored in the duffle bag and quickly dropped to my knees to cram it all back inside so I could try to seal the damn thing. Tugging on the zipper until the bag was closed, I hoisted the duffle bag up onto my shoulder, grabbed the leather binder from the top of the locker and shut the door. I had to get the hell out of dodge before someone stopped me, so I raced to the exit with the heavy ass bag hanging from my shoulder.

The moment I barreled through the second door into the main part of the gym, Grayson spotted me and quickly came over to where I was heading for the door. "Here," he reached for the bag. "Let me help you with that."

I quickly latched my hand down on the handles to hold it securely to my shoulder. "It's okay, Grayson, I've got it." I forced a friendly smile and kept walking.

"Well, at least let me grab the door for ya." He hurried to the large glass door and held it open so that I could pass through.

"Thank you, Grayson!" I called back over my shoulder as I raced to my car.

I popped the trunk and tossed the duffle bag inside before slamming it shut. My chest was heaving from not only exertion, but stress too. "What the hell, Thomas!" The words ripped from my lungs before I could stop them. Afraid someone might think I was crazy, I quickly surveyed the area, my eyes darting around parking lot, before slumping into my car and driving off.

The entire ride home was a blur. My mind was working on overdrive after seeing the contents of that duffle bag. I was at a loss for words, along with a loss of just where in the hell it all came from. I threw the car in park and hauled ass inside as fast as I possibly could, locking the front door behind me and leaning against it for support. The duffle bag hit the floor with a thud, and I stared at it, my chest heaving and on the verge of dying for something to drink. I pushed off the door and frantically walked to the refrigerator and grabbed a beer. It wasn't the time for the hard stuff, but I needed something to take a wee bit of the edge off that was weighing down on me.

Twisting the cap off of the bottle, I pressed the cool glass to my lips and turned it up, swallowing every bit of the beer before taking a breath. "Ahhh…." I sighed and tossed the empty bottle into the trash. My taste buds begged for another, but I refrained from grabbing one as I made my way back into the living room where the duffle bag sat, beckoning me to open it again.

I stood with my hands on my hips staring down at the charcoal grey bag. "What have you done, Thomas?" I repeated a couple times as I pushed the heavy bag with my foot over towards the sitting area. Flopping down on one of the couches with the bag between my legs on the floor, I bent down and unzipped it. Stacks of one hundred dollar bills, along with fifty dollar bills, stared back at me. My nerves were shot, and the level of adrenaline pumping through my blood stream was making my entire body shake. I wanted to count it to see exactly how much it was, but then again I was afraid to touch any of it. My fingerprints were already on the bag, so if it was illegally obtained I was already royally screwed.

My first instinct was to call Julian and tell him to get his ass over to my house, but instead I reached inside the duffle bag and began pulling each bundled stack out one at a time. From the looks of it, I was going to be counting it for way longer than I had ever spent counting money.

Numerous minutes and close to three hundred thousand dollars later my stomach was churning while I tried my best to hold back everything I had eaten during the day. To say I was sick was an understatement. Every inch of my body felt like it had been run over and back again at least fifty times. I was on the brink of tears when I finally picked up my cell phone and shot Julian a text asking him if he could stop by. As I anxiously awaited his response I sat there staring at the stacks of money on my coffee table. I had never seen that much cash in my entire life. My phone buzzed beside me as Julian's response popped up in our text thread.

Julian: Yeah, I'll be there in a few.

My palms were clammy and my heart was on the verge of bursting through my ribcage, not only from the money but from the fact that Julian was on his way over. I was pretty damn sure that my body was about to give out from all of the stress and the rollercoaster of emotions I had been experiencing. Something had to give…

"Did you rob a fucking bank?" Julian all but yelled as I quickly shut and locked the front door behind him.

"Seriously? Do I look like I could rob a damn bank?" I shoved his shoulder as we both stepped closer to the mounds of money on the coffee table.

"How much is that exactly?"

"Two hundred and ninety thousand."

"Where in the hell did you get that, Kenzie?" The accusation in his voice was palpable. I couldn't believe that he would accuse me of robbing a bank. If I was the robber type I sure as hell wouldn't have told him about it after the fact.

"First off, don't talk to me like I stole this shit, because I didn't." I pointed my index finger at him. "You should know me better than that, Julian! Come on!" I huffed.

Julian exhaled a long breath and closed his eyes. Once he opened them again they had softened. "I'm sorry." An apologetic smile tipped the corner of his lips. "Where did it all come from?"

"You might want to have a seat." I gestured towards the couch, but Julian shook his head no.

"Just hit me with it." He crossed his arms over his chest as he waited for me to spill the story behind all of the cash.

"I was boxing up Thomas' stuff to donate when I decided to tackle the study upstairs. I don't go up there much because it was always his place. I was digging through the filing cabinets and getting rid of all the unimportant stuff when I found a slip of paper that had a combination and an address on it.

Julian covered his face with one of his hands and groaned. "Please tell me you didn't go by yourself."

Completely ignoring his question I continued. "I searched the address online and found that it was a gym that offered storage lockers so I did what anyone else would do, I went to the place to see just what in the hell Thomas had stored there." I shrugged my shoulders nonchalantly. "That," I motioned towards the stacks of cash. "is what I came home with."

"You carried all of that cash out of the building without anyone stopping you?" Julian looked at me like I had grown an extra head.

"No!" I face palmed. "It was in that duffle bag," I pointed to the bag lying on the floor. "There were a few other items I left at the gym; boxing gloves, bandages, and so on, but that bag and a leather binder came home with me." The thought hit me that I hadn't had the chance to look inside the binder. But I wasn't sure if it was a good idea to bring it up to Julian, knowing he would want to see it, so I kept that tiny bit of information to myself so that I could investigate its contents later on my own.

"What was in the binder?" He hit me with the question I knew was coming.

"It was empty."

Lie, lie, lie.

I kept my best poker face on as I waited for the subject of the cash to come back around, and thankfully it did. "What are you going to do with all of this cash?"

"I honestly have no fucking clue," I huffed as I flopped down on the couch and stared at the insane amount of cash stacked on the coffee table. "That's why I asked you to come by. I thought you would have some kind of idea what to do with it."

Julian took a seat on the couch opposite me, much like the night we had argued about music and drank quite a few beers. He scrubbed his hands up and down his face before leaning over and bracing his forearms against his thighs. "I—" He started to say something but stopped and shook his head back and forth.

"Whatever you were going to say, say it." Julian wasn't one to keep things to himself. He let you know exactly how he felt about a situation without holding back. But for some reason, he was staying quiet.

"I don't know what to say." A laugh that was far from humorous left him. Pausing for a moment, he leaned forward and picked up a stack of hundreds. Flipping it over a couple times he then fanned through the bills that were still wrapped in the yellow money wrapper indicating that it was a stack of ten thousand dollars. "They're real."

The thought of them being fake didn't even cross my mind. "That's…uh…good I suppose."

"I honestly don't know what to do here, MacKenzie." Julian rarely used my full name, but when he did I knew it was pretty serious. "I feel like we should tell the police about this, but I don't want it to blow back on you."

I jerked back like he had slapped me. What had he meant by it blowing back on me?

"Don't look at me like I kicked your puppy." He could see right through me. "I didn't mean you were involved in gathering all of this money, I meant that they would investigate you. Your entire life and what all happened with Thomas. His infidelity would be on full display for the entire world to see, not to mention whatever else they can stir up."

"Why would they do all of that?" My nervous stomach was making me sick.

"Because Thomas was a Sergeant in the Marines is why. It would become a headline in no time. Do you want the world to know about something you don't fully know about yet?"

Julian was right. There was no way I could take the money to the police. Everything that I knew about the lies Thomas had lived would be blown wide open, and there was no telling what would arise from the ashes. "So what do I do?" I pushed up from the couch and paced the floor behind us. My hands clasped against the top of my head with my elbows out as I forced myself to steadily breathe.

Julian pulled me to a stop by placing his hands on my waist. I hadn't even realized he had moved until we were merely inches apart. His minty breath danced across my face as he spoke, "First, you need to take a deep breath." I did as he asked. "Now, let's put the money back in the bag and put the bag somewhere that you find to be safe."

"Okay." I dropped my hands from my head, brushing his hands that were still gripping my waist with my fingertips on their way down to my sides. The feeling that settled in my core had my heart thumping wickedly within my chest. The connection I felt with Julian was unlike any I had experienced before, and pushing him away would be an inevitable task as long as we were around one another.

After what felt like an eternity of staring into each another's eyes, Julian took a step back. I watched as his hands dropped to his sides and the left corner of his lips tipped up just slightly in a small smile that vanished quickly as he moved past me and started loading the money back into the duffle bag. Without saying another word, I followed his lead. It only took a few minutes to get the money back in the bag and zip it shut, then Julian followed me up the staircase in the garage to the study.

The lights came to life as I flipped the switch just inside the door. I had left the study a complete and utter mess. "You weren't lying about boxing stuff up," Julian commented on the disarray.

Some boxes were stacked on top of one another while two others were half full of stuff from throughout the room. One was designated for paperwork, while the other held personal items and awards Thomas had received over the years. Julian walked around the room before stopping at that box and staring at its contents. "You're getting rid of all of these?" He didn't bother looking up at me as he asked.

"I don't want any of it." It was easier to admit than I had thought.

All things Thomas Cole were tarnished to me. Where they used to hold honor and pride, they held a heavy reminder of the man I had once thought he was; before I found out he was as far from that man as anyone could be. So any reminders of him were laced with a helluva lot of heartache and a failed marriage that I didn't even realize was failing.

"Maybe you should get a storage unit. You can put all of the things in there and later on down the road decide what you want to do with it all. Making decisions while under a lot of stress usually turns up being a mistake."

Julian was trying to be the voice of reason yet again, but I wasn't feeling it. My brows furrowed as I shook my head back and forth, letting him know I wasn't agreeing with him before I actually spoke the words. "Naw, I honest to God don't want any of it. And why in the hell would I want it later on down the road?" I placed my hands on my hips. "No matter how much time passes I will always feel anger and heartache when it comes to him. I spent too many years of my life with a man I loved only to find out he didn't love me as much as he proclaimed on our wedding day, if he even loved me at all. I don't want any inkling of a reminder of this heartache in the future. I just want to move past it all and find my happiness."

"Avoiding it won't make you feel better."

"How in the hell would you know?" My words echoed through the room, the tone dripping with venom as I tossed my hands up in the air.

Julian's eyes narrowed as his jaw clenched tightly. He ran his hands roughly through the closely cropped brown hair that adorned his head. "Do you honestly think you are the only person who has dealt with heartache?" The anger in his voice sent a chill through my body. "Well? Do you, Kenzie?" He yelled even louder, causing my eyes to flood with tears and my bottom lip to quiver, but he didn't stop there. No, he kept yelling at me until the truth about the redhead in the photo at the beach house was thrown into the conversation.

"Heartache is a part of life, MacKenzie! Try being thousands of miles overseas when you receive a letter from the man your fiancée is fucking with photos of the two of them in compromising positions. Try having to go home after being gone for almost twelve months to find she up and left the home the two of you had owned together, leaving all of the bills piling up and not even a fucking bed to sleep in. It's a helluva lot easier when the person isn't alive, you don't have to run into them every time you turn around like I did with Danielle and that sorry motherfucker."

Julian's words hit me hard in the face, chest, and heart. Tears slipped out of my eyelids and raced down my cheeks as I listened to the crappy hand life had dealt him. The one thing that hurt worst of all was hearing him say that I was pretty much lucky that Thomas was dead so I wouldn't have to see him and Sara together. I knew it shouldn't have enraged me like it did because the loss of my husband didn't sting as much as it had when I first found out about her, but the fury racing through me from Julian speaking to me the way he had sent me straight over the edge. "Get the hell out of my house, Julian!"

Julian stepped back in shock as my angry outburst registered with him. "Are you serious?" His eyes narrowed as he awaited my response.

"Please," I hiccupped as the last bit of the wall I had up to hold my emotions at bay crumbled, "just leave!" I screamed as angry tears flooded my eyes, making it hard to see clearly.

I felt him step closer to me before I could fully see him; I took a step back. "I'm sorry I got so upset." Julian was being sincere, but I was hurt too much to accept his apology.

"Just go…" My shaky plea was the last thing I managed to say as I crumbled onto the floor beside the filing cabinet in a heaping mess of tears.

The sound of the door closing let me know Julian had left without another word.

Chapter Twelve

I wiped away the last remainder of tears from my cheeks. My body and mind were beyond exhausted so dragging the duffle bag behind the computer desk was the only option for me. This way it wouldn't easily be seen if someone was in the study. My reaction to Julian created a pain deep in my chest, but my pride wouldn't allow me to contact him. I had no idea how long ago he'd left, my cell phone was still inside the house and the study had no clock. After securing the duffle bag behind the desk, I packed up a few more of Thomas' things and decided to make myself a hot bath in the spare bathroom since the master bath didn't have a bathtub in it.

My eyes burned from the massive amount of tears I had shed as I flipped the light off in the study and locked the door shut behind me. I turned to walk down the steps to go back into the house and stopped dead in my tracks. "What are you doing?" I crossed my arms over my chest and waited for his response.

Julian jumped up from the steps, "I didn't want to leave with you so upset with me so I gave you space."

I descended the stairs and was going to walk right on by him, but he put his arm across the staircase so I couldn't pass. "Julian," I warned.

"I don't like you being upset with me, MacKenzie. I'm sorry for being a dick earlier...you beating yourself up about the shit Thomas put you through just struck a nerve today."

"Well, I don't want to be the person to *strike* a nerve for you, Julian." I tried to move his arm so I could pass but he moved to the center of the stairs and held my hands in his.

"You're taking it wrong. I was trying to make you see that you aren't the only person who has been left with the shit end of a stick. I thought Danielle was it for me, but she was actually just the beginning. She scarred me pretty good..."

"I can tell," I mumbled and he shot me a warning glance.

"Today's the anniversary of me finding out the truth about Danielle," Julian blurted out.

I hadn't expected that. "I'm sorry."

"Why are you apologizing?" Julian shook his head back and forth, still holding my hands.

"I felt like I should for the way I yelled back at you."

Julian gently rubbed his thumbs under my eyes, "They're swollen," he said, and then pulled me against his chest, wrapping his arms around my back. I snuggled deep into his chest as he spoke again. "Everyone has scars from their past, I don't want to be one of yours, Kenzie. I want to be someone that brightens your day, someone whose name instantly makes you smile. I'm sorry for making you cry and being a pompous asshole earlier, you didn't deserve that—you never deserve to be treated like that, and I'm ashamed of my actions."

Julian's words had tears pooling in my eyes once again, not from anger but from happiness. "I know you're a good man, you don't have to justify yourself to me, Julian. Just like the scars everyone has, everyone also has bad days and moments that send them over the edge no matter how hard they try to fight them. But thank you for apologizing…and I'm sorry as well." I gave him a little squeeze and he did the same to me. I felt comfortable in his embrace, like everything around us wasn't a bother, and we were exactly where we were meant to be.

Taking a step back Julian grabbed my hands. "Did you get everything taken care of in there?" He nodded towards the door of the study.

"Yeah, I did a little more packing, too."

"I was beginning to wonder if you were ever going to come back out."

I laughed as we headed down the stairs and into the house. "I had no idea you were still here."

Julian pulled the door to the garage closed behind him. "I figured if you knew you'd for sure run me off."

With a full-blown smile on my lips I laughed. "You're probably right."

"I know I'm right," Julian teased, leaning against the counter beside me.

"Do you now?" I teased back by moving so close that our lips were almost touching.

Julian's voice dropped an octave, "Don't start something we can't finish." His statement danced across my lips, almost like it was begging me to defy him, and start the something he warned me not to. And boy did I want to start it. Instead I gave him a little shove and walked away laughing.

"What happened to this?" I turned back around to see what Julian was talking about and found him holding Thomas' lifeless cell phone.

"Well…" I rocked back on my heels. "I kind of got angry and threw it at the wall."

Julian laughed. "Do I need to put you in anger management classes?"

"Hey now…" I paused, deciding whether or not it was a good idea to tell him about my conversation, or should I say the yelling spree that transpired between Sara and me. "To be honest with you, I smashed it against the wall because I talked to Sara."

"You did what?" Julian's mouth almost hit the floor with shock.

Squeezing my eyes closed, I let the secret conversation between Sara and myself out of the bag. "She called the other night and I answered it. Not sure why, but I did. She kept calling out for Thomas because I didn't say anything at first, but that's when I told her he was dead."

Julian gripped the counter, "MacKenzie…"

"What!" My eyebrows stretched up my forehead. "I couldn't listen to the woman sobbing over *my* husband. She had no idea that he was gone, nobody had told her. I wonder why that is…" When Julian didn't respond, I did so for him. "Because no one knew she existed is why! She tried to tell me I was being cold for not considering her feelings because they have a son together." I began pacing the kitchen while throwing my hands around in the air as I continued on my rant. "Can you believe the nerve she has? She tried to put a guilt trip on *me*." My chest heaved from the anger coursing through me just thinking of my conversation with that woman.

Julian was standing before me with his hands on my shoulders and his eyes peering into mine. "Take a deep breath." I inhaled so deeply, my lungs burned before I slowly exhaled. "Good." Julian let go of my shoulders and put some distance between us.

"What are you doing?"

"I moved so you don't try to slap me for what I'm about to say." *Definitely don't like the sound of that.* "Put yourself in her shoes, even if you knew about the wife, you've built this connection with a man who was supposed to be leaving her for you. The two of you were expecting a baby, which would be his first child. But instead of him being overseas fighting for his country, he's six feet under from a raid gone wrong and you had no clue about any of it."

I wanted to be angry at what Julian was saying, but I couldn't be. He made a good point about me putting myself in her shoes. You can't help who you love, but you can go about being with that person in a better manner than Thomas had done to me. Sara was shattered from the loss of a man, just like I was. Except I knew as soon as it happened, and she was only finding out after the fact. Guilt pained me as I thought about how I had treated her, but there was no way I could contact her again to apologize because Thomas' phone was destroyed.

"You're right," I admitted.

"I am?" Julian questioned. "I am." He smiled.

"Why do you sound so surprised that I agree with you?"

"Because I am surprised." Julian ran a hand through his hair. "I was expecting another fight. Mainly because most women wouldn't see the truth of the matter. A scorned woman is not something you want to mess with."

"Did you just call me scorned?" I placed my hands on my hips.

"I was saying in general…not you." He quickly back-pedaled his statement, not knowing I was only kidding with him until my smile spread widely across my face, and he relaxed as he realized it. "You're playing dirty." Julian smiled as he shook a finger at me.

"You know I'm only messing with you."

"Oh, I know." The double meaning of his response didn't go unnoticed by me.

Julian was sound asleep on the couch as my legs rested in his lap. A throw blanket was draped over my lower half, covering him as well. We had snuggled together underneath it as we watched television and ate Chinese takeout. I hadn't expected him to stay most of the night, but he fell asleep looking all peaceful so I had no choice but to let him, right?

I was selfishly digging around the leftover bit of shrimp lo mein for pieces of shrimp while some horrid infomercial about a new workout DVD played over and over again. The remote was on the other side of Julian who looked way too comfortable with his head resting back against the cushions and his hands on my ankles for me to move to get the remote, so I didn't bother.

A night on the couch like we'd had made me wonder what the future held for me. Could I have a love that burned so fiercely it would never go out? Was that a true possibility? What I had with Thomas was love, I never doubted that, but it wasn't the type of love that made you yearn for that person every waking hour of the day. *That* kind of love was what my heart was searching for. *That* kind of love was what my body and soul needed to become whole again.

I sat the almost empty box on the floor since I couldn't reach the coffee table and slid my feet out of Julian's lap. My bladder was about to pop. I tiptoed to the spare bathroom, trying my best not to wake Julian or bump into anything faintly illuminated by the glow from the television. Even though I knew I'd have to wake him up at some point to go home, I wasn't ready to do that just yet. After using the restroom and washing my hands, I quietly opened the door and silently maneuvered my way back to the couch. Julian was still sound asleep, just not in the same position he was in before. He had somehow managed to lie completely down on the couch with the throw blanket wrapped around his waist. I pulled his tennis shoes off one by one and grabbed a bigger blanket from the hall closet to cover him up with for the night. There was no need for him to drive home, especially seeing just how tired he must've been. With one last look at Julian sleeping soundly, I flipped the television off and went to tuck myself in for the night.

Chapter Thirteen
Julian

My body was bound from the waist down and felt like it was on fire. I gripped the material and pulled, opening my eyes to take in my surroundings. A blanket had somehow managed to wrap my legs tightly together, along with rendering me motionless because the ends of it were shoved down beneath the couch cushions; grey cushions to be exact…I didn't have a grey couch. I yanked the blanket from the cushions and quickly unwrapped myself as I took in the room I was sleeping in. MacKenzie's living room; it was all beginning to come back to me.

I hadn't meant to fall asleep, let alone stay the night. Apparently she hadn't wanted to wake me, or she tried and failed. The past four nights had been sleepless ones. Between her running through my mind, the feel of her in my arms, the taste of her lips on mine, and the smell of her hair. I sounded like a love sick fool, but I couldn't fucking help myself.

Grabbing the collar of my shirt I pulled it off; there was no way I could fall asleep in Kenzie's hot as hell house again. The clock on the cable box below the television read almost twenty after five in the morning. Not sure what time I had fallen asleep, but she had cleaned up our dinner mess and tucked me in. I felt like a jackass for falling asleep on her, but however many hours I'd slept was more than needed. I felt refreshed for once, not like a sluggish sloth. Lying back down on the couch I stared up at the ceiling, thinking about Kenzie and everything she was dealing with. It wasn't fair of me to put her in the position I had with my feelings towards her. Being selfish had never been in my blood until her, and selfish was the only thing I wanted to be. I wanted her to be mine, to be the woman that stood by my side day in and day out, and vice versa. But I was afraid that she wouldn't be able to fully take that step, not because of Thomas' death per se, but because of who I was to him. We were brothers-in-arms, together every single day while overseas. It was a hard pill to swallow for me, so I could only imagine how big of a pill it was for her.

Instead of lying on the couch until MacKenzie woke up, I decided to preoccupy my mind by finding something to cook for breakfast for the two of us. It was the least I could do after unexpectedly crashing on her couch. She wasn't the best at grocery shopping, at least that is what I had gathered after running into her in the grocery that one time, but I was lucky enough to find a dozen eggs and some turkey bacon, along with some fresh fruit and a tomato. Either she was too stressed to be grocery shopping when I had run into her or she was trying to start a clean eating regimen, because her entire refrigerator and freezer were full of healthy foods.

Gathering the items I needed, I scrambled the eggs and cooked the turkey bacon. I washed and cut up the fruit and the tomato and sat the table. The sound of the water running somewhere in the house let me know that Kenzie was awake. I quickly placed the food on the table, and then grabbed the orange juice from the refrigerator and two glasses from the cupboard just as she passed the threshold into the kitchen. Her hair was wild, but sexy.

"You cooked?" A smile spread across her face, brightening her flawless skin even more than it already was.

"Good morning to you, too." I smiled back. "It's the least I could do. I hadn't meant to fall asleep on you last night, let alone stay the full night here."

"It's fine." She waved me off as her eyes trailed down my chest and I realized I was still shirtless.

Placing the glasses on the table I motioned for Kenzie to sit and excused myself. I slid my shirt back on and headed back into the kitchen as she was loading her plate with eggs. "I hope you like your eggs scrambled."

She took a big bite. "Mmm…these are so good, Julian," she moaned with a hand over her mouth full of eggs.

"Thanks." I sat across from her and filled my own plate. "I like to cook. I did it a lot for the guys."

"Really?" Kenzie replied as she put some turkey bacon on her plate and poured both of our glasses full of orange juice. "Thomas never cooked. Mainly because I wouldn't let him."

I laughed. "I know how bad of a cook he was."

She looked up at me and laughed as well. The sound went straight to my heart, just like every other time she laughed. It was the most musical sound I had ever heard. "He tried cooking for me on our third date and I actually got food poisoning." She continued to laugh.

"You're serious?" I took a bite of bacon and continued to watch her face full of laughter and happiness from the memory.

"Completely serious." She took a sip of her orange juice before continuing, "I'm not even sure what happened, but I ended up in the hospital for a few days because of it. He vowed never to make chicken parmesan again, and I was thankful for that."

"Wow." I shook my head laughing, "Talk about a shitty date."

"Tell me about it." She chuckled some more and we fell into a silent spell of simply enjoying breakfast together.

"That was the best breakfast I've had in a while." She got up from the table and began cleaning up the dishes and leftovers.

"What have you been eating every morning?" I hopped up from my chair to help her. I wasn't one of those guys that would sit back and watch the woman do the cooking and cleaning, I'd rather give a helping hand.

"A quick breakfast bar, or a lot of times I skip breakfast all together." She shrugged her shoulders as she loaded the dishwasher with our dishes.

"MacKenzie."

"Don't give me the spiel about breakfast being the most important meal of the day, Julian. Did you see my groceries in there? I'm trying to turn over a new leaf and eat healthier. You just beat me to the punch of making breakfast this morning."

With the palm of my hands facing out, I suggested, "I wasn't going there. I was just simply going to say that if you ever need a breakfast companion you could call me."

She glanced up, still bent over, and smiled knowingly at me. "Sure you were."

Shortly after we cleaned up the mess from breakfast I headed out. I didn't want MacKenzie to feel overwhelmed by my presence when we had just started being around one another again. The last thing I wanted to do was have her push me away just as soon as I had her back. We were both walking on eggshells, hoping the other wouldn't break them.

On the way home I called a fellow I had met at the gym I had recently joined. Ben seemed like a cool guy and offered up his number in case I needed some help around town or wanted someone to hang out with on the weekends since I was new and had pretty much nobody…well, except MacKenzie, that is. Since it was Saturday afternoon I suggested we grab a couple of beers later in the night and he agreed, informing me that some guys he knew had planned on hitting up a local bar. It would be the first time I had gone out on a weekend since before I had gone on my last tour of duty. Usually I was a homebody, but I knew deep down in my gut that I couldn't keep revolving my days around Kenzie. She didn't need me to shadow her every single day, so I knew it was time to get out again; I needed to be a single thirty-two year old man and stop hoping for something to evolve with my deceased best friend's widow.

After cleaning up my place I tossed the last load of laundry into the washer and decided to take an early shower. I hated being home for very long, mainly because of the silence and loneliness. When you've been overseas for so long you get used to the craziness of the day so the calmness of being in a house by myself seemed off. I knew with time it would probably line itself out, but I still hated the feeling so I found ways to stay busy or away until it was time for bed.

The warmth of the water pelting down on my body was relaxing. My muscles were sore from over working them, which I hadn't done in a couple months due to the injuries I endured during the raid. The thought had me running a hand over my side where shrapnel had embedded itself deep into my flesh, leaving a thick, gnarly-looking diagonal scar about four inches long that finally seemed to have healed. Numerous small raised scars decorated the area of my side below it, stopping just above where my pants rested. Those scars were a reminder of the pain and suffering that not only myself, but my fellow Marines had endured battling for the freedom of so many. Would I do it again? Hell yes, I would. It was in my blood. My father had spent much of his life in the National Guard, only to retire not long before he lost his life to cancer. Being an only child I took it upon myself to enlist, knowing it would make him proud, but little did I know I would find a whole new life by taking that leap into the Marines.

I'm not sure why it hit me, but the thought of something I had seen on the wrappers around the money that MacKenzie had from Thomas' storage locker flashed in my mind. "Son of a bitch…" I growled as I finished washing the soap from my body and turned the shower off. It was a small black symbol that was all too familiar to me. Mainly because the same damn symbol was used on certain missions that different sectors of my group would do. "I don't know why it didn't register until now," I grumbled out loud as I moved my towel angrily back and forth over my head, drying my hair as I thought about the last mission Thomas had been on that would get that stamp.

Fury was blocking my mind from being able to think back to all of my past missions. All the missions Thomas was involved in, I was involved in, so it wouldn't be hard to pinpoint the exact one. I just needed to take a breather and figure it all out. My mind was a little fuzzy from all of the shit I had gone through in the raid; certain things I put together didn't go together, while others I couldn't grasp at all. The doctors told me over time I would most likely remember everything as it truly was, but there was a slight possibility that I wouldn't. I didn't have time to lollygag around; I needed answers as soon as possible. Where to find those answers was going to be the tricky part.

Chapter Fourteen
MacKenzie

Thanks to my reaction in the moment of anger, Thomas' phone still wouldn't turn back on. I knew a guy who was pretty good at fixing phones, so I was pulling a Hail Mary by taking it to him. The "open" sign wasn't lit up but I decided to try the door anyway. Wrapping my hand around the handle I pulled it and the door opened. The bell above it rang out alerting Jonathon that I had arrived, but the silence of the building was all I heard.

"Hello?" I called out but got nothing.

As I walked farther into the building I saw light coming from beneath a door past the counter that was labeled Employees Only. I knocked a couple of times and the door flew open, and I jumped back and hit my lower back against the counter.

"Shit! I didn't know you were here." Jonathon grabbed my arm and pulled me back upright.

"I called for you, guess you didn't hear me." I rubbed the sore spot in agony.

"Are you okay?" He nervously rubbed the back of his hand as he stood there with his eyebrows furrowed.

"I'll be fine," I smiled.

"I forgot I had already unlocked the front door for you when I first got here."

"It's no biggie," I waved him off and pulled the cell phone from my purse. "Here it is."

Jonathon flipped it over in his hand and pushed a couple of the buttons before taking the back off of it. "You did a number to this bad boy." He ran his finger down the screen that was full of cracks and chips of glass missing.

"Yeah…me and anger don't mix so well."

"I know how that is." He turned and walked back into the room I had found him in when I arrived. The room was packed full of totes on metal shelves that were labeled for certain cell phone types and parts with a fold up table occupying much of the wall on the right-hand side of the room. The table was full of tools and parts from phones. Jonathon noticed me looking around as he took a seat at the table. "This is where I work my magic."

"I sure hope you can work some magic on that thing." I nervously bit at my fingernails.

"Even if I can't get it to boot up, as long as the insides are good I can put them in another phone and everything should be fine."

"Really?" I almost *literally* jumped for joy.

"Yeah, *really*." Jonathon pulled some kind of magnifying glasses down from the top of his head and went to work. "Give me about an hour and it should be fixed."

I ran to the folding chair he was perched on and squeezed his shoulders in a half-ass attempt at a hug. "Thank you, Jonathon! You're a lifesaver. What do I owe ya?"

"Yeah, yeah." He patted my arm in return. "Bring me a case of beer and we will call it even."

"I feel like I'm getting a deal here."

"Okay, make it two cases then."

"Deal." I was out the door and off to waste the hour until the phone was ready.

"You've reached Julian Cooper, please leave your name and number after the beep and I will get back to you as soon as I can."

"Hey, Mister Busybody. Just thought I would see what you're up to. I'm wasting time, trying to get this damn cell phone fixed. Why? I'm really not sure…it's the only form of connection to Sara we have, and I feel like we might need it down the road. Hell, maybe I'm crazy…anyway, give me a call back when ya can. Bye."

Julian not answering was odd to me; he rarely missed a call. But I couldn't expect him to answer every single time I called him, it wasn't like we were an item or anything, and even then that would've been quite ridiculous. I slid my phone into my purse and grabbed a quick deli sandwich, bag of chips, and large bottled water from the gas station I had stopped at. The public beach wasn't far away so I went there and took a beach towel from my trunk, along with my lovely lunch down to the sand and made myself a little picnic.

The weather couldn't have been better. The sun was bright but would hide behind the white fluffy clouds that were spread out in the sky every so often, giving my body a break from its heat. The ocean wasn't frantic but calm; the light brushing of the water on the shore was relaxing as I sat there and enjoyed the food from the gas station. It wasn't the best I had ever eaten, but it wasn't bad either. A group of girls were hitting a volleyball back and forth over a net they had put up, providing pretty good entertainment; their laughter made me smile. I had never been lucky enough to be surrounded by numerous close female friends; the last time I had a close girlfriend was so long ago that I couldn't remember exactly when it was. Maybe high school? I really needed to stop being a loner and find a group of friends again, but I had no clue where to start. My life had been the same for so long that all of it crumbling down at once was a major slap in the face to my routine.

I shoved my lunch trash into the plastic bag from the gas station and put it under my purse so it wouldn't float away. The volleyball game had ended so my entertainment was officially over, leaving me with the sound of the ocean. I closed my eyes and the sun warmed my face with the soothing sounds of the ocean infinitely moving about. My skin was beginning to twinge from the sun, letting me know my time was up on the beach since I lacked sunscreen and wasn't ready for another hellacious sunburn. My skin was still grossly peeling from that. Gathering my things I headed back to my car. With everything thrown in the back seat, I slipped into the driver's seat. The small blue light flashing on my cell phone in the cup holder caught my attention. It dawned on me that I hadn't realized I had left it in the car.

Two notifications awaited me; one from Jonathon and one from Julian. The phone rang twice before Julian's voice filled my ear. "Sorry I missed you calling earlier." He was apologizing even though there was no need; it made my heart swell just a bit before I quickly gathered myself.

"No need for an apology." As I turned the key in the ignition, my car sprung to life and pulled out towards Jonathon's shop. "I left my phone in the car while I ate lunch on the beach."

"That sounds nice."

"It was, actually." *Except the part about being so damn lonely anymore.*

Without missing a beat he jumped right into the reason I had called him earlier, Thomas' phone. "I'm surprised you decided to get that cell phone fixed."

Julian wasn't the only one surprised about me getting that thing fixed, I was surprised I had decided to do it as well. "You're not the only one. I wasn't going to; I was going to turn the service off and move on, but I feel like there is more to the story than I—we know. I guess

I'm not ready to close that chapter until I feel like it's the right choice. Does that make sense? Or have I lost my damn mind?"

What seemed like a long pause ticked away before Julian's voice came back on the line. "You're not crazy. I understand what you're saying and wanting to do with the cell phone, I just don't know if it's the healthiest thing to do, Kenzie. But that's your call. When you're ready to move past it all and start a new life you will, and I'll be right beside you with whatever decision you make."

Julian made perfect sense. The healing process was one each individual had to take at their own pace; it couldn't be pushed to happen, it took time. My time hadn't come, but it would…eventually.

The fact that Julian proclaimed he would be by my side no matter the choice I would make was comforting. He was a caring man that always seemed to have my back, even if we hadn't known one another very long. It was nice to have him as a friend, even if I was struggling with wanting him as more. With that being said, I gave him the truth of it all. The truth of just how thankful I was for him. Minus the depth of my feelings. "Thank you for being so understanding, Julian. When I was first told about Thomas' death I had no idea what I was going to do next, but even with all of the crazy shit that's been thrown in the mix I feel like you have been my savior through it all. There's no telling what kind of shape I would be in right now if it wasn't for you."

"You have way too much faith in me, MacKenzie. You've brought yourself to where you are, not me." I wanted to beg to differ but I left it at that. Julian was also one that never took credit for the things he'd done; I learned that very quickly about him.

"We'll agree to disagree. Do you have any plans later? I'm pulling in to pick up the cell phone right now, so if you don't maybe we can get together."

"I might be able to come by for a little bit before I head out with a guy I met at the gym."

Disappointment reared its head. "It's okay, maybe tomorrow then."

"Yeah, tomorrow sounds good." I knew he could hear how disappointed I was by the change in my voice, even though I tried my damnedest to hide it. "I'll give you a call in the morning."

We said our goodbyes and I placed my phone back in the cup holder, leaving it there as I went inside to talk to Jonathon.

"Did you get my message?" Jonathon piped up as soon as he saw me pass through the front door.

"Umm…yeah, but I didn't listen to it yet." Jonathon looked at me like I was crazy. "I just assumed the phone was ready…" I raised an eyebrow as I walked up to the counter he was standing behind.

"Oh, it's ready all right." He took off into his workroom and came back holding a cell phone that I assumed was housing the insides of Thomas' old phone. "As soon as I powered that bad boy on it sprang to life with about twenty text messages. That's exactly why I hate text messages." I wasn't sure where he was going with his statement, but I kept quiet hoping he would finish. "Did you know some woman was sending your—err—husband provocative photos?"

Mentally face palming myself about ten times, I took the phone from his hand, slipped it into my back pocket and slid the two cases of beer that I had placed on the counter towards him. "Thanks, Jonathon." He didn't even comment that I'd completely ignored the question he had asked. That's one thing I adored about the man, he let it go if it wasn't something I was going to give him the answer to. We'd had that type of relationship for years, making him the easiest man I had ever had to deal with.

Jonathon Paxter was tall and skinny with brownish-red hair and deep brown eyes; he was the first person I became friends with, I guess you could say, when we first moved to Shallotte. He was the only person I still kept contact with off and on as well. The story of meeting him was one for the books. Thomas was on leave when moving day came, which left me having to move all of our belongings into the house with some of the military personnel after the furniture and appliances were delivered. I had gone down to Grant's Deli for lunch and was chatting up Grant, who still worked there at the time when Jonathon came in. Apparently they were related some way or another and Grant told him to take his happy ass to my house and help me with whatever I needed done. I refused at first, mainly because I didn't know them at all, but the persistence of old man Grant had me caving since a couple of Thomas' superiors were on their way with the last round of boxes from our old house, and I didn't want them to feel obligated to do more than that. The moment Jonathon opened his mouth about having to set up some kind of networking system I knew I needed him to do my router and wireless stuff around the new house. He was more awkward than anything at that point in time, not that he had grown out of it much, but he was officially more comfortable around me than he had been before. Thanks to him, every piece of wireless equipment in the house was working perfectly fine; if it had been left to me it would have never worked, not until Thomas had come home and had someone sent over to set it up.

The first thing I did once I was seated back in the driver's seat was push the power button on the side of the phone. Within seconds it sprang to life, looking exactly like the previous phone had, minus all of the cracks and crevices I had put into from it becoming one with the wall. A shaky breath left my lungs. The text message notification read twenty, just like Jonathon informed me, while the missed call indicator was housing a smaller number, twelve. Scrolling through the missed calls was easy because every single one belonged to Sara. Apparently she thought I was avoiding her, or had shut the phone off; as I moved into the text messages to read what she had sent, I braced myself for what her words might do to me.

A lot of it was skimmed through, she was ranting about how Thomas and she had a child together and if I couldn't understand any of what they had I should at least understand how the little boy would feel when he got older and learned that his father was killed overseas. She was using the poor boy as a mechanism to try and make me feel sorry for them yet again. My heart was indeed hurting for the little boy; I wasn't that big of a coldhearted bitch for it not to be. It was just hard to feel sorry for a woman who knowingly slept with a married man thinking that he was going to have a life with her once he left his wife by shattering her heart with the news. I wasn't sure which was worse though, it getting to the point of Thomas leaving me or it unfolding like it had with him passing and the news being unexpectedly thrown at me by my discovering it on my own. It was one of those situations where I wanted to yell and scream at him for what he did to me. I wanted to punch him in the arms and beat on his chest so that he could feel the heavy weight of heartache that I had been feeling, but in reality I couldn't.

Closing out of the messages I hit the voicemail button. Several of the voicemails were hang-ups, but the last one had my heart pounding out of my chest. Sara wanted to meet up with me. I hit the button to repeat the message four times before I allowed the phone to drop into my lap. Time had passed by me without a bit of acknowledgment on my part, until a rap of knuckles against my window brought me out of the shocked daze I was in.

"MacKenzie…" tap, tap, tap, "Are you okay?" I turned my head and found Jonathon leaning down with his face inches from the glass of my window. I pushed the button for the window to roll down without saying a word. "You've been sitting out here for almost thirty minutes." His brows were furrowed as he took me in. "It was something in that phone, wasn't it?" He pointed to the cell phone resting in my lap.

"Yeah, I'm okay though." I plastered on a smile hoping he would drop it, I wasn't so sure he would.

"Don't do anything stupid. Whatever you just read or listened to, take a deep breath and think it through before you do whatever it is that you are feeling you need to do." He covered one of my hands with one of his own and gave it a gentle squeeze. "If you need me don't hesitate to call either."

A genuine smile made its appearance, "Thank you, Jonathon. I'll be fine, I promise."

"Take care of yourself, MacKenzie." Jonathon tapped his hand against the window frame and headed to his own vehicle. A heavy sigh escaped me as I placed the phone in the cup holder beside my own and headed towards my house. The day had already been a long one, I was only hoping the remainder would be a bit better.

The drive home was quiet, I didn't even bother turning on the radio to drown out the silence. Sara's last message had thrown me for a loop. The pros and cons of meeting her were playing on repeat in my head, and I couldn't decide which the better choice was. To meet her or not to meet her, that was the question.

Calling Julian was out of the question, I didn't want to hinder the outing with his new friends that he had told me about; instead of calling him I flopped myself down on the couch face first and grumbled into the throw pillow. My phone was blaring from its spot in my back pocket so I reached around and retrieved it, hitting the answer button without taking a glance at who was calling. I wasn't in the best of moods, but once Loren's peppy voice filled my ear I couldn't help the smile that formed on my lips.

"Hey, girl! Do you have any plans tonight? Please tell me you don't."

"I'm completely free." I rolled over and kicked my shoes off.

"Thank God!" she huffed. "I'm going crazy in this house today. Want to grab a drink or two?"

A drink sounded like something I needed. "Sure. When and where?"

"I haven't made it that far in the planning process," she laughed. "But I'll come to your place around eight? Does that sound good?"

"I'll be here."

"Cool, see you then!"

Loren was giving me a reason to push myself off the couch and get ready for a night out. The decision that revolved around Sara was going to have to wait, because I was going to drown my sorrows in a few well-mixed drinks.

Chapter Fifteen

The music from the live band playing at the Driftwood Tavern danced through the air as we entered the front doors. People were gathered around the small stage, dancing to the melody of the upbeat song the band was grooving to. I couldn't help bobbing my head to the music as I moved around the establishment.

"There's two open spots at the end of the bar," Loren called back to me as she maneuvered us through the throngs of people.

We both slid up onto the tall bar stools. The bar was a beautiful dark wood; you could tell it was antique from the distressed looked it had to it. Mirrors lined the back wall of the bar behind the bottles of liquor on the shelves that stretched taller than the bottles, leaving space to see what was going on behind you. Loren ordered each of us a margarita on the rocks as I continued to watch the crowd behind us through their reflection in the mirrors. I hadn't been to a bar at night in quite some time. The interaction of the patrons was not only comical at times but rather provocative as well. Being thirty-one didn't make me an old lady, so why in the hell had I been closing myself off like one?

"What are you thinking about?" Loren's voice caught my attention as the margarita was placed in front of me on the bar.

"Just why in the hell I haven't been at bars—or out in general—more often. I've been living like an old woman. Hell, I bet there are old women that get out more than I do!" I took a large gulp of my drink as I turned my stool towards Loren a little more.

"You've been through a lot." She shrugged. "Sometimes it takes baby steps to get back on course."

She was right, but I still felt like I hadn't truly been living. It reminded me of having a movie on pause because something interrupted you watching it. My life was on pause, waiting for the interruption to pass so that the play button could be pushed again. "I've been moving like a snail; baby steps haven't even been an option." Tipping the margarita up, I sucked down the remainder and motioned towards the bartender for a second round. Talking about my life was never an easy subject, especially when I couldn't *fully* talk about it to anyone but Julian.

Loren watched the crowd while perched on her stool while I faced the bar. She was all about people watching, not that I wasn't, she just enjoyed it a little more than I did. She was leaning back with her elbow resting against the bar while holding the straw of her margarita up to her mouth, taking slow sips of her first round as I started on my second. It was looking like a night for a cab ride home, unless she laid off after her second drink that was awaiting her on the bar, because from the looks of things I wasn't going to be able to drive home.

"Hottie at twelve o'clock, heading this way," Loren mumbled, trying to make it look like she wasn't actually warning me.

"How are you ladies tonight?" The man's smooth voice was like warm honey. I turned in my stool so that I was facing the same way as Loren and took in the man. He was a few inches taller than Thomas and Julian and had dark brown hair that had natural highlights to it. His hazel eyes were an odd shade of brown and deep green mixed together with a hunter green ring around them. His angular jawline and strong chin screamed for attention, and mixed with his high cheekbones the man was gorgeous. Absolutely *deliciously* gorgeous.

"Pretty good, I suppose." Usually I would run off any man that came up to me at a bar, but I couldn't help talking to him. Loren looked over at me in surprise as I smiled widely and crossed my black skinny-jean-covered legs.

"I'm Gabe Tully." He extended his hand to me and I slipped mine into it, shaking hands lightly.

"MacKenzie Cole."

My eyes traveled down from his eyes to the snug fitting navy blue polo he was wearing. It stretched nicely across his broad chest and the dark wash jeans hung on his hips like they were made for him. Gabe was most likely a dangerous man to get intertwined with, I could tell simply by the way he carried himself; full of just how much he knew he looked good.

"I knew that had to be you."

Excuse me?

It felt like a bucket of ice cold water was poured over me; a chill ran through my body from his words. "Do what?" I leaned back, putting a bit more space between the two of us.

"I served with your husband." He smiled sadly and pushed his hands deep into the front pockets of his jeans.

"Oh." My erratic beating heart pained as it slowed its pace.

Awkward silence hung in the air for many seconds as I tried to think of something to say but came up short.

"Who wants a shot?" Loren piped up, trying to break the awkwardness floating in the air.

"Sure, why not." I turned towards her. "No vodka though."

"Vodka gets you down?" Gabe questioned.

A throaty laugh escaped me almost instantly. "It does more than get me down. It's like a Mack truck slammed into me and backed up again about twenty times. We have a *very* love-hate relationship. I'm loving it in the moment, and hating it after the fact."

Gabe was laughing as Loren ordered us all a round of shots. I hadn't heard what they were so I was hoping she heeded my warning. "I have the same relationship with Tequila." His admission made me laugh right along with him.

"Everyone has that one alcohol that isn't very friendly, huh?"

"Whiskey!" Loren announced as she spun around on the stool and handed Gabe and me each a shot glass.

"Cheers!" Gabe held his shot glass up as Loren and I clinked ours together with his before we all threw the amber liquid back our throats. Loren shivered as I coughed and Gabe laughed at the both of us.

"I'm not usually a heavy drinker," I admitted through my coughs from the burn of the whiskey.

"Let me guess…you're a wine kind of girl?" A playful smirk tipped up his lips as he leaned against the bar on the opposite side of me than Loren.

Was he flirting with me? Or were these his usual antics?

"Actually," I took another pull from my margarita, "I'm more of a beer girl, but wine is next on my list."

Gabe's eyebrows shot up in surprise. "I wouldn't have pegged you for a beer girl. You seem more…" he paused, thinking of the next word he was going to use, "of a classier type of woman."

"I'll take that as a compliment."

"You should." His full-blown smile was to die for. Either Gabe was indeed absolutely gorgeous or my hormones were working in overdrive from the alcohol consumption at a steady pace.

"Shouldn't you get back with your friends?" Loren inquired.

Gabe leaned around me to see her. "Are you trying to run me off?"

Loren's face turned pink from embarrassment. "Oh my gosh, I didn't mean it like that! Never mind…" She threw back another shot she had ordered for herself. There was no way either of us were going to be driving home.

Somehow they had managed to drag me out onto the dance floor. Gabe had a couple buddies with him who were giving Loren a run for her money. What was odd to me was that she didn't seem to mind. I had never gone out with her before, but one would think she wouldn't be so flirtatious with other men since she had a husband who was about to come back from being overseas. But who was I to judge? She was having a good time and wasn't crossing any lines.

Gabe wasn't a bad dancer either. His moves were on beat and sexy as hell. I kept my distance as I moved right along with him and the music. As the upbeat song transformed into the first slow one since I had been on the dance floor, Gabe extended a hand towards me. "May I have this dance?" The smile stretching across his face made it hard to resist, so I took his hand and allowed him to pull me in close against his chest, resting both of his hands on my lower back while mine were wrapped loosely around his neck. We moved to the slow sensual sounds of a man singing about living with and loving someone until they were old and grey.

The door chimed and the sound of men chatting and laughing roared almost louder than the music itself. My back was to them as Gabe and I swayed along, but his attention was no longer on me, it was on the people who had come in the door of the place. "I'll be damned."

"Something wrong?" I looked up at him as his eyes looked over my head in the direction of the door still.

"Someone I haven't seen in quite some time just walked in." A large smile broke out as a familiar voice caught my attention.

"Gabe Tully! You've got to be shitting me!"

That voice…

I would know that voice anywhere.

"Julian Cooper!" Long time no see, man!" We stopped dancing as Gabe extended a hand to Julian, of all people.

My back was still turned to Julian when Gabe introduced me. "This is MacKenzie Cole." He motioned towards me as I turned, placing a tight smile on my lips.

Julian moved back just slightly, but enough that I saw it. "Kenzie, what are you doing here?" His eyebrows were pulled down deep between as he took me in.

"Loren asked me to come out for a couple drinks tonight." I motioned towards Loren who was back sitting at the bar.

"You two know one another?" Gabe looked back and forth between Julian and me.

"Yeah," Julian spoke up before I could, keeping it short and sweet.

"We met at Thomas' funeral," I managed to throw in.

Gabe shook his head in understanding. "How have you been, Julian? I hadn't seen you in years."

"Since the tour before that last one; it has been a while. Just living day-to-day." Julian's eyes were still fixated on me.

"Let me grab you a beer." Gabe patted him on the shoulder.

"I'll let you two talk, I really need to get back to Loren. She looks lonely over there." I smiled at the both of them. "Nice to meet you, Gabe, and enjoy your night, Julian."

As I moved through the crowd towards Loren the door opening caught my attention for some reason. It was as if my intuition was screaming at me to look at the damn thing in the exact moment the brunette that had been chatting it up with Julian at the deli sashayed in. My steps faltered as my thoughts went directly to whether or not Julian had asked her to meet him. I knew I had no right to even care, but it bugged the hell out of me.

"Is that…" Loren started to say but I cut her off.

"Yeah, it's the chick from the deli that Julian was with." My annoyance was on display as I motioned for the bartender.

"Yes ma'am?"

"Two shots of tequila, please." Loren's eyes were large as she listened to what I had ordered.

"I'm done. I can't take another shot even if I wanted to."

"Good, because they are both for me." The bartender came back and placed them both before me as I slid him a twenty and told him to keep the change. The first one was down my throat before Loren could say a word and the second was right behind it.

"You're going to have one helluva hangover tomorrow." She shook her head at me.

The brunette quickly found Julian at a table with four other guys, including Gabe. A literal growl erupted from my chest. "Did you just growl?" Loren asked as her laugher bubbled through her words.

"Shut up," I groaned.

"You have a serious thing for Julian, don't you?" She poked me with her index finger to try to get me to look at her instead of the shot glass I was swirling my finger around the rim of.

A heavy sigh released from my lungs. "Would it be bad if I said yes?" My eyes were squeezed shut as I awaited her reply.

"Honey, it wouldn't be bad at all. He's an attractive guy and you're a widow. It has to be hard not having someone there for you. Believe me, I know."

"What do you mean you know?"

"I'm filing for a divorce."

It was like a bomb exploding. I couldn't believe what she had confessed. "What? You were super happy about him coming home when we got lunch the other day. What the hell happened?"

She sighed. "I'm lonely, MacKenzie. He's been gone for so long it makes it hard to be at home alone." I knew exactly what she was saying, but my husband wouldn't ever be coming home. I would be lying if I said I hadn't struggled the same way with Thomas being gone so much. It made life hard and lonely.

"I've been there. I struggled with the same loneliness before Thomas passed. But if you truly love him when he's home, you have to love him while he is gone."

Loren dropped her head in her hands. "I'm not even sure that I am still in love with him."

"Then maybe you should wait and see how things go when he comes home. Talk to him about it, because if you're not sure about things you shouldn't make a decision until you are."

"You're completely right." She looked up at me with tear-filled eyes. "Even though I hate what you've been going through, I'm thankful that you chose me to be the person you lean on."

I pulled her into my arms and gave her a squeeze. "I'm thankful, too."

"We need to get our drunk asses home before a weeping fest takes place," Loren said as she closed out her bar tab.

I laughed, "I agree."

We slid off our stools and pushed through the front doors only to be stopped moments later by Gabe. "MacKenzie! Wait!" I turned around to see why he was calling after me.

"Yeah?"

He stopped just in front of me and quickly caught his breath. "Do you all need a ride home?"

"No, we're just going to call a cab."

"It's no problem, really. I can take you."

Gabe wasn't a scary guy, but I didn't feel comfortable having him take us home, mainly because we had just met the guy. Even though he knew Thomas and Julian, it didn't sit well with me allowing a complete stranger to give Loren and me a ride home. Turning down his offer was the only way to go about it.

"Thanks, Gabe, really. But I already called for a cab and it should be here any minute. Plus, you've been drinking just like us," I smiled sweetly at him.

"My buddy hasn't been. He's the driver. I insist." He linked his hand with mine.

I pulled my hand away quickly as our cab pulled up to the curb. "I really appreciate it, Gabe, I do. See you another time." I gave him a small wave as I climbed into the cab behind Loren and shut the door. I watched as Gabe walked back into the bar as the cab began moving.

The last thing I saw as we drove away was Julian standing on the side of the building with that damn brunette too close for comfort and a cigarette in her hand.

His eyes were locked on mine in the darkness, or at least that's what I told myself.

Chapter Sixteen

Loren had crashed at my place and left early in the morning before the damn rooster had time to crow. I, on the other hand, hadn't had the urge to even move from the bed hours later. When she had woken me to tell me she was leaving I asked her to lock the door behind her because my butt wasn't moving from the comfort of my sheets. She thought that was the funniest thing ever, but my head didn't agree. Apparently the excessive amount of drinks I had mixed together had got the best of me because a drumline was playing a horrific beat against my skull.

The thought of Sara's request to meet hit me out of nowhere; I rolled over and groaned from the decision that was to come. It would be a helluva lot easier to just ignore her request, but then I knew that it would beat down on me for a long time afterwards. The only thing I could do was actually meet her. Unfortunately, I was unsure whether or not I should bring Julian in on it. I wanted to, I really did, but after everything else I wasn't sure if it would be the best idea to bombard Sara with the both of us.

Finally getting my ass out of the bed, I padded into the kitchen securing my silk robe around my almost naked body as I poured myself a glass of water from the tap and tossed back four headache pills and a pill for nausea. Drinking in excess was never my forte; I wasn't sure why I allowed myself to drink as much as I had, but I was sure paying the price for my antics. I braced a forearm on the counter and squeezed my eyes shut as I massaged my right temple. If the headache didn't release its hold I was going to end up back in bed for who knows how long.

After my head started to clear a little bit, I grabbed Thomas' phone off the counter and went into the living room. With a throw pillow positioned under my head I stared up at the ceiling while I thought about what to say back to Sara. It took me thirty minutes and numerous typed and then deleted messages before I actually sent one.

To Sara: All bullshit aside, I'm willing to meet. I'm not fully sure why you feel the need for us to talk face to face, but I'll hear you out.

I set the phone on the coffee table and closed my eyes. The last thing I had thought I would do once I found out about her was have a face-to-face conversation with the woman. But much like everything else in my life, it wasn't an average situation. Stuck in my own thoughts as I was, the sound of the text notification going off made my heart rate spike.

This is it...I'm actually going to meet the woman that turned my life upside down.

Sara: Does tomorrow around noon at the Ocean Isle Beach Park work for you?

To Sara: Works just fine. See you then.

A heavy, shaky breath left my lungs as I sat up on the couch. The feeling of bile rising up my throat from my nerves was hard to choke back down, but I managed to. What the hell was I getting myself into? I wasn't fully sure. It was either going to be a step in the direction of closure, or a catastrophic mistake. Either way, there was no turning back. I had less than twenty four hours until I would be before the woman who turned my entire life upside down and tarnished the memories of my deceased husband for all eternity.

I had managed to clean the entire house yet again. Apparently when my nerves were on the fritz cleaning was the only thing that seemed to calm them. As I finished mopping the kitchen floor I heard loud knocking coming from the front door. No one was expected to stop by so I was truly unsure as to who it might be. Positioning the mop against the doorframe I went to see who it was. The peephole only showed the back of a man's head as he faced out towards the street, but it wasn't hard to tell who the tall dark-haired man was. Even if I had only met him once, I knew Gabe's stance instantly.

The locks clicked as I unlocked them and pulled the door open. Gabe turned around with a breathtaking full-blown smile on his lips. "Hey."

"Hey," I replied, a little shocked to be seeing him on my front porch.

"It's probably a little weird that I showed up at your house without asking for your address, huh?" He ran a hand through his hair.

"Just a bit." I bit down on my bottom lip and cocked a hip against the door I was holding open. "Actually, how in the hell did you know where I lived anyway?" I stepped out on the porch and closed the door behind me.

"Okay," Gabe held his hands up, palms facing outward. "Before you think I'm some psycho stalker, I looked your name up in the phone book."

Well, that definitely falls under psycho stalker.

"Why would you do that?" The uncertainty was very evident within my voice. Gabe seemed nice, but why would he go above and beyond to hunt me down? Something was off, I just couldn't decide what that something was.

"I wanted to see you again, and since I didn't get your number I thought it was a good idea, but now that I'm saying it out loud I sound like a damn crazy person. I would completely understand if you told me to get lost." He nervously rubbed his hand through his hair again and smiled an unsure smile.

I couldn't help the laughter that bubbled up from my chest and erupted out of my mouth. It was the kind of laughter that made you bend over from exertion and brace your hand on your knees. "I'm sorry." I held a hand up as I apologized and attempted to stop the laughter that wouldn't *actually* stop. After a few minutes I managed to compose myself and found Gabe standing there with that same huge smile on his face and his arms crossed over his broad chest.

"You done?" he laughed on the end of the question.

"Yeah," I held back another laugh. "I believe so."

He shook his head while still smiling. "I really did sound like a stalker, though."

"Yeah, you kind of did," I replied as I opened the front door and motioned for Gabe to join me inside.

Much like Julian had, Gabe took in the living room studying every inch of the place. It was either a Marine thing or they were just nosy boys. Either way, the photos of Thomas and me were all missing except one that sat on the mantel beside the flag I had received during his funeral. Then it hit me, why hadn't Gabe been at the funeral if he was friends with Thomas?

Gabe stepped up to the mantel to examine the flag and photograph. "Were you at the funeral?" With his back to me his response was a simple head shake no. "How come?"

He cleared his throat before speaking. "I was in Afghanistan. Thomas and I were on the same mission the time before this last one overseas. I hadn't seen him but a couple times on base since then, and that was before he shipped out."

"That's how you know Julian, too, I guess?"

"Yeah." Gabe turned to face me. "Julian and I never really saw eye to eye very often. Honestly, most people didn't see his point of view on things. He seemed to second guess a lot of the things that would go down. Even Thomas had doubts about how trustworthy Julian was."

What he was saying about Julian didn't seem like the Julian I knew. He was never one to second guess or be untrustworthy, he seemed straight forward. In all honesty, I would trust my life with Julian without hesitation. But just like Gabe, I didn't honestly know a whole lot about Julian.

"That doesn't sound like the Julian I know."

Gabe shrugged his shoulders. "Maybe it was just being in the Marines that made him that way. I honestly don't know the guy other than those nine months I spent with him."

Doubt. Gabe had planted that little seed of doubt into my mind regarding Julian, and I *hated* it. Was Julian really the man I thought he was? Or was he someone completely different who was just hiding his true self remarkably well? It wouldn't be the first time a man pulled one over on me; look at how completely I had been fooled by Thomas.

"Everything all right?" Gabe pulled me from my inner thoughts.

"Yeah, I'm fine." I forced a smile to prove that I was fine, even though I was actually far from it. My life was one big jumble of what I thought existed, what actually existed, and whether or not I could honestly trust the people around me. It was like standing on the edge of a cliff and expecting someone to catch you when you fell, but you honestly didn't know if someone would be there to do so or not.

Doubt, I fucking loathed it.

"So what did you come by for?" A change of subject was a good idea. I didn't think I could handle much more about Julian not being the person he portrayed himself to be. I was teetering on the edge of either locking myself away from the world or up and leaving Shallotte altogether. Starting a fresh new life in a town I'd never heard of where no one knew who I was and what had happened to me sounded like the perfect plan.

"Honestly," Gabe rubbed his hands together before sliding them into the front pockets of his jeans. "I just wanted to see how you were doing after Thomas' death. I didn't have a chance to make it to the funeral and I felt like I should pay my respects to you and him somewhere other than at a bar."

A twinge of sadness hit me in the heart. Even though Thomas was going behind my back with another woman, it still hurt to think about what we had. It hurt to have those that cared about him come by, like Gabe had, to show their respects, too. It was a gaping hole in my heart and soul that was being picked at instead of being allowed to heal. It was going to leave one gnarly scar that could only be covered up by something that was most likely unreachable for me: a love that would smooth the jagged ridges and cracks as it plastered together the pieces to make me whole once again.

Staring out the front window I shook the thoughts away and turned to find myself in the living room alone. Gabe was missing, but I hadn't heard him leave or even state that he was leaving. "Gabe?" I headed for the kitchen and found it empty as well.

Turning to go back into the living room I ran smack dab into his chest and yelped.

"Sorry! I had to use the restroom. I thought you heard me say that." His hands were holding my biceps as he gazed down at me.

"No, sorry, I was thinking about Thomas…" I dropped my head to avoid seeing the intensity of his eyes.

Gabe tipped my chin back up with his hand. "No need to apologize, MacKenzie. I understand." A small smile tugged at his lips as he let go of my arms and took a step back. "I should be going." He walked around me and picked up my cell phone off the counter. After a few pushes of buttons he set it back down. "Now I have your number and you have mine."

"Less stalker-ish," I laughed.

Gabe laughed right along with me. "Yeah, sorry about that." I waved him off as we walked towards the front door. "I hope to hear from you soon, MacKenzie." He smiled widely as he passed the threshold onto the front porch.

"Goodbye, Gabe." I waved from the doorway as he got into his truck and drove away.

My morning had been thrown off by Gabe stopping by. I needed a shower and a change of clothes after cleaning the house, so I did just that. Rummaging through my closet for something to wear for the day, I settled on a simple navy blue spaghetti strap knee-length sundress with gold bangle bracelets and simple gold stud earrings. I slid my feet into a pair of gold strappy sandals, grabbed my purse, keys, and phone off of the counter, and headed to Loren's house.

Why I hadn't called before I showed up at her door was beyond me because she wasn't home. I sunk down on the concrete steps of her front porch and took in the peace and quiet of her neighborhood. It was a beautiful one with numerous types of flowers planted in the freshly cut yards with large shade trees. Children were laughing and playing a couple houses over while an older couple were gardening directly across the road. Loren's neighborhood reminded me of something you would see in a romance movie. Families that seemed oh so perfect on the outside, but you never knew what was hiding behind closed doors. Yes, I had to go there, mainly because my own life was far from perfect thanks to Thomas and his wonderful piece on the side.

I pushed off of the steps and headed down the walkway to my car as Loren pulled into the driveway. Waving like a mad woman she threw the car in park and hopped out. "Hey, girl! What are you up to?"

I waved back as she met me on the sidewalk. "Sorry for unexpectedly showing up. I had to get out of the house."

She waved me off. "No problem at all! I just ran down to the store to get some gas. I have to pick Derrick up from the airport bright and early in the morning so I didn't want to have to worry about getting gas beforehand."

"He's coming home early?"

"Yeah, big surprise to me, too." She was nibbling on her bottom lip with her eyebrows creased down the center. "I don't want to spring everything on him as soon as he gets home, but I don't want to act like everything is fine either, you know?"

I knew all too well what she was saying. "I do."

"Come on inside, it's too humid out here to stand and talk." She walked past me and I followed her up the steps and into her beautiful ranch style brick home.

Her house was even more breathtakingly beautiful on the inside. Everything was in perfect condition, spotlessly clean; it almost looked like not a single soul lived there until I noticed the shoes by the door and a slight tear in the arm of the recliner. Much like I had until I smashed the frame, Loren had a photograph from her wedding hanging on the wall just before you turned down the hallway towards the bedrooms. Her wide, beautiful smile was as bright as her husband's. It's sad how people can be so happy in certain moments, or throughout so many years, only for it to change with time. I had officially became a person who believed people weren't meant to stay in your life for long periods of time. Apparently everyone that had been in my life hadn't been meant to stay because I was lonely, searching for companionship; whether it be friendship or simply someone to talk to. Life was a never ending roller coaster ride full of twists and turns that I never saw coming.

I took a seat on a stool at the island in her kitchen as she pulled a container of lemonade out of the refrigerator. "Want some? I promise that it is one hundred percent virgin." She laughed as a wide grin spread across her face, obviously joking about the massive hangover I had endured.

"Funny." I playfully narrowed my eyes at her as my smile stayed firmly in place. "But, yeah, I'll take a glass." A moment after she filled a glass and placed it in front of me I took a large drink. The lemonade was refreshing, not over-or under-sweetened, just right. "This is probably the best damn lemonade I have ever had."

Loren was smiling widely when I looked up at her. "It's my grand-momma's recipe. Thought I would try it out since it's been tucked away in the recipe book my momma gave me at my wedding." The sadness in her voice made my heart ache for her. She cleared her throat and fanned the tears in her eyes away with her hands. "Sorry, I didn't mean to get so emotional over lemonade." She laughed a small, unsteady laugh.

"You don't have to apologize to me." I covered one of her hands with one of my own.

"Thank you," she mouthed, but the words didn't physically come out. She cleared her throat again. "It's not even the fact that the recipe was my grand-momma's that upset me, it's the fact that it was tucked away in a damn recipe book I got at my *wedding*. A wedding that might end up being pointless." Loren braced her forearms on the counter and dropped her head between them. Taking a couple deep breaths she looked up at me with red, tear-filled eyes. "How have you survived Thomas dying, MacKenzie? I'm trying to survive the possibility of a divorce, and I'm barely hanging on."

If she only knew everything that had been happening in my life…

"Well," I took another sip of the lemonade, "you have to take it day by day. If you need to cry, then cry. If you feel like you need to get away from everyone, then get away. Holding in your emotions is the worst thing you can do right now. You have to let it run its course before you can learn to move on or even attempt to fix what's been broken." Giving her the advice Julian had given me was close to cheating, mainly because I hadn't fully abided by the advice myself.

Loren rounded the island and pulled me into a strong hug. "What is that for?" I managed to choke out.

"Because you are the strongest and most knowledgeable woman I have ever met. I needed to hear what you just said to me. Most people would simply just say that it'll get better or that everything happens for a reason, but you didn't. I love you for that, MacKenzie."

Her words had me choking back my own round of un-spilled tears. "I love you too, Loren, and I'm beyond grateful that I have you to lean on when need be." I just wished I could lean on her fully, give her every ounce of the crazy going on in my life and ask for assistance in what I should do. But I couldn't.

Chapter Seventeen
Julian

Seeing Gabe Tully in town last night had been totally unexpected. Hell, I honestly hadn't seen the guy in years or knew where he lived for that matter. But the moment I had realized that he had MacKenzie wrapped in his arms on that dance floor was the same moment I thought I could rip his head off. Jealousy was a new emotion for me; no one had ever brought it out before. Not even when I found out about Danielle and her piece on the side. Yes, I was pissed as a motherfucker, but I wasn't jealous of what they had; I wasn't jealous of the fact that he was trying to make a life with the woman that was supposed to only be mine. No, I was pissed that she would go behind my back like that. One thing I've always been about is honesty, and Danielle wasn't one to be honest it seemed.

Andi, the granddaughter of the old man I had met at the deli wouldn't leave me the hell alone either. She practically begged me to screw her brains out when we were outside the bar towards the end of the night. I had gone out there to clear my head from all of the shit swimming around in it after seeing Kenzie when she came up out of nowhere. Her tight red tank top was pulled down lower on her chest than it had been when she sauntered up to our table inside, exposing even more of the swells of her breasts, and she held a lit cigarette in her hand. The cigarette alone made me want to puke. I wasn't a fan of a woman, or anyone for that matter, smoking. It was an unattractive trait in my book, so if she had an inkling of a chance before, that shit went out the window the moment I saw the cherry burning bright in the darkness of the night as she sucked the poison into her lungs. Andi was upset about the fact that my attention was on the interaction between Kenzie and Gabe before she got into the cab and not on her, but it didn't stop her from running a hand down my chest and cupping my junk. Never in my life had I had a woman I barely even knew do that. I stood there in shock as she massaged me until I couldn't take it anymore. I was growing hard by her touch, but I was envisioning it to be Kenzie's hand working its magic, not Andi's. She wasn't a very happy camper when I smacked her hand away and ripped her a new ass for the lack of dignity she had. It didn't take her long to find someone new inside the bar once she stomped her way back inside. When I had calmed down enough to go back inside she was perched in the lap of a much older man in a suit tucked away in a corner booth. I was yesterday's news.

    My feet slammed against the pavement beneath them at a steady pace as I rounded the corner onto the street behind mine. When I woke up with a clouded mind I knew I needed a good long run to clear it. Even though I had been friendly to Gabe at the bar, he wasn't one of my favorite people. The few years I was around him in the Marines, he always had me questioning the type of person he was, mainly because he always seemed to have an ulterior motive behind his actions. He didn't simply help others without wanting something in return. That wasn't what the brotherhood was built on, but to him it was. The idea of him and Kenzie spending time together didn't sit well with me. No, I couldn't be selfish and keep her as my own if it wasn't what she wanted, but I could voice my opinion about Gabe. Or at least that was the conclusion I had come to. She might not like it, but if it saved her in the long run I wouldn't feel like a dick about it. My mind was a fog when it came to that girl. A fog that I didn't mind as long as she was feeling it too, but was it my place to always try to keep her safe?

My feet moved faster and faster against the pavement as I pushed myself harder. My lungs were burning from the exertion, and I felt like I could drink about a gallon of water. I needed to tell Kenzie that I wanted to try something between us, that I would wait until she was ready to take the next step. But the thought of rejection was weighing down heavily on me. We had crossed the line a couple times, nothing too drastic, and after each time we seemed to back track about a hundred steps. I knew she wasn't ready; there was no doubt about that, and she shouldn't be. Thomas had died and a world of lies and bullshit was thrown in her face before she could wrap her head around the loss of him. No one deserved any of what she had been dealing with, especially someone as kind hearted and genuine as Kenzie.

Once I reached the back door of my house, I shoved it open and plopped down on the wooden bench just inside. I kicked my running shoes off and discarded all of my clothes into the washer beside the bench. I was drenched in sweat from my run, so I headed straight for the shower. My phone started buzzing on the dresser as I passed it, and I contemplated picking it up but settled on a shower first. The warmth of the water pummeling my body helped relax my spent muscles. I hadn't pushed myself that hard while running in quite some time; the burn deep in my lungs felt refreshing.

My cell phone continued ringing off the hook the whole time I was in the shower. Something was definitely off so I quickly scrubbed my body and rinsed before doing the same to my hair and shutting off the water. Before I could get a towel to dry myself off and wrap it around my waist someone was banging on the back door. "I'm coming!" I yelled as loud as I could, knowing they probably couldn't hear me. I secured the towel around my waist as well as possible and headed for the door.

The sound of it creaking open sent my senses into overdrive. I grabbed the gun from its holster on my dresser and slowly moved towards the back door. As I rounded the corner I secured my hands on the Glock and positioned my trigger finger in just the right spot.

"Christ! Julian! It's me…MacKenzie!" She was standing stark still in the mud room behind the kitchen, and her beautiful bright green eyes were huge as she held her hands up in surrender.

"Fuck, Kenzie." I lowered the gun as I watched a tremor run through her body from the fear of me having the gun pointed at her. "How in the hell did you get in here?" The safety clicked back into place, and I sat the Glock on the kitchen counter.

"I—I'm sorry," she stuttered as she lowered her hands, still shaking. "I couldn't get a hold of you, and when I saw your car here I knew you were home and that you had mentioned leaving a key under the mat around back. So I..." She paused momentarily as a round of tears rolled down her rosy cheeks. "I had nowhere else to go, Julian." Another round of tears pooled in her eyes and flooded over before I could get to her. She collapsed into my arms as soon as I reached out to pull her body against mine and the sobs racked through her body. "Someone broke into my house..."

She wasn't shaking because of the gun; she was shaking because some piece of shit had broken into her house. "Please, tell me you weren't home, sweetheart." I caressed her hair as she sobbed against my chest. Her head moved back and forth telling me that she wasn't home and I exhaled, completely thankful for that.

Her sobbing paused and her even greener eyes pierced into mine from beneath her tear-clad lashes. "The bag is...I'm not sure if it's still there." Her words were whispered so quietly that I almost didn't hear her.

"It's okay, I can go back with you and check."

"I can't—I can't go back there, not right now." Her body shook with trepidation so I scooped her up into my arms and carried her into my bedroom without saying another word.

Lowering her onto the bed I climbed onto it beside her and cradled her against my side. She snuggled against me as she cried. Without another word passing between the two of us, I held her as she poured out her emotions until her cries subsided and her breathing evened out. MacKenzie had cried herself to sleep.

Low whimpering pulled me out of my slumber. I couldn't move due to the weight of MacKenzie wrapped around my left side. I ran a hand up her bare arm and her whimpering ceased. She was sound asleep, dreaming of who knows what. But whatever it was, her eyebrows were creased deeply in the center, and a frown was pulling her lips downwards. "Kenzie…" Her name left my mouth on a whisper as I continued to rub the soft skin of her arm.

She gently stirred in her sleep enough for me to slide down the headboard so that I was lying flat on my back just as she was. Her leg hooked over my waist pushing the towel off of my lower half and leaving me completely bare. Thankfully she was still asleep as I tried to move her leg so that I could cover myself, but her foot was hooked behind my calf making it a lot more difficult. My eyes were fixated on her face as I slid my hand down to her ankle and pulled it from behind my leg. Her eyes fluttered open, and I quickly dropped her leg and jerked the blanket that was bunched up around my feet over our bodies so that she couldn't see all of me. There was no way around her realizing that I was naked beneath the blanket.

She stretched her body against my side as she yawned. "I didn't mean to fall asleep on you." The embarrassment in her voice made me grin.

Before I could reply she moved her leg up until her foot touched my dick and it twitched in response. Her eyes grew wide as realization washed over her.

"I need to put some clothes on." I sat up, but she stopped me by rubbing her foot up and down my shaft that was growing harder by the second. "MacKenzie," her name fell from my mouth in a guttural moan that was meant as a warning; it failed miserably.

She slid onto my lap, positioning my erection perfectly against her core. Her chest was heaving as she slid each strap of her dress off of her shoulders, allowing it to fall and pool around her waist. My mouth was slack as she reached around her back and unsnapped her strapless nude-colored bra. I focused my eyes on the ceiling as I heard the material hit the hardwood floor beside the bed.

"Look at me." The words were a needy whisper that hit me in all that right places. I lifted my head and focused on her eyes, wanting so badly to drop my focus onto her bare chest but refused to do so.

"You shouldn't be doing this," was all I could manage to say as she grabbed my hands and placed them over her breasts so that I was cupping them. Her nipples pebbled against my palms as she squeezed my hands trying to get me to do it. My dick was throbbing so intensely that if I didn't do something I was going to end up with a massive case of blue balls. "Are you sure about this?" My thick voice caused her nipples to harden even more than they already were.

"Yes," she breathlessly replied.

Hearing her say that one word was all it took for me to throw my reserve out the window. I massaged her breasts, causing her to throw her head back and release the sexiest sound I had ever heard. My lips quickly found hers, and I devoured her like my lungs needed her lips on mine to breathe air deep into them. Kenzie began rocking her hips against me, searching for the friction she needed to find that euphoric release we were both desperately craving.

"Slow down, sweetheart," I spoke against her damp, swollen lips, and she smiled before slowing her pace.

MacKenzie pulled her dress up and over her head before tossing it somewhere on the floor, leaving herself in nothing but a pair of skimpy nude-colored lace panties. Never did I think I would have her like that in my bed. Her body was a beautiful thing: curves at her hips, slim waist, and heavy, perfectly shaped breasts with pale pink nipples. The redness from her previous sunburn had faded into a slight glow of a tan, leaving lighter lines where her clothes had been. My hands moved down her sides, curving with her body as I rounded them around her lower back and over her firm bottom.

Her vibrant green eyes were boring into mine as the only sound coming from either of us were our heavy breaths. She stood just enough to pull her panties down one leg and then did the same with the other. Both of us were completely bare as I swallowed the little bit of saliva

I had left in my dry as hell mouth. The feel of her hot, slick skin against my shaft was driving me mad. As if she could read my mind she moved forward just enough for me to slide right inside of her with ease. A strained groan moved up my throat and slipped from behind my clenched teeth. She was soaked. I wasn't expecting her to do that, but the feeling of being inside of her almost sent me straight over the edge. "Fuck…" The heavy word left me without warning.

Kenzie began rocking her hips slowly, gradually picking up the pace as her walls squeezed me tightly with each stroke of my dick. The last time I had sex was a blur to me, much like every other time, but what was happening between the two of us was beyond sex…it was a deeper bond being made.

My hands gripped her hips as she continued to rock back and forth. Her tits bounced to the rhythm she had created, and I leaned up just enough to capture each of them, one at a time, in my mouth. I sucked her hardened pink nipple before roughly flicking my tongue against it and moving on to the next one. Her head flew back as her mouth fell open and the sexiest long moan released from deep within her chest. That sound was one I would never forget. If I was only going to get one chance to explore all things MacKenzie Cole, I was going to make it one time I would *never* forget.

My lips peppered loving kisses up her body to the curve of her flushed neck until I captured her mouth with my own. The taste of her skin was almost as mesmerizing as the taste of her lips. One of my hands was buried deep into her silky brown hair, tugging just enough to give a little bit of tension against her scalp. Kenzie sunk down hard on me as her rhythm went off beat, and I knew it was time to take matters into my own hands. With my free hand I gripped her waist and quickly flipped us so that I was buried deep between her milky smooth legs and she was laid on her back. Her eyes were locked on mine as she worked her bottom lip back and forth between her teeth.

Her legs were quivering against my sides as I pumped in and out of her. She felt good...no, fuck that, she felt a-fucking-mazing; better than I could have imagined her feeling. "Oh, God...I'm almost there...Oh, Julian..." My hand weaved between our bodies as I picked up my pace, my thumb found her swollen clit easily, and I applied the pressure her body was aching for. Not even a second later a strangled cry echoed throughout the room as her release exploded around me, coating my dick even more than it was, soaking the both of us.

She could no longer hold her legs up against my sides so I pulled them up onto my shoulders and pushed deeper into her. The familiar tingling at the base of my spine started to form and Kenzie's fingernails found my shoulder blades; she dug them deep into the flesh as I pumped three more times with all I had into her before pulling out and releasing onto her lower stomach. She looked from me to my release coating her and laid back, closing her eyes. In that moment I knew she was second-guessing what had happened. It was more than evident. I leaned forward and kissed her lips gently before sliding out of the bed to get a cloth to clean her up with.

Chapter Eighteen
MacKenzie

My senses were on overdrive, and the sound of Julian's footsteps as he walked away from the bed echoed loudly within his bedroom. My eyes were squeezed tightly shut as I thought about what had transpired between us. I hadn't shown up looking for a roll in the sheets with him. I had shown up because someone had ransacked my house. The thought of it made my chest ache and caused my breathing to pick up. A panic attack was trying to grip onto me until the feel of a warm washrag rubbing across my stomach caught my attention. My eyes fluttered open and I watched as Julian cleaned me up. His chocolate brown hair was disheveled and his body was shiny from sweat; he was so sexy in all his glory.

My forearms pushed deep into the mattress as I held myself up. "Julian…" I reached a hand out and rubbed the back of it across the scruff that ran across his strong jawline.

He sighed heavily and brought his eyes up to mine. So many emotions were swimming within their depths. "Please don't tell me that what we just did shouldn't have happened. If you regret it, I understand, but let me have this one moment to hold onto without having it tainted by the words you're about to say."

Thick emotions clogged my throat as I tried to choke them back down. Regret was something I *thought* I would feel, but I didn't. My heart was full of some indescribable feeling that I couldn't shake. My body felt relaxed, more than it had in a very long time, while my mind was running a million miles a minute.

"I don't regret a thing," I admitted with my hand cupping his face as our eyes searched one another's.

Julian's frown turned into a wide, beautiful smile just before he crashed his lips to mine. "You don't know how happy hearing you say that makes me," he murmured between placing kisses against my lips.

My teeth caught his bottom lip before he could move back again, and I sucked it into my mouth so that I could get a full blown, earth shattering kiss from him. He tasted like my future, wrapped with a hint of peppermint. "That was not my intention coming here."

Julian's face was mere inches from my own as he spoke, "I don't believe either of us intended for that to happen, but I wouldn't change it for the world." His hand smoothed around my jawline and into my hair as he pulled my head back to his for another deep earth-shattering kiss.

I felt alive. My bones, my soul, along with my heart were humming from the feelings Julian had awoken within me. It was like my soul was taking a breath of fresh air that it had been deprived from for far too long.

I pulled back just enough that our lips were still brushing together so I could whisper the question that was weighing me down, "Where do we go from here, Julian?"

I needed to know the answer to that almost as much as I needed to breathe. My life had been a giant ball of a mess, but I wouldn't allow the only good thing I had left to get thrown into chaos as well. It would be my full-on breaking point, and I was teetering on the ledge as it was.

Julian sat back, giving each of us space and ran a hand through his disheveled hair. "We take it one day at a time." That one sentence pierced my heart deeply. The uncertainty of whether or not he wanted 'us' to happen reared its head in those short moments before he spoke up again. "I want you…" He cupped my face. "God, do I want you, MacKenzie. But I also don't want us to rush into this and have it be tarnished by what has happened to you, and me for that matter, in the past. Neither of us has fully dealt with what life has thrown at us; I'm farther ahead than you are, but that isn't saying much." Julian held up his hands as he said, "Don't get me wrong about saying I am farther ahead than you, I meant it as you have been dealt a much more difficult hand than I have been. So let's take it one day at a time until we close all the doors on our pasts so that we can move forward the right way, without any burden or heartache constantly knocking at *our* door."

His over-enunciation of the word 'our' caused a happy smile to dance across my lips. "I agree." Julian placed a chaste kiss against my lips before standing from the bed in all of his naked glory. My eyes scanned his body; the scars on his side stood out sharply as he stretched to run his hand through his hair. An image of Thomas flashed before my eyes, one I hadn't actually seen: his lifeless body with those same scars but in other places and in mass quantities. For a split second I felt a tinge of pain for what Julian and I had done, but I shook it away as I focused again on the beautiful man standing before me. In reality we were simply two human beings without companions, and even though we had each gotten to that point in our lives in different ways, we were both at that point. Nothing about what we had done, or what I still wanted to do, was illegal or morally wrong. A widow and a single man, both searching for that someone to help piece back together their torn-apart lives.

"Kenzie?" Julian's voice broke through my thoughts.

"Yeah?" I smiled up at him as he walked back over to the bed and leaned down, bracing his fists into the mattress so that his face was right in front of mine.

"You're an amazing woman, don't you ever think otherwise." His lips pressed firmly against my forehead before he moved to stand back up.

My hand grabbed hold of his, and I pulled him back towards where I was sitting on the bed. "Then make me feel amazing once more," my husky plea only took a moment to settle in before Julian's lips found mine, and we tangled ourselves with one another and the sheets for a second round.

As we pulled into the driveway my nerves kicked into overdrive. I was afraid of stepping back into my own home, which should never be the case. You should feel safe in your home, no matter what, and the fact that someone had ransacked mine threw my feeling of safety off a cliff.

My hands were clasped tightly together, and Julian reached over to cover both of them with one of his, soothing me with its warmth. "Don't be nervous. Whoever did this, we'll find out and they will get what's coming to them."

"I know."

His fingertips gently pulled my chin around so that I was looking directly into his eyes. "I mean it, MacKenzie. Whoever did this is going to pay. You shouldn't have to feel unsafe on top of everything else going on."

The right side of my lips tipped up in a small grin and wavered just slightly before I asked the elephant in the room question. "What if it's all connected? The money, the affair, and the break in; what if one person connects it all? What if that one person is Sara?"

"You can't think like that."

"Why the hell can't I?" I tossed my hands up in the air. "Nothing surprises me anymore. I have to second guess everything…and I mean *everything* that happens. There is no way it's coincidental that my house was broken into not long after I found that bag of money in Thomas' storage locker at the gym, Julian. There is just no way."

Julian sat back in the driver's seat and rubbed the light scruff on his chin before turning his head back towards me. "Then we need to keep an open mind about it all. If we let it get the best of us, then we'll be blindsided by anything that comes at us. Now take a deep breath and let's see if anything had been taken during the break in. Okay, sweetheart?"

"Okay." I let out a deep breath and handed over the keys to my home.

Julian opened the door and paused. "Stay behind me, just in case." He reached beneath his shirt at the waistband of his jeans and pulled out the same gun that he had pointed at me the night before.

I followed closely to Julian as we canvassed the entire house, leaving the study and the garage as the last two places that needed to be checked. "The garage is clear," Julian spoke in a low voice as we climbed the stairs to the study. The knob wouldn't turn, letting us know that it was indeed still locked, so he undid the lock and shoved the door open. The light was out but the light from the garage was bright enough to illuminate the study, allowing us to see that it was empty. Julian reached around and flipped the switch on. Everything looked exactly how I had last left it. I quickly rushed to the desk and pulled it out enough to see the duffle bag still securely behind it.

"Thank God," I sighed.

"You might not agree with me, but I think we should move the cash." Julian stepped to my right and grabbed hold of the duffle bag to pull it out from behind the desk.

He was right. We needed to move the duffle bag. My house had already been broken into for who knows what, which meant the person might be back. "Where could we take it?"

Julian unzipped the bag and inspected the contents. "I have a large safe at my house. We can put the entire bag in there until we decide what to do next."

"It would be safer at your house in a safe than shoved behind this desk."

"Do you have a large trash bag?" Julian's question threw me for a loop.

"Umm...there are a few down in the garage. Why?" I raised an eyebrow in curiosity.

"Because I don't want to carry a duffle bag of cash out of your house when someone is obviously after something you have. It would be easier to put it in the trash bag and then put it in my trunk."

"I like the way you think." A smile pulled the corners of my lips up.

"Or we can wait until later tonight to take it out. It's almost noon, so a lot of people might be out."

"Did you say it's almost noon?"

"Yeah. Why, what's up?" Julian furrowed his brows, confused about why I was freaking out.

"I'm supposed to meet Sara at noon!" I took off out of the study, down the stairs, and into the house to quickly change. Julian was on my heels, shooting off a million questions as I stripped my clothes off and slid into a pair of cut off jean shorts and a simple grey tank top, not caring that Julian was standing right behind me.

"Kenzie! Stop!" Julian's voice bellowed through my bedroom as I came to a halt and turned to face him. The intensity of his eyes almost swallowed me whole as the realization hit me. I hadn't told him about my meeting with Sara.

"Yeah?" My bottom lip was sucked into my mouth just enough for me to nibble on the plump pink skin. My nerves were at an all-time high as I awaited what Julian was about to say in regards to me meeting up with Sara.

"Did you say that you're going to meet Sara?" He shook his head in disbelief as I shook my head up and down. Julian groaned as he ran his hands through his hair. "Why am I just now finding out about this?" He was upset, not just a little bit, but a lot.

I sighed as I slipped my feet into a pair of grey flip flops and checked the time on my phone. I had less than fifteen minutes to get to Ocean Isle Beach Park; I'd be pushing it if traffic was at a minimum. "I was unsure about whether or not I should tell you until it was over with. I knew you would want to come, and I didn't think it would be the best idea to bombard Sara with the both of us." My words were more a rambling mess than a smooth couple of sentences.

"MacKenzie, if you didn't want me to go I'd be okay with that, but I need you to be honest about things...at least tell me what's going on. I don't want to have to worry that you are out trying to take on the world when I think you're at home."

"I know, and I'm sorry." I closed the distance between us and rubbed the palm of my hand across his scruffy jaw. "I've really got to go. Can we talk more when I get back?" My eyes were pleading with him.

"Of course." He kissed my lips gently. "Come back here when you're done, I'm going to try and clean up the mess from the break-in."

"You don't have to do that."

"I know I don't *have* to, I want to." His lips gently touched mine again.

"I can't thank you enough, Julian." I squeezed his hand and kissed his cheek before I took off sprinting through the house to gather my things and then hurried to the car. The last thing I wanted to be was late when meeting Sara.

The car ride was a breeze. I drove well over the speed limit while silently praying the entire time that I wouldn't get pulled over. Those prayers were answered as I pulled into the parking lot that was designated for Ocean Isle Beach Park with time to spare. I had no clue what she was driving so I parked my car and walked over to a line of picnic tables that overlooked the beach. I sat with my body facing the parking lot so that I knew the moment she got out of her vehicle. It was twelve on the dot as I watched a sleek black SUV pull into a parking space two down from where I had parked.

A slim almost black-haired woman slipped from the front seat. At first I was unsure that it was her. Her hair was longer than in the photo; it laid more than halfway down her back and was loosely curled. She seemed shorter than I would have thought. But the moment she pulled a car seat from the backseat I knew it was her. Large sunglasses covered her eyes much like my own as she made her way directly towards me. I would have to find out how she knew that it was me, because she shouldn't have known what I looked like unless Thomas had shown her.

"MacKenzie?" she asked nervously. Her voice didn't have an annoying pitch like I had deep down hoped for it to be. I wanted every reason possible to hate her, but the gentle tone and smoothness made me realize that it probably wasn't going to happen.

"Yeah. Sara, I'm assuming?"

"Yeah." She sat the car seat on the bench beside where she took a seat. "This is Thomas Junior." I leaned over the table to take a peek at the sleeping dude. I couldn't help the thoughts of what my baby with Thomas would have looked like, if we had become pregnant that is.

"He looks just like his father." Bile was trying to rise up my throat from the sight of Thomas Junior. He looked identical to Thomas' baby picture. The peacefulness of that baby sleeping made me jealous. He was so innocent and had not a single idea about the chaos and heartache that he lived within.

Clearing my throat I took a deep, lung-burning breath and began picking a stray string at the end of my cut-off shorts. "Why am I here, Sara?" I was done with the small talk. Answers were needed before I flew off the rail on the crazy train.

Sara removed her sunglasses. "First, I don't want to fight with you, MacKenzie." Starting the sentence off with that automatically put me on alert. My nerves were flowing rapidly through my body as I tried to keep my anger at a minimum. "Thomas was a good man." I scoffed and she held up a hand. "Hear me out, please." She had some nerve. "You can't sit here and tell me that the life the two of you shared wasn't a good one. He loved you, I know that for a fact."

"I'm going to stop you right there." I leaned across the table with my index finger pointing directly into Sara's face. "You have no fucking right to act like you know how my relationship with Thomas was. If I am correct, *you* were the woman on the side; the woman he went to when he needed whatever in the fuck he was searching for outside of our marriage. You are in the category of women that ruin marriages and people's lives by laying down with married men!" My voice was rising as I continued laying it out there for her. "If you are here to try and make me feel sorry for you, then you better think again, Sara! The only people innocent from all of the heartache and bullshit that has been unraveling are that little boy right there and me!" I swung a leg over the picnic table and started to get up when her hand caught mine, stopping me. My eyes were full of anger as I slid my sunglasses up onto my head and jerked my arm free of her hold. "Don't you *ever* touch me again." My words were like venom being spewed from behind my clenched teeth.

"I deserved every bit of that." Sara's admission wasn't what I had expected her response to be. "But this little boy deserves to know how his father died and where he is buried. He deserves to be able to go to his grave when he gets older if he wants. He," she pointed to Thomas Junior, "had nothing to do with the horrible situation we are all in. He's a victim by association, not by choice." She stood from the bench seat. "You can hate me, MacKenzie, that is completely fine. But please don't hold a grudge against this sweet little boy. He's far too innocent for that."

I took a deep breath and turned my back to her, looking out at the ocean not far from where we were sitting. "You're right." I turned back to her. "I have every right to hate you, but not that little boy. I'll tell you how Thomas died and take you to where he is buried as long as you promise me one thing."

Shock was plain as day on her face. "What is that?"

I had a feeling she wasn't going to like what I had to say, but I was going to say it anyway. "When you tell him about his father and how he died, if he has questions about how the two of you ended up together…make sure you tell him the truth. He deserves to hear the truth about that just as much as he deserves to hear how his father died."

"I'm not sure I can do that." She sat back down.

"Why is that?"

"Because it will paint Thomas in a way that isn't the man he was. It'll make his son believe that he was a horrible man, that he traded his life with another woman for me. It'll make me look bad," she stated matter-of-factly.

"You're kidding me, right?" I laughed a humorless laugh. "You *do* look bad. When it all comes out, you will look even worse. So it would be better for you to tell him the truth when he gets older than for him to hear it from someone else. Thomas was a great man to me, I won't even lie about that, but the fact that after his death I have his affair tossed in my face after stumbling upon cell phone photos…that changes my outlook on him, along with my entire life. The life *we*, Thomas and myself, had built together. How can you sleep at night knowing you were having an affair? And how in the hell did you know who I was when you pulled in today?"

"Do you want me to be honest with you about how I met Thomas?"

"Obviously!" I plopped back down on the bench of the picnic table.

"I was on base one day, interviewing for a possible position in one of the offices over there as an office assistant. They had placed me in a seat just inside the door of this tiny house as I awaited the woman who was interviewing me to come out and get me when a man walked in. His presence captivated me; he carried himself with pride and when he smiled, it was breathtaking." She paused and smiled widely herself. My stomach was rolling and my heart was aching from her story, but I needed to hear every last bit of it. Why? I wasn't sure. But I knew that deep down I needed to hear it all, so I didn't say a word as she continued. "He wore his dark hair in the usual military cut, but what really caught my attention was the overwhelming feeling I got when his eyes connected with mine. They were a deep blue with lighter specks throughout them." She cleared her throat. "But you already know that—I'm sorry…I don't know if I can finish this." She wiped away the tears that were frantically streaming down her face.

In that emotional moment I realized that I needed to let go of the pain I had. She was hurting just as badly as I was. Yes, she was his woman on the side, and yes, she knew about me, but would that make her heartache less important than my own? I reached across the table and took her hand in mine. "Take your time. I do want to hear this." A small smile pulled up the corners of her lips as I let go of her hand, and she wiped away the remainder of the tears that were moistening her face.

"Thank you." Her bottom lip quivered as she spoke. I knew how she felt, at least when it came to the loss of someone you loved. She cleared her throat again and leaned over to check on Thomas Junior before continuing on with her story. "Thomas was friendly, a super nice man. He never wore a wedding band, which made me think for quite some time that he was indeed a single man. It wasn't until I was three weeks pregnant that I found out he had a wife." My eyes were squeezed shut as I thought about how Thomas hated to wear jewelry. He couldn't wear his ring a lot during missions so I agreed that it was okay if he simply didn't wear it. But just because he chose not to wear his ring, and I agreed upon it, doesn't mean I should feel like it was partly my fault. He made his bed full of cheating and lies, I did not. "Are you sure you want me to continue on?" Sara asked nervously.

A heavy sigh left me as I opened my tear-filled eyes. "Yes, please continue." She knew how badly hearing all of it was hurting me; I gave her credit for having a heart because I wasn't sure she had one previously.

"Thomas had rented a room at the Sunset Inn Bed and Breakfast for a couple nights right after I found out that I was pregnant. So on the last night we were there I decided to surprise him with the news. Being beyond ecstatic about having a baby with the man you were so in love with was a wonderful moment of my life. That is, until I told him about the pregnancy. Thomas freaked out…and when I say freak out I mean he was yelling and cussing. Totally out of his normal character. That's when he dropped the bomb." She sniffled. "He was sitting on the edge of the bed, rocking back and forth and mumbling something I couldn't understand. The moment I put my hand on his shoulder he jerked away and yelled that his wife wasn't going to understand…" Sara looked me directly in the eyes. "That's the moment I found out about you."

My emotions were on overdrive as I took in what she had divulged. Even with the warmth of the sun radiating my body I had chills covering my skin. Sara hadn't known about me, until she was stuck. "I had no idea."

She smiled sadly. "Of course you didn't. I was Thomas' best kept secret, apparently." A humorless laugh left her. "By the end of the Bed and Breakfast stay it seemed that everything was fine, Thomas was onboard with the baby. He made it seem like we would be together soon. He would constantly tell me that he was going to talk to you, but he got his next duty overseas and was gone before anything else was mentioned. I was left with a phone number to get a hold of him on and a growing belly."

"So the affair had only started a few weeks before you found out you were pregnant?" Her timeline was confusing to me.

She shook her head back and forth. "No. The affair, that I had no clue I was involved in, had been going on for almost a year before I found out that I was pregnant and he was married."

My head jerked back like I had been slapped. How in the hell had they been seeing one another so much without anyone catching on? Especially me. "I'm sorry," I held my hand up. "But how in the hell did he pull all of this off? I don't get it." Doubt was beginning to rear its head about the story she was telling me. Was she painting herself innocent so that I gave her the information about Thomas that she wanted?

"You're not going to understand everything, MacKenzie, because *I* don't understand it all."

"You never went to his house?"

"No."

"Didn't you think that was odd?"

"No."

"Who in their right mind wouldn't think it was odd that the man they were dating wouldn't take them to his house? I sure as hell would."

"He told me he didn't have a house, that he shared an apartment on base with a couple guys. That's why he never took me there and I never questioned it."

I needed to know if people on base saw them together because everyone knew he was married. I had met everyone that surrounded Thomas on that Marine base. "Did you get that job you applied for on base?"

"I didn't."

All the pieces of her story were almost too perfectly in place. But there was nothing I could do to find out any more of it without going onto base and asking questions. I needed to talk everything over with Julian, pick his brain to see if he remembered any little thing that would raise a red flag. Back then it might not have seemed weird or important. I decided to cut our meeting short by giving Sara the information she wanted.

"Do you want to follow me to his grave site?"

Sara looked surprised, like she didn't expect me to offer it. "Of course." We both stood from the picnic table and went to our own vehicles. The meeting itself wasn't as awkward as I thought it would have been, but I had a feeling that the grave site would be.

Chapter Nineteen

I pulled my car into the gravel lot just off of the main circle in the cemetery and shut it off. Sara was parked almost directly behind me as I stared back at her through the rearview mirror. A heavy sigh left my lungs as I shook off the uneasy feeling that had settled over me during the drive. As I got out of the car I waited for Sara to at least start walking in the same direction as me before I started off towards Thomas' resting place. Being back in the cemetery was unnerving. After they had laid Thomas to rest I had come by almost every day for weeks, but once the truth about everything started unfolding I couldn't bring myself to visit.

"It's right up here on the left," I called back to Sara. We had been walking for a couple minutes and with her hauling around Thomas Junior I knew her arm had to be killing her.

The marble headstone was decorated with a small American flag sticking up out of the ground on the side of it, with a black outlined cross at the top, and his name and information below. I stopped dead in my tracks and pointed towards where Thomas was laid to rest. "It's that one." My voice was thick and dry. "I'll give you some time."

"You don't have to." Sara wiped what I assumed to be a tear from her cheek before turning her back to me and stepping closer to the stone.

I didn't say anything in response as I turned away from her and Thomas Junior, giving her privacy to have her own moment without me hovering over them. As I moved about ten feet away from them I took in the cemetery. Hundreds of headstones just like Thomas' were in perfect rows; seeing just how many soldiers were buried in the cemetery alone was heartbreaking. So many men and women had given their lives to fight for the freedom of our country, leaving loved ones behind for the greater good. I clutched my shirt above my heart and let out a shaky, deep breath when the sound of Sara sobbing caught my attention. Turning back towards where she was I found her almost lying on the ground with Thomas Junior perched in one arm and a hand placed on Thomas' headstone. The sight had tears forming in my eyes for the devastation I knew she was feeling. I couldn't help but question why the scene affected me so much, but I knew deep down that she had been a victim of his just as much as I had been. Neither of us knew the truth until our lives were so intertwined that there was no way to escape heartache in the end, and it was all because of one man.

Sara placed Thomas Junior back into his carrier and dusted herself off as she stood, wiping away the tears beneath her eyes as she pulled her sunglasses back down to shield them and headed in my direction. The sadness on her face was evident, even with her sunglasses covering her eyes. As she reached me I began explaining what had happened to Thomas. "All I know about his death is that he and the rest of his team were trying to infiltrate a location in Iraq when he and his partner Julian went into a different part of the compound right before some type of explosion. Thomas was killed instantly while Julian was taken to a medical hospital after they rescued him along with a couple others who were outside of the compound. Any other information from that day is far too classified for me or anyone under a certain ranking to know about it." Giving her part of the truth was better than giving her it all. I remembered when they told me about Thomas' body being burned beyond recognition and how they were only able to identify the remains by the dog tags that were still around the neck. I had refused to believe that it was indeed Thomas until several days had passed without any different news, and his body arrived for the funeral. That's when it all sunk in. It was better not to tell Sara how badly Thomas' body was mutilated so that she wouldn't have the thoughts I had regarding what happened to him. No one needed those images in their head, not even someone's worst enemy.

 Sara stifled a cry with her free hand over her mouth, "Thank you, MacKenzie," she managed to choke out.

 "Why are you thanking me?" I'm sure I sounded just as confused as I felt.

 "For telling me what happened and bringing me here, you didn't have to but yet you did. I don't think I could be as compassionate to someone like me if I were in your shoes."

 Her statement hit me hard in the chest. She had called me compassionate when I felt farthest from that.

Deep down I wanted to hate her for what had happened, but after hearing everything and seeing with my own eyes the pain she was feeling, I just couldn't do it. I was raised better than that, you shouldn't hold someone accountable for their actions when they didn't know they were crushing someone else's life by being with someone they assumed to be single.

"I'm not going to lie to you; I wanted so badly to hate you with every inch of my being. But hearing your side of the story, and seeing your pain as evident as my own, I can't hold on to that anger I had towards you when I first found out. I'm not saying what happened is okay, because Lord knows it was far from it, I'm just simply saying that there is no need to hold on to such a toxic emotion when we both need to heal."

Sara stood there in silence for quite a few moments before clearing her throat. "Why Thomas would ruin a marriage with someone like you is beyond me. I am so sorry that I was the person on the other side of that. If I had known…" She choked on a sob before gaining composure again. "If I had known, I would have never stepped over that line with him." Sara reached out with her free hand and grabbed hold of one of mine, giving it a squeeze. "I hope you find the happiness you deserve, MacKenzie, I truly do." She quickly turned and took off towards where we had parked, leaving me standing a couple graves down from Thomas' with a heavy heart for the woman who was responsible for ruining my marriage to a man who was no longer with either of us.

Turning the car off, I rested my forehead against the steering wheel and exhaled a lung-burning breath. The events of the day were swirling around in my head like a massive tornado ripping through a town, leaving bits and pieces of memories in its path of destruction. My eyes stayed shut as I replayed different parts of my conversation with Sara in my head. Some made complete sense while others didn't seem to fit the more I thought about them. I knew I needed to just let it all go. Sara knew everything, where Thomas was buried and how he had died, so there was no need to bother with her anymore. It was time to move on and find the life I had been desperately wanting for quite some time.

Light tapping on the driver's side window caught my attention. My head felt heavy as I lifted it enough to see who was bothering my private internal battle. When my eyes focused on his concerned face a genuine smile tugged the corners of my lips up enough to let him know just how happy I was to see him. I hadn't noticed how long his hair had grown. The full, chocolate brown locks were slightly wavy and laid haphazardly on his forehead, curling slightly around the contours of his ears. Julian looked good with longer hair, better than the usual military cut he had been sporting. I motioned that I was getting out of the car and he took a step back, giving me enough space to open the door and slide out without knocking him over.

Throwing my purse over my shoulder I slipped from the car and closed the door behind me. "How'd it go?" Julian asked the moment the car door shut, but instead of replying I went directly into his arms and squeezed him tightly against me. His strong embrace sent warmth through my body as we stood there. His lips gently brushed against my forehead, and I snuggled my face deeper into the crook of his neck. The smell of his cologne and natural scent mixed together; thankfully it wasn't still the same cologne Thomas used to wear; this time it was a woodsy, masculine scent that danced around my nostrils in a soothing manner.

I looked up at Julian from beneath my mascara-clad lashes, "Take me inside and make me feel something other than sorrow and heartache," my voice wavered as thick emotions crept their way up my throat, threatening to ravage my entire composure. Julian noticed that I was about to crumble into a million pieces, so he took my hand in his and led me into my house, shutting and locking the door behind us.

A sob passed my lips as I took in the place. He had put everything back like it was before someone had broken in and ransacked it. My house looked like nothing had transpired that night, like everything was normal and okay. Julian stepped into my view, smiling a loving smile that reached his beautiful light brown eyes. Without a thank you I cupped his face and feverishly pressed my lips against his as I slid my hands beneath his black fitted shirt, running my hands across the defined curves of his abs and chest. His lips trailed from mine, down my jawline, and around to my ear where he nibbled my earlobe before speaking. "I need to feel you, all of you," his husky voice caused chills to dance across my skin in anticipation of what was to come.

My head fell back against my neck, aiming my face towards the ceiling. "Then feel me, Julian. Have your way with me; let's get lost in one another." My chest was heaving as he lifted me up, my legs enclosed around his waist as his lips found mine again; devouring one another, searching for the escape we both needed from life. We were closing out the world and simply revolving around making one another feel how much we craved each other.

Once we reached the bed I dropped my feet back down to the floor and quickly pulled his black shirt over his head. I placed my hand in the center of his chest and pushed him back until he fell onto the bed. His elbows were shoved deep into the mattress to hold his upper body up so that he could watch me as I slipped off each item of clothing that I was wearing except one, one at a time. Julian's eyes were full of desire; he wanted me just as badly as I wanted him. Standing before him in nothing but a pair of sheer navy blue panties I stepped between his jean-clad legs and leaned over, grabbing the button that was securely holding his jeans shut; I pushed it through the hole to unlatch them and slowly slipped his zipper down. His erection was instantly tenting his grey boxer briefs; my eyes found his as I pulled them and his jeans off of his legs. Julian sharply sucked air through his teeth as I leaned down and ran my tongue up his length before taking him into my mouth. I wrapped my hand around the base of him as I moved my head up and down, pulling groans and curse words from him with each stroke of my mouth and tongue against his pulsing shaft.

"If you don't stop I'm going to go in your mouth," Julian groaned the words out through clenched teeth as I smiled to myself.

One last bob of my head and I lifted up so that I connected my eyes with his as he wrapped a hand around my forearm and pulled me up so that each of my legs were on the outside of his thighs with his dick positioned directly against where I needed it the most. The warmth and pulsing of it was driving me mad as I began rocking my hips against him. "Julian…" I moaned as he leaned forward and sucked hard on each of my erect nipples.

    His hand slid down my stomach and into my panties. Once he found my sweet spot he applied pressure and began making small circles against my clit, igniting a spark low in my belly that sent tingles throughout my entire body. In one swift moment Julian tore my thin sheer panties from my body and quickly pushed himself inside of me to the hilt. A long seductive cry escaped my chest as he stilled, allowing me to become acquainted with his size. Without giving me full reign he flipped us over and began pumping in and out of me at a slow, agonizing rate.

    The slow build burning deep within me was intoxicating. My body was yearning for its release, making me feel like I could combust into a million tiny pieces once it was granted. Julian's head lowered so that his lips and tongue could tangle with my own. He grunted and groaned with each thrust of his hips upward, sending him deep into me. "Roll me over," I breathlessly moaned as Julian dragged his teeth across my swollen bottom lip before letting go. He pulled out of me and I quickly rolled onto my stomach; his hands gripped my hips and lifted me so that I was on my knees with my chest flush with the bed. With one knee he scooted my legs father apart, creating tension between my thighs as he slipped back into me with one quick, fluid thrust. The intensity from the newly found angle almost sent me crashing over the edge as I screamed his name loudly. His pace quickened and with each pull of his shaft dragging out of me almost completely before slamming back inside, I was getting closer and closer to the ledge that I desperately craved to fall from.

Julian towered over me as he reached his hand from beneath me and began teasing my clit again. A few strokes along with the fast pace of him pummeling into me and I was shattering around him. My legs gave out so he gripped my hips with his hands and continued until he groaned out my name and lost himself within me. Once he let go of my legs I collapsed fully against the bed again, completely spent. Julian dropped down next to me and placed a gentle kiss to the end of my nose before sliding from the bed and retrieving a warm cloth to clean the both of us up.

Once we were clean he padded back into the bathroom and dropped the cloth into the hamper. With the angle of my bed I could see almost my entire bathroom, which gave me a glorious view of Julian's naked backside as he walked away from me, along with another glorious view of his naked front as he walked back to the bed. His body was strong and beautiful. As he slid into the bed beside me the raised scars on his side were on full display for my eyes to take in. Julian made himself comfortable with his arm behind his head as he rested his back against the headboard of the bed. It was then that I realized we had just had sex in the bed I had shared for years with Thomas. Things were changing, that was for sure…the fact that I hadn't even second guessed about having sex in that bed made me realize that Thomas was slowly fading into the past for me; I would always hold on to the good memories of us together but it was time to move forward. And that moving forward would hopefully be with Julian.

I snuggled against Julian's chest as I locked a leg around one of his. It was something I was growing fond of doing while lying with him. My hand moved lazily across his damp skin and around to the scars on his side. My heart squeezed tightly in my chest, almost making it hard to breathe as I took in the angry flesh up close, all while Julian kept quiet. I glanced up to find his eyes on me as I moved my fingertips gently against the markings that could have taken his life in the same misguided raid that took Thomas'. The thought hit me, if Julian had died that horrible day with Thomas where would I have ended up?

Would I have known about the infidelity on Thomas' part?

Would Sara have come into the picture?

Would I be lying in bed with a different man as happy as I was with Julian?

They say everything that happens would be altered if you changed one little detail of how things unfolded. I was thankful for the way this scenario had unfolded, minus Thomas losing his life. I would never wish that on anyone. But, what if he lived? Would he have left me shortly after returning home like he had promised Sara, or would he have continued to be unfaithful to me by spending time with her? All of those thoughts muddied my mind as I continued to caress Julian's skin until his warm hand covered mine, stopping it on the largest wound.

"Penny for your thoughts?" his voice was soothing and laced with concern.

I grinned up at him as I rolled my hand over and interlocked our fingers. "I was just thinking about how one little instance could have changed this entire path."

"What do you mean?"

"What if you had died right along with Thomas? Where would I have ended up? Or what if Thomas had lived…would he have continued to cheat on me without me knowing, or would he have left me high and dry with a shattered heart and broken soul?"

Julian's facial expression softened as he cupped one side of my face. "You shouldn't think like that. We're in this moment of our lives together, so don't think about the 'what ifs'. Enjoy the now, MacKenzie, and stop overworking that pretty little mind of yours on things that don't amount to a hill of beans."

He was right. Thinking about what could have been was only adding unneeded stress to my already stressful life. "You're right." My lips pressed against his bare chest as he pulled me in closer to his side. Julian made me see all sides of scenarios that I might not have seen otherwise. He was the rational one in the relationship, and I was grateful that he had been thrown into my crazy-as-hell life. Even if it made some things more complicated.

Chapter Twenty

Julian had managed to talk me into packing a bag and going on an adventure with him. He was good at getting me to go places without knowing what we were actually going to be doing. I'd be lying if I claimed it didn't excite me, the unknown of what he had up his sleeve. Since we had officially become a couple it was going to be the first real getaway for us.

"All packed?" Julian's voice came from the doorway of my bedroom. I turned and found him smiling widely with his arms folded over his broad chest and aviator sunglasses sitting on top of his head. A white T-shirt hung loosely at his waist and was paired with camo cargo shorts and flip flops.

My bottom lip was sucked into my mouth as I tried to hide the huge smile tugging at my lips. "Yep. Now if you will only tell me where you are taking us." I raised an eyebrow at him as I tossed the strap of my bag over my shoulder.

Julian crossed the room, kissed me gently on the lips, and pulled the bag from my shoulder only to strap it over his own. "Not happening, beautiful." He tapped the end of my nose with his index finger and I playfully scoffed.

The car was still running in the driveway as I shut the door behind us and locked it securely, checking it twice. Ever since someone had broken in and ransacked my house I always double checked, or triple checked, the locks.

The sound of the trunk shutting and Julian hollering for me to come on, that the house would be fine made a silly grin spread across my face as I readjusted my purse strap on my shoulder and headed for the car. Once we were both buckled in he backed out and headed for destination unknown.

"Kenzie." The feeling of my leg being shaken slowly woke me up. I stretched my arms above my head as well as I could in the car and rolled my neck so that I was facing Julian in the driver's seat. "Have a nice nap?" He gave my thigh a gentle slap as I smiled.

"Yeah, I did actually." The anticipation of our trip had kept me up most of the night, but I felt bad about falling asleep on him. "I didn't mean to fall asleep."

"It's a good thing you did because we have a nice full day ahead of us."

The car came to a stop in front of a bright teal blue house with white shutters, perched high on stilts with a parking area underneath. It was cute and perfect for its spot on the beach but I was unsure why Julian would have brought me to a beach house when he already owned one just outside of Wilmington. We definitely weren't in Wilmington by the looks of things. "Where are we?" The question came out in a yawn.

"I rented this place for a couple nights." Julian was smiling proudly with excitement.

"Julian! We could've just gone to your beach house, you really didn't have to do this."

Julian was chuckling at my protest as he slid from the driver's seat and went around to the trunk to retrieve our bags. I followed him to the back of the car and he extended his hand with what I assumed to be the keys to the place dangling between his fingers. "Go open the door, I've got the bags." I snatched the keys and took off up the white painted wooden steps and quickly unlatched the door and pushed it open. The place was beautifully updated with the kitchen and living room adjoining but divided by a long bar with a white marble top and pale yellow painted tiles on the front side. Four white stools sat on the living room side of the bar and the pale color scheme continued into the living room with sea shells and paintings of the ocean for decoration. It made for a very relaxing feel.

"What do you think?" Julian dropped the bags just inside the door before closing it and turning back towards me.

"It's beautiful." I crossed the room and wrapped my arms around his neck. "You really didn't have to do this, Julian. I would have been fine at your beach house."

He leaned forward and pressed his lips to mine. "Stop it." He placed a finger over my closed lips. "I wanted to give us a getaway to somewhere we hadn't been before and found this place. Now let's put our bags in the bedroom and get changed." He slipped his finger from my lips and replaced it with his own. "I want to spend time with my woman in her bikini on the beach." A sly grin spread across his face as he smacked my butt. "Get on, woman!" He playfully raised his voice. A yelp escaped me as I took off in the direction of where I assumed the bedroom was.

Rounding the corner into the room that was indeed the bedroom—the house only had one—laughter echoed as Julian chased me. His arms wrapped around my waist as I screamed with laughter and he turned me to face him, picked me up, and tossed me down on the bed before climbing over me. We were both smiling widely as our chests heaved from our playful escapade. Julian's eyes focused on my smiling mouth as the air between us changed. It was filled with want and need as his lips connected with mine. At first our lips danced in a slow, needy rhythm until we lost control, throwing the steady rhythm out the window and devouring one another. Nothing ever stayed slow between the two of us. Every time our bodies connected in any way it quickly escalated from one to one hundred in no time. The connection between us was magnetic and burning strong like a wildfire.

"Julian...We've gotta stop or we won't be making it to whatever you have planned for the day." He pulled back, disconnecting his lips from their spot midway down the curve of my neck and rested his forehead against the same spot.

"I can't keep my hands or lips off of you." The husky growl of his response set that familiar burn ablaze deep in my stomach.

Just hearing his voice was a damn turn-on.

He pushed up from the bed and said, "I'll give you ten minutes to get changed. If you're not out there before then I'm coming back after you, and we won't be leaving this beach house for a while." Julian's promise had chills creeping across my skin; it was *very* tempting to keep my happy ass in the bed until he returned, but I knew he had planned out our entire trip so I didn't want to spoil it. Doing the only other thing I could do, I changed into my bikini with a white V-neck sheer cover-up and met him on the porch.

Julian lifted his sunglasses from their perched position on his nose and asked, "What is that?" His eyebrows scrunched together in the center as he took in my choice of clothing.

"It's a cover-up," I explained.

He shook his head and repositioned his sunglasses where they had previously been. "There is no need for that thing. I know you hate wearing a bikini, swimsuits, or whatever you want to call them, but babe, your body is beautiful and definitely doesn't need to be hidden." He waved his hand up and down motioning towards my cover-up.

The chuckle that escaped me had a large smile spreading across Julian's face. "Well-" I grabbed the cover-up by the bottom hem and slowly pulled it up and over my head before tossing it onto the porch and heading down the stairs to the sand. He had already seen every inch of my body, to be afraid to wear my bikini in front of him after all of that would've been a bit ridiculous. "Is this better?" The last of my sentence was spoken with my back to him as I sashayed my backside a little more than usual.

A primal growl rumbled from Julian behind me as the corners of my lips spread widely and tipped up in an accomplished full-blown smile. MacKenzie, one; Julian, zero.

I fanned the two beach towels I was carrying out side-by-side on the sand, overlapping slightly, before I stretched out on my half with my palms flat on the ground behind my back so that I could look out at the beautiful waves crashing gently against the sand.

"You did that on purpose, didn't you?" Julian questioned as he took a seat beside me, with his sunglass still shielding his penetrating brown eyes. The only response I could give him was the witty grin that adorned my lips.

"You're bad...very, very *bad*." His deep voice rumbled against the shell of my ear, sending chills across my warm, sun-heated skin as he leaned into my personal space.

"Mmhmm..." My body instinctively leaned towards him as his tongue swooped out and seductively ran down the shell of my ear before his lips found the soft skin just behind my earlobe. A heavy sigh fell from my lungs as every inch of my body ignited with a burning desire for Julian to take me back into that beach house and make me scream his name over and over again. Just as soon as I was on the verge of begging him to do just that, his lips were gone from my ear and he was headed down to the water, leaving me sitting in a heap of sexual desire.

My huff was swallowed by the breeze as I lathered myself up with sunscreen so that my easily burnt skin hopefully wouldn't get as toasted as it had been, before I laid back on the beach towel. SPF five million was what I needed, but apparently the stores didn't carry something that strong so I had to settle on a SPF of fifty. The soothing sounds of the ocean, along with the gentle breeze blowing, had me drifting into a peaceful relaxation. I closed my eyes and removed my sunglass so I wouldn't end up with those pesky tan lines that made one look like they were related to a raccoon and rested my arms at my sides. The warmth of the sun felt amazing, like it was massaging my body and getting rid of the tension from the days prior.

Lying there had my mind shutting off all of the hurt and mounds of questions that had been floating around in there for quite some time. It didn't take me long to start zoning out and falling closer to sleep, but instead of allowing myself to do just that I rolled over on my stomach so that I wouldn't burn to a crisp. My hand blindly searched for the strings of my bikini top and undid them. If I was going to be tanning on the beach where hardly anyone was around, I was going to do it with a minimum of tan lines. I tucked my arms under my head to make a makeshift pillow, resting my forehead against my overlapping hands with my face down towards the beach towel beneath me.

Smooth hands ran up my bare back, "You're going to get us kicked off this beach if you don't tie this thing back." Julian informed me as he massaged his fingertips deep into my muscles. A satisfied moan fell from my mouth as I turned my head towards his side and smiled.

"What if I rolled over?" One of my eyebrows rose in question as I acted as if I was going to roll over so that my chest would be facing him.

Julian shook his head back and forth with a grin on his lips. His fingers made quick fluid motions tying my bikini top firmly back in place before he rolled me over and scooped me into his arms. As he stood cradling me to his chest, I yelped from all of the unexpected movement. "Fuck beach time. I'm going to be the one to make your ass red, not the sun." A fit of giggles echoed through the air as Julian jogged up the beach house steps, pushed the door open, and took me into the bedroom. He wasn't lying about being the one to make my ass red, he did just that and so much more.

The sun was setting, cascading a beautiful array of colors across the once bright blue sky. Julian had his hand interlocked with mine as he rubbed ever-so gently in small circles on the back of my hand with his thumb. The boardwalk was booming with all walks of life. A Ferris wheel with different colored bucket seats had lights flashing and dancing throughout it as it went in a slow circle, giving its occupants a chance to look out over the boardwalk and ocean before returning back to the ground so others could take their turn. Small, slightly ramshackle buildings were placed in different areas throughout the boardwalk, each painted a different bright color, and all with a snarky name displayed on the front just above the door or service window; some offered food while others offered souvenirs and swimsuits.

We came to a stop where part of the dock reached out over the ocean. "This place is beautiful, Julian." I was in awe of Carolina Beach and how down-to-earth everyone was. We hadn't encountered a single person that seemed to be having a bad day or was full of a horrible attitude; it was refreshing.

He stepped behind me so that his chest was flush with my back and caged me in with his arms. "I had a feeling you would like it here." His voice sent chills dancing across my skin, noticing them he ran his warm hands up and down my arms. "Cold?"

I twisted in his arms so that we were facing one another and shook my head back and forth. "Not at all. Those were the good kind of chills." I smiled up at him from beneath my eyelashes and a mega-watt smile stretched his lips in return.

Before another word was spoken between us the sounds of fireworks started going off, and different colors and designs danced throughout the sky behind me. I turned around and leaned back into Julian's chest as he locked his hands together, securely holding me in place as we watched the beautiful array of fireworks with the rest of the growing crowd. My off-white, strapless, knee length dress danced around our legs as the breeze came in, carrying with it the scent of the salty ocean and food. My stomach growled from the aromas as the fireworks continued to explode one after the other.

"Hungry?" Julian chuckled.

"You heard that?" I gasped with embarrassment.

Julian laughed as he shook his head. "No, I felt it." He gave his hands a gentle squeeze, reminding me of them being locked around my waist.

The rumbling of my stomach must have been a helluva lot more intense than I had thought it was for Julian to have felt it. I couldn't help but laugh. "Yeah, you have me there." I shrugged. "So what's good to eat around these parts?" A thick southern accent rolled off my tongue, causing Julian to erupt with laughter.

"Well, ma'am." He faked like he was tipping his hat to me as he dialed in his own thick southern accent. "There's this little place called Pippy's that sits on a stretch of the dock all its own, they have the *best* seafood that will ever pass through your pretty little mouth." His lips found mine as he finished his perfectly-pitched fake southern charm.

I moaned in acceptance of his lingering kiss and spoke quietly against his lips. "That sounds perfect."

Julian wasn't kidding when he told me Pippy's had the best seafood to ever pass your lips. We sat on a picnic-style table out on the deck that stretched above part of the ocean. A long canopy covered most of the large deck, keeping possible rain, bird droppings, and other *wonderfulness* off of the patrons and their food. Strands of round light bulbs draped around the deck, giving just enough lighting to see your meal while also creating a romantic atmosphere at night.

As I finished off the last bite of my fish sandwich I glanced up at Julian who was grinning from ear-to-ear while stifling his laughter. "What's so funny?" I managed to say around my mouth full of food while covering it with my hand.

He leaned over the table and swiped the pad of his thumb across the left corner of my mouth before sucking it clean. "You had a little something on your face."

"What was that little something?" I teased.

"Tartar sauce." He knew exactly where I was going with my questioning. "But it could be something else once we get back to the beach house later." His eyebrows waggled up and down playfully as I laughed at his suggestion.

"Typical man." I waved dismissively at him. "Always thinking with your lower member." My smile was so big that it was causing my cheeks to hurt from it hanging around so much throughout the day. I hadn't smiled to that extent in a very long time, and it felt good to have someone in my life that made me do that. Julian was my breath of fresh air from all of the pollutants my life had been contaminated with.

"If you understood the woman I have the chance of calling mine, you'd always have your mind in the gutter as well." Julian winked just as the waiter placed the bill on the table in front of him and wished us a good night. I tried to snag the bill before he got his hands on it. He had spent enough money on the two of us, it was my turn. "What do you think you're doing?" He quickly picked up the piece of receipt paper before I got close enough to grab it.

"Let me pay for our meal. You've spent enough money on the beach house and everything else." Julian was having no part of my attempt at paying.

"I don't think so, beautiful." He quickly pulled cash from his wallet and handed it to the waiter as he passed by again. "Ready?" Julian stood and extended his hand, palm up, for me to take. I slid my hand into his and he threaded our fingers together at our sides as he guided me through the building and out the front door of the cute bright yellow shack.

"What's next on the agenda?" I questioned as we headed down the boardwalk.

Many carnival games came into view the closer we got to the Ferris wheel. The familiar excitement of being a kid at the county fair hit me as a wide smile pulled my lips up with anticipation. "First-" Julian unlatched our hands and dug some cash out of his pocket. "I'm going to win you the biggest damn bear this place has." A giggle fell from my lips as I envisioned us carrying the thing around. I *really* hoped he would win me a giant bear.

"Try your shot! Hit three targets and win your choice of one of these great prizes!" The man from behind the counter called out to passersby as he waved his hand beneath the hanging prizes for everyone to see. "How about you, kind sir, want to win your girl an animal of her choice?" the man propositioned Julian.

He turned to me and kissed my forehead. "Let's get you that bear." He walked up to the counter and I stepped up to his side as he handed the man a ten.

"You have six shots. Good luck!" The man took a few steps to the left and leaned an elbow on the counter to watch.

Julian crouched forward so that the feet of the gun were positioned correctly on the counter before taking a deep breath and exhaling slowly as he pulled the trigger. I squealed with happiness as target one went down with ease. Julian turned towards me and smiled widely at my over-enthusiasm for him to win the game before he turned his attention back to it. I watched as he took another deep breath before letting it out just as slowly as the first one, but this time he missed the second target by a fraction it seemed. "Damn," he growled before taking his shooting stance again. Without a second of pause he pulled the trigger once more and laid the second target down, followed by the third almost simultaneously. I was jumping with joy as I wrapped my arms around Julian's neck once he stood to his full height. The man behind the counter congratulated us as he moved front and center of the counter.

"You're a good shot," he praised Julian. "Military?"

"Former Marine," Julian replied proudly as the man nodded in acknowledgement.

"Thank you for your service." The man behind the counter extended his hand and Julian took it. They shook firmly before letting go.

"No need for thanks, I was just doing my duty as an American." Julian seemed a bit embarrassed by the man praising him over being a Marine; I found that to be a cute attribute of his.

"Which animal would you like?" The man turned his attention to me as I scanned my options with the goofiest grin on my face.

"That one." I pointed to the large chestnut brown bear that held a heart with its paws. The man pulled it down and handed it over. The fluffy bear was almost as big as I was as I squeezed him tightly in my grasp and smiled at Julian.

"Here-" Julian took the bear from my arms. "Let me carry it back to the beach house for you. It's almost carrying you instead of vice versa," he laughed as I playfully smacked his shoulder. "I'm just trying to help you out, Kenzie." His laughter picked up as I crossed my arms over my chest and pretended to pout as we walked back down the boardwalk.

"Yeah, yeah." I walked ahead, making him think that I was truly upset about the lack of the giant bear being in my arms.

"Hey!" He called after me and I stopped dead in my tracks, allowing him to catch up before I turned to face him.

Julian positioned the bear on his hip so that his face wasn't blocked by it. Concern was etched across his eyes and lips as he raised his free hand and gently dragged it across my cheek. "Are you really upset with me?" The question made me internally fist pump the air as I smiled and Julian's concerned morphed back into laughter.

"Of course not, goof! I was just messing with you." I quickly grabbed the bear and took off running the best that I could down the boardwalk, laughing hysterically as I went.

"You sneaky ass!" Julian called after me as the sound of his heavier-than-mine footsteps pounded against the wood walkway as he ran to catch me.

My hysterical laughter became even louder as I continued to push myself as fast as I could run with the giant bear locked against my chest with my arms squeezing it as tightly as possible.

"MacKenzie!" Julian yelled. "Stop!" I wasn't sure why he was yelling for me to stop until the terrain beneath my feet changed, causing my sandal to buckle sideways. The bear went flying forward out of my grasp as I tumbled towards the sand face first.

"Shit!" I heard Julian growl as my face hit the sand. The burn from the grainy sand singed against my cheeks and forehead as I came to a stop. My palms pushed deep into it as I lifted myself from it and sat back on the heels of my feet.

"I'm okay!" I lifted a hand in the air as Julian dropped down in front of me.

His hands quickly began examining me before dusting my face off and cupping my cheeks with his hands. "Your face has a few red scrapes on it, but no blood or anything." The look in his eyes hit me straight in the heart. "You scared the shit out of me when you fell, I thought you were going to be pretty banged up from the way it looked as you went down."

A shaky breath blew from my mouth as I erupted into a heavy laughter that slowly morphed into tears. My knees, palms, and face were stinging from the fall. I pulled my legs from beneath me and stretched them out to view the damage that had been done; sure enough red scrapes covered both knees, with blood pooling lightly in spots on my left knee while the right knee was torn open pretty good.

"MacKenzie…" Julian sucked in a sharp breath as he pulled me to his chest, soothing the embarrassment and pain that was radiating through my fresh wounds. No, they weren't too horrible, but they still ached like a son of a bitch. "Let's get you to the beach house, those need to be cleaned before they get infected." He helped me to my feet and draped my arm over his neck so I could walk. The bending of my right knee was killing me as Julian snatched the bear up with his free arm; we slowly made our way back as the tears finally stopped falling from my eyes.

Once we got inside Julian left the bear sitting on the couch and helped me to the kitchen, since the bathroom was too small for the both of us to have much room. Moments later he returned with a first aid kit. I felt like a kid that hadn't listened and ended up with shitty circumstances afterwards, not the woman I actually was.

"Here." Julian helped me back to my feet from my resting spot in a chair at the table. His hands gripped my hips as he lifted me into the air and placed me gently on the counter. "This is a better angle for me to clean your knees up." He pushed my dress up just enough to fully expose the area and its surroundings, but I gripped the hem and hiked it up, bunching it at my waist so he had more space to work.

His attention was on my knees first, gently rubbing a wetted cloth to clean the scrapes before rubbing ointment onto them. The burn ached but soon began to fade, leaving an almost soothing feeling in its place. Large bandages covered my knees as he moved onto my palms, gently rubbing them clean was enough. Thankfully my face got the least of the fall, even though it planted firmly into the sand, so the scrapes were minimal and would easily be covered with makeup.

"You did a pretty good number on your right knee." Julian's eyes found mine as he dusted off the remainder of my face with the damp cloth.

My hands quickly rose and covered my face. The embarrassment of falling like I had in front of so many people—and Julian—was horrid. "How embarrassing." My words were muffled as I groaned.

Julian gently removed my hands from my face, placing a kiss to each palm before pressing his lips against mine. "It wasn't *that* bad." His eyebrows dipped low, telling me he was being nice about it.

"Ugh..." My groan was cut short as he took my mouth again, slowly caressing my tongue with his own. All train of thought about my fall had ceased as I lost myself in the depth of Julian's deep, core-burning kiss. A moan echoed in the silent beach house as he bit down on my bottom lip, sending a surge of desire coursing through my body, raising goose bumps in its wake. Julian knew exactly how to evoke a yearning for pleasure within me, he was a master of my body, and I prayed he would be the only one for me the rest of my life.

"I'm sorry you got hurt today." His husky voice was hot against my skin as he dropped his mouth to the soft skin behind my ear and trailed kisses down the curve of my neck. In one swift motion Julian pulled my strapless dress up and over my head, leaving me sitting before him in nothing but a simple white thong.

My chest was heaving from the anticipation of his next move as he stepped back to drink me in with his desire-filled eyes. His heavy lids raised as his eyes met mine again before dropping to my mouth where my teeth dug into the plump flesh of my bottom lip. I wanted him *badly*, so badly that the thin piece of material covering my most sensitive area was beginning to moisten simply from watching the way he was looking at my almost naked body. I straightened my back, lifting my chest a little higher as my breathing became even more erratic.

"You're so fucking beautiful." Julian stepped between my legs, pushing them wider as he made his presence known. His hands smoothed up my waist until he was cupping both of my breasts within them. The rough surface of his palms rolled against my nipples, causing just enough friction to elicit another moan from my lips as my head dropped back on my neck, aiming my face towards the ceiling with my mouth slacked. "I love when you make those sounds." His lips kissed down the column of my throat before giving each nipple its own attention.

My hands found his hair and gripped it roughly, pulling a groan from deep in his chest. Julian hooked his fingers into the band of my thong and pulled it off my legs, letting it drop to the floor on its own. With me completely nude he spread my legs wide on the counter as I leaned back into the palms of my hands that were secured against the counter behind me. The path of his kisses moved down the valley between my breasts to the hollow of my rib cage and past my navel without stopping until the warmth of his tongue swept against my folds. My body bucked as he kissed my sensitive flesh passionately, dipping his tongue into my entrance before sucking my swollen bud into his lips.

His fingers clutched my hips in their grasp as he continued the sweet torturous rhythm against me. The mewling cries that left me seemed to push him into even more of a frenzy; two of his fingers pushed deep into my channel repeatedly as his tongue lapped at my folds and clit. The burning sensation deep in my core was building by the second as he hooked his fingers upward, hitting the exact spot I needed him to and the world around me faded away as my release crashed down heavily. Julian groaned as he removed his fingers and lapped my release with his tongue, flicking my even more sensitive bud once again with his thumb.

My hands could no longer hold me up as I collapsed on the counter, my legs spread wide open and my eyelids heavily shut from the euphoric feeling seeping through my body from Julian giving me pleasure. The sound of a belt hitting the floor barely registered as his hands pulled me to my feet and turned me around so that my breasts were lying on the counter top. Without a moment's notice Julian had pushed fully into me and was holding my body up with his left arm wrapped around my waist. His other hand was spread out wide on the counter beside my head as his thick hot words at my ear sent tingles down my spine. "This is mine…" He pulled out slowly before hastily pushing back in. "So fucking good…" Julian's primal groan sent me over the edge for a second time as his pace quickened. His rhythm was so fast that my nipples were rubbing against the counter top at a painful rate, but the pain barely registered as he reached around to dance his fingertips against my clit. His name fell loudly from my lips as he placed his lips at the base of the back of my neck, biting and licking the skin before releasing into me.

"Fuck," he breathed as his hands rubbed down my hips, massaging the red spot created by the force of him pushing me into the counter. "Did I hurt you?" The sincerity in the question had me lifting my head just enough to look back at him.

"Hell no." My chest was still heaving from exertion. "That was…if I wasn't so tired I'd ask you to do it all again." A lazy smile spread widely across his face as he gently slid out of me, scooping me up into his arms and carrying me into the bathroom.

Julian sat me on the toilet as he ran a warm bath. "You deserve more than just a warm bath, but this will have to do for now." He kissed my bare shoulder, turned the water off once the tub was filled, and picked me back up so that he could slide me into the nice-sized tub. It was the main reason the bathroom seemed so small. Apparently the owners loved their baths.

As the warm water covered my body I relaxed, letting my limbs float in the water. I rolled my head on the rim of the tub so that I could look at Julian. "You're a beautiful man, Julian. Inside and out." Pure admiration was laced in my words.

He dropped the rag in the sink for the time being and came back to the tub; leaning over the edge his lips found mine in a gentle, loving kiss. "I am who I am because of you." My throat clogged with the emotions of his words as he sat back and took one last look at my smiling face before running his heated eyes down the length of my body and back up again. "Enjoy your bath, beautiful." He kissed me again before leaving me to the silence and soothing warmth of the water I was lying in. Julian was beyond anything I could have ever hoped for in a man.

Chapter Twenty One

It officially marked one month since Julian and I had jumped into a relationship together. Things were beginning to calm down quite a bit with Sara out of the picture and Loren's divorce finalized. She and Gabe had actually been coming over to spend time with Julian and me; I wasn't sure if the two of them had anything going on, but it seemed they connected pretty well.

Not long after we'd returned from our trip to Carolina Beach Julian had gone to base, leaving me home alone for the first time in the month we had been together. The silence wasn't as deafening as before, now it was nice and peaceful. I hadn't realized how much I needed a day to myself until I had a couple.

The day was spent planting flowers in the gardens in front and back, followed by lounging on the deck with some homemade lemonade. It felt good to relax. As night fell I curled up on the couch and started catching up on some of the shows that were quickly filling up the DVR. It had been a while since I had the chance to do that, and some horrible reality shows were beckoning me to watch.

It didn't take long before my eyelids were too heavy to keep open, but I kept fighting the battle to finish the last bit of the season finale of a police show I had been pulled into since day one. With a throw blanket pulled up to my chin I propped my head up on the side of the couch with one of the smaller decorative pillows and tried to rally myself awake for the ending.

A loud bang caused me to jump up, suddenly wide awake. My heart was racing a mile a minute as I slipped from the couch with my cell phone in hand. I knew I shouldn't have been heading towards where the bang had come from, but I couldn't stop myself either. If someone was breaking into my house again, they were going to have to deal with me.

I quietly made my way into the kitchen and slipped a knife from the butcher block where numerous ones were resting. The light above the sink was the only light on in the house besides the TV, but my eyes had adjusted enough to be able to tell what I was near as I maneuvered myself towards the garage. The sound of something crashing to the ground caused me to yelp and jump involuntarily, so I slammed my hand holding my cell phone over my mouth to try and muffle myself. Terror ripped through me at the thought of the person hearing me, but I pushed on.

My sweaty palm gripped the door knob as I slowly turned it so the sound of the door unlatching wouldn't be so loud. I gradually pulled the door towards me, opening a path into the garage. In my crouched position I peeked around the corner towards the stairs that led up to the study. What I saw had my heart dropping into my stomach out of fear. The door was cracked open just enough to see that the light was on, and a figure was walking about up there. A scream threatened to escape me, but I clamped my shaky hand down tightly to smother it if it tried. My finger found Julian's name on the screen and quickly pressed it, letting the sound of ringing flood my ears. "Pick up…come on, come on…" I whispered to myself as I slouched back against the wall and silently tried to close the door to the garage. Once the door was shut I hopped up from the floor and took off running to the opposite side of the house and into my bedroom. I quietly closed the door as my phone call to Julian went to his voicemail.

"You've reached Julian Cooper, please leave your name and number after the beep and I will get back to you as soon as I can."

"Dammit!" I quietly cursed, hitting end to keep from leaving a message. I switched the phone to silent so if he called back, or anyone else called, it wouldn't alert the intruder. My heart was slamming so hard within my ribcage that it was causing me to shake horribly. Then it hit me. Thomas had kept a handgun attached to the back of the bedpost. I quickly made my way over to the bed and found the gun exactly where I had thought it would be. The last time he had been home he had taught me how to use it. I hadn't been to the range in quite some time, but I knew if need be I could pull the trigger.

My hand gripped the gun as I slid it from the holster and took a deep breath. "You can do this, MacKenzie." The quiet pep talk I was giving myself was cut short by the sound of something being knocked over. Instead of fear pulsing through me, rage took over. The thought of some piece of shit ransacking my home again made me livid. I cocked the gun and slowly reopened the bedroom door before slipping into the living room. The TV was still on as I crouched down behind one of the couches and slowly slipped around it, trying to keep the shadow I cast in the illumination from the TV off of the wall. If the intruder was in the kitchen they could easily see a shadow on the wall, and the last thing I needed to do was alert the person that I was in the house.

The thumping of my heart picked up the closer I got to the kitchen. The sound of a drawer being hastily pulled open and its contents being dumped onto the counter had my body involuntarily jumping at the loud crashes and bangs. Whoever it was in there was on a mission to find something. That was obvious, but what could they be after? The bag of money wouldn't fit in that drawer so there had to be something else that I hadn't run across myself. A steady, deep breath left my lungs as I tightened my grip on the gun. In one swift motion I rounded the corner into the kitchen. "Freeze!" I yelled with conviction as I held the barrel of the gun towards the tall man dressed in black with his head aimed down at the counter. In the darkness of the kitchen I couldn't see his face. The light above the sink was casting light only on his back, but from what I could tell he wasn't carrying a weapon.

He stood stark still and lifted his head, still not looking my way. "What the *fuck* are you doing in my home and what are you looking for?" The words spewed from my mouth with venom before I could stop them. Apparently I wasn't going to tread lightly, even if I was in danger myself.

Without replying he turned towards me with his face low enough for me not to be able to tell just who he was in the darkness. As his feet moved him closer to me I warned him to stop twice as my hand shook with my finger hovering over the trigger of the gun. "One more step and I'm going to shoot." The warning was stern as the man stopped and sighed.

"It was only a matter of time before you found out."

Chills rose on my skin as I took in his words, his voice, and finally his face. My eyes and ears had to be betraying me because there was no way it could have been him. There was no way in hell…

No. Way. In. Hell.

My hand holding the gun, but not the trigger, slapped against the wall in search of the light switch. Once it was found I quickly flipped it on and snapped my hand back in its place on the gun as a gasp echoed through the kitchen when my eyes focused on the man before me. Tears flooded my eyes, running relentlessly down my face as I lowered the gun.

The clogging of my throat from the abundance of emotions made it hard to speak, "It can't be you…"

Chapter Twenty Two
Julian

Staying on base for three days had put me back in the mindset of wanting to be out in the field again. After I had been on leave for so long they approved me to receive my pension along with working a limited number of hours if I wanted. There was no way I could stay at home and do nothing all of the time, so working on base was the best choice for me. My body wouldn't allow me to go back out in the field, let alone the Marines themselves, but I couldn't even fathom leaving MacKenzie for long periods of time anyway.

My locker clicked as I dialed in the last number of the combination before opening it. I grabbed my overnight bag and placed the clothes I needed to wash along with the other personal items I wouldn't leave on base in it. The vibration of my phone on the top shelf made a loud noise as it scooted across the metal. As I checked it the screen showed one missed call from Kenzie around eleven the previous night. Either something was up or she was bored. Since there wasn't any voice message to go with the missed call I assumed the latter of the two.

"See you later, Brighten," I saluted him as we passed. He was the guy over me, the man who helped me rehabilitate after the explosion that put me in hospital and killed Thomas. Brighten was a man that would go above and beyond his duties to help his fellow Marines, along with his country.

"See you next week, Cooper."

"Yes, sir." My hand latched onto the bar and pushed open the door that led out into the parking lot where my car sat. It felt good to be heading home to MacKenzie, it had been three long days of not being able to feel her skin or kiss her lips. Remedying that was first on my agenda.

The leather of my seats made noise as I slid into the driver's seat and shut the door. I pushed the button to crank the engine and hit MacKenzie's name on the missed calls list; I needed to hear her voice way before I got to her house. The ringing ceased as her voicemail picked up, the voicemail box that she apparently hadn't set up. *Way to go, Kenzie.* I tried one more time only to hear that her voice mailbox hadn't been set up once again. My hand moved the gear shift into reverse when a knock sounded on my window. Brighten was standing there.

Pushing the automatic roll down button I nodded at him. "Yes, sir?" He handed me a slip of paper through the window seal.

"Patsy forgot to give you this phone call slip. MacKenzie Cole left a message for you to meet her at your house instead of hers." Brighten raised a questioning eyebrow. Hardly anyone on base knew about me being with the widow of Thomas Cole, especially Brighten. "Do I need to ask what's going on between the two of you?"

"It's complicated." My eyes diverted towards the windshield as I took in how I had described MacKenzie and me. We actually weren't complicated, but to the outside world the situation would seem to be just that.

"I don't think it is, Julian." The fact that Brighten used my first name threw me off. "Thomas would be happy that she is with you, simply because of the type of man you are. You're a protector, you'd walk through hell and high water to keep someone safe. That's the kind of man Thomas would have wanted her to end up with."

I nodded in affirmation as he tapped his hand against the hood of my car. "Go see your girl, I'll see your ass next week, Cooper." And with that he was back to his normal self. Giving him a salute I closed the window and backed out of the parking space. Kenzie was waiting for me at my house and I couldn't wait another minute to get to her.

As I pulled closer to my house I noticed MacKenzie's car parked half-ass in front of the place. Not sure why she would have parked like that, but it looked like a drunk had done the parking job. Surely to god that wasn't the case. Once my car was in park and shut off I quickly got out, leaving my bags and shit in it. My feet quickly took the front steps as I pushed the unlocked door open, "MacKenzie!" My voice carried through the house as I scanned the living room.

Empty.

"MacKenzie! Are you here?" I frantically called out again, but I was met with silence. After scanning most of the house I came up short. The only room left was the master bedroom. I pushed the door open and passed the threshold, and my eyes instantly landed on her curled up in the center of the bed wearing one of my Marines T-shirts.

Her legs were tucked up so that her knees were pressing into her chest, revealing the bottom of her ass due to the shirt being pulled up just slightly. Her hair looked damp, like she had freshly showered. The redness of her cheeks, eyelids, and nose caught my attention the closer I got to her. I kicked my boots off and slid onto the mattress beside her, gently nudging her shoulder with my hand. "MacKenzie, baby…" She whimpered and I gently shook her again. "Wake up, sweetheart."

Her legs stretched out as she stirred awake, rolling onto her stomach. The T-shirt had ridden up against her panty line, giving me a full view of her perfect round ass. My hands were itching to grab hold and massage the globes; the thought alone had my dick stirring in my pants. I repositioned myself as I watched her eyes flutter open. At first she looked confused before her eyes fully focused and a sigh of what seemed like relief passed her lips. She pushed up quickly from her lying position and wrapped her arms around my neck. "Julian…" Her voice cracked on the end of my name as she broke into body-wrenching sobs.

Confusion washed over me as to why she was crying. I stroked her hair with one hand as I held her close. "Baby, what's wrong?" I questioned softly, which only seemed to make her sob even harder. My hand rubbed her back soothingly as I listened to her cries fade away. Her body expanded as she inhaled a deep breath and let it out. Her body tensed as she pulled away from me. That's when I knew that whatever she was about to hit me with was not going to be something I would be happy about. Perspiration beaded across my forehead from the stress of what she was about to tell me, the tension in her demeanor was nerve wracking.

"What's going on, MacKenzie?"

She dipped her head, dropping her eyes to the hem on the shirt—my shirt—she was wearing. The sadness etched across her face was tearing me up, I wanted to pull her back into my embrace and hold her until it was gone. By the looks of things, that wasn't going to happen.

She released a shaky breath, which was something she would do when she was about to lay something important out there for the world to hear, and lifted her tear-filled green eyes to meet mine. "We need to spend some time away from one another." A crack ran down the center of my heart. "Everything's becoming too much, and I need to wrap my head around what in the hell is going on right now. You being gone for the past few days made me realize how crazy I have been. We jumped head first into a relationship, without any notion of the massive dark cloud hovering over us."

What she was saying made sense, but parts just didn't seem like her. Something was going on, I wasn't sure what it was but allowing her to push me away without finding out wasn't going to happen. "What brought this on?"

A sad smile pulled at her lips as she shook her head back and forth. "Life." One simple word was all she gave me before climbing into my lap and sealing my mouth with her own. Her kisses were frantic, like she had to taste every inch of me because her life depended on it. Our tongues moved against one another as she fisted my hair and my hands gripped her bare thighs, pushing my fingertips deep into the milky flesh. Her body shook as I felt warm tears touching my face from hers.

My lips stopped moving as I pulled away to find her crying uncontrollably. Kenzie was hysterical as my hands cupped her face, my forehead resting against hers, "Please talk to me, don't shut me out. Whatever is going on we can work through it together. I can't lose you when I've barely had you, MacKenzie. I'll fight like hell to prove that to you."

Her lip quivered as her big green eyes focused on mine. "I—I shouldn't have come here." She tried to slide off my lap but I gripped her waist, not allowing her to move. Running was not an option.

"*You* made it a point to call me on the base and leave a message for me to meet you at *my* house. I called your cell phone but you never answered, so I came straight here. I deserve some answers, and I'm not letting you leave until I get them." My eyes bored into hers with the conviction that I meant what I was saying. "Now tell me, MacKenzie, why are you so upset and springing this 'we need space' shit on me now? Everything was better than fine; we were great before I left. So tell me...what the hell happened?"

MacKenzie scooted up until her back was flush with the headboard of the bed and slipped her knees into the shirt, stretching it out as she wrapped her arms around her legs. She looked terrified as her own internal battle took place. So many emotions flashed across her eyes before she spoke, but the words that slipped off her tongue weren't ones I would have ever expected in my entire life.

"Thomas is alive."

Chapter Twenty Three
MacKenzie

The trembling in my hands intensified as I watched Julian's reaction to the news. I had no idea why I had come to his house, why I had bathed in his shower, and why I had put on only his T-shirt and a pair of panties. My mind was on the fritz even more than it had been. Thomas being alive evoked emotions from me that I didn't know were still there.

Yes, he had cheated on me with Sara.

Yes, he had a son from the infidelity.

Yes, my heart still held the love I had for him within it.

But the clusterfuck of emotions inside my heart was tearing me apart limb by limb, and I wasn't sure if I would survive it. How can one be torn between two men, two completely different men that shared a career…and a woman? Everything I had done with Julian and felt for him felt wrong with the news of Thomas being alive. I was married, no longer a widow. In reality, what I had done with Julian was just as bad as what Thomas had done with Sara. No, I'd had no idea that he was still alive, whereas he had intentionally slept with Sara behind my back.

My head was aching and the hollow feeling of wanting to vomit churned in my stomach. "Did you hear me?" Julian's eyebrows dipped low in the center as he leaned closer to me.

I shook my head back and forth.

Julian's hand covered mine that we clasped around my legs. "How do you know that he is alive, MacKenzie?"

My eyes flooded with tears once again as I focused them on Julian's sandy brown heartbroken ones. "I saw him." Julian relaxed just a bit, not understanding exactly what I was saying; assuming that I meant I saw him in passing or someone that might have easily been mistaken for him. But that wasn't the case. "Last night someone broke into the house, that's why I called you. But instead of calling the police, I was pissed off and grabbed the gun that Thomas kept on the back of the bed post." I unlatched my hands and gripped Julian's hand tightly in mine. "It was Thomas, Julian! Thomas was the intruder last night. I know this sounds crazy, but it was him!"

He sat there in complete shock as I nervously waited for him to say something…anything. Something changed in his eyes from heartache to hurt. "You're pushing me away because of him, aren't you?" Julian stood and roughly raked his hands through his hair as I sat in silence. The truth of the matter was that I *was* trying to push Julian away because of Thomas.

The entire situation made me sick. I loved Julian in ways that I hadn't loved Thomas, but Thomas was my *husband*; the man I declared my vows to before my family, friends, and God. I cradled my head against my knees as another round of hellacious tears wracked through me.

Why couldn't my life be easy?

"You're probably thinking that you should feel bad, that what we have is no different than what Thomas had been doing with Sara behind your back…but you're wrong, MacKenzie." My head lifted from its resting spot against my knees as the tears continued to run down my face relentlessly. Julian had his back to me as I listened to what he was saying. "We both thought Thomas was dead, that he wasn't ever coming home. Neither of us thought we would end up in a relationship, we were two people that had a mutual connection that found peace within one another. There is no cheating involved. You were a widow, not a married woman who was intentionally going behind her husband's back to sleep with another man. I can't allow you to believe that anything you have done is even remotely close to what Thomas put you through. He has a son with another woman for fuck's sake! That son was conceived while he was married to *you*! Don't you see the difference there?" My head bobbed up and down in affirmation as he turned towards me with tears of his own pooling his eyes. "I belong to you, MacKenzie Cole. No matter what you decide is the best route for you, I want you to know that. This-" His knees hit the side of the bed as he got as close as possible to me without sitting on it. His hand covered the part of my chest that was just above my heart as his other hand mimicked it on his own chest. "Is a connection that will never be lost. No matter if you run, or if you stay."

My lips were quivering as I tried to hold back the sobs that were attempting to overtake me. "Why?" I managed to choke out through the tears.

Julian's face softened as he took a seat on the bed, reaching his hand out to cup my cheek; my face instinctively turned into his warm palm. "Because I love you." A couple of tears rolled down his cheeks as he pushed up from the bed and quickly exited the bedroom, leaving me sitting there all alone with my thoughts and aching heart.

They say your heart knows what it wants, even if your mind doesn't. Not knowing how true that statement was makes it hard to go with what your heart tells you over your mind. Thomas was supposed to be my forever guy, the person I spent my entire life with until death did us part, but he didn't see it in the same light. His infidelity with Sara tainted the chance of a happily ever after. Whereas Julian came barreling into my life when I least expected it and threw me completely off kilter. My heat beat wildly for Julian, and my mind told me conflicted stories between the two; that I shouldn't feel that way for one man while being legally married to another.

As I sat there in Julian's bed I knew what I needed to do. Julian was the man for me. He was meant to be my one and only, not Thomas. No matter how much I had thought beforehand that Thomas was it for me, his actions shattered any chance of that. His being alive didn't change the fact that he had a son with another woman that he had slept with on repeated occasions; it was his choice to live two separate lives, but my choice was not to stay. Did I love him? Of course. It's hard to stop loving someone even after they shatter you. But was I *in love* with him? No. Love was a tricky word, especially in my life, but I knew one thing for certain…I was in love with Julian Cooper, not Thomas Cole.

Hastily getting out of Julian's bed I took off down the hallway and into the living room, but there was no sight of him anywhere. My feet carried me into the kitchen, which was empty, and then through the two spare bedrooms. Julian was nowhere to be found. My heart sank at the thought of him leaving me alone in his house. I had hurt him enough to push him away, literally. How I had managed to allow myself to do that was beyond me. The sound of a toilet flushing caught my attention as I turned back towards where the bathroom was and watched as Julian stepped over the threshold, wiping a hand down his face. When his eyes connected with mine sadness swam within them. I quickly crossed the room and wrapped my arms around his waist. "I don't want Thomas, I want you, Julian, only you! I'm tired of what life has dealt me…so damn tired." The material of his shirt muffled my voice as I turned my face into his chest and inhaled the scent that was one hundred percent Julian Cooper. "You came into my life when the darkness was consuming me day-by-day, and I don't want to live a day without you by my side. You've been my constant. The person that would walk through shards of glass or blazing fire to make sure I was okay. Thomas isn't half the man that you are, Julian. I want you to know that I wasn't questioning us…I was questioning *me*. All of the decisions I had been making were on the fly, without thinking twice about the situation at hand. I was afraid of screwing things up worse than they had been, but I'm not afraid anymore. If you want me, I'm yours; mind, soul, and body."

    The silence was deafening as I awaited his response. My stomach was churning while my entire body was shaking from my overabundance of nerves. My arms loosened their hold on his waist and I took a few steps back, putting distance between the two of us. As I lifted my eyes to his, he turned his head ever so slightly to the side and took me in. A heavy sigh left his lips as his hands hung loosely by his sides. "When I first met you I knew that there was something different about you, at least to me. You weren't like every other woman I had laid eyes on or interacted with, you had a fire inside of you that tried its damnedest not to be put out. I watched you throughout the entire funeral, and the sadness and heartache that you were handling better than most would made me feel protective of you." He laughed as he raked a hand through his hair. "Once most of the people had left I made it a point to sit down with you. I needed to let you know that I would be there whenever you needed someone, even though you had no idea who I was other than by my name. It was your eyes that captivated me when they connected with mine. The emerald green was even greener from the tears you had shed, but the beauty of them—of you…" Julian paused with his eyes on mine as a small smile tipped the corners of his lips upward.

"That moment was enough for me to know that if I didn't tread lightly I would be completely screwed when it came to you. The feeling that was evoked within my heart from the simple interaction we had that day was one I had never felt before. Guilt ate away at me for many nights because of the way I was thinking about you. You were my partner's wife…we had each other's backs every fucking day without hesitation, so having feelings for his wife after his death was something that I couldn't grasp."

"Julian…" My heart ached because I knew exactly what he was saying, mainly because I had been feeling the same way about having feelings for him since I admitted that they were there.

He held up a hand to stop me from going any further with my words. "Let me finish." I nodded in understanding. "You were the reason I rented a house here in Shallotte. I couldn't admit that to you in the grocery store that day, but something deep down in my soul told me that you needed someone to keep you safe; whether or not you would move on with your life with someone else down the road, I had to be that person to keep you safe until you were emotionally okay again. Call it a Marine's duty or instinct…but my number one priority was to make sure that you were going to be okay. I couldn't keep Thomas safe, or so I thought at the time, but I was going to do my damnedest to keep you out of harm's way. The more time I spent with you the harder it became to keep it strictly a friendship. Your smile, the way you scrunched your nose if I said something you found to be completely wrong in your opinion, the smell of your hair when you hugged me tightly, the sound of your laughter and even the heart-aching sound of your cries. Every little piece of what made up MacKenzie Cole captivated me to the point of no return. But if you have even the slightest inkling of thought that you being with me isn't the right choice for you, I won't hold it against you. All I want is for you to be happy, and if I'm not the person that can make you one hundred percent happy then I can't fault you for that. Just think about this decision you are making, MacKenzie. Think long and hard because I can't keep going back and forth when things are thrown off balance by life, I need you one hundred percent because that is exactly how much I want to be with you and make us work."

My legs wavered as his words sank in. Julian had felt something deep for me for longer than I had anticipated. I was hurting him just as much as I was hurting myself with the back and forth bullshit my mind had been dishing out. Selfishly, I hadn't realized it until he made it clear as day with his words. My chest expanded as I sucked in a hefty amount of air, holding it momentarily until my lungs burned before letting it out slowly. "I don't need any time to figure out what I want. I'm done thinking about what is the right thing to do and what is not. My heart wants you…I want you one hundred percent, Julian. Please believe me when I say that I love only you, I'm in love with only you." Tears pooled in my eyes as the air between us morphed from the mixture of heartache and tension to something soothing and full of love.

Before I could take in what was happening Julian had lifted me into the air. My arms instinctively went around his neck as my legs circled his waist tightly before his mouth molded with mine. "I love you, MacKenzie…so damn much." His hot breath danced across my lips between kisses.

"I love you too, more than my shitty words can explain," I countered, pulling a throaty laugh out of him.

As Julian's laughter faded his mouth found mine again. His tongue swept deep into mine as the passion of his feelings towards me poured out of him. A moan rose up my throat as my back slammed against a wall. "I'm sorry..." Julian breathlessly apologized. "I couldn't see the doorway."

My head fell back against the wall, as I laughed. "Just get me in the bedroom. I'm fine," I reassured him as he pulled me back towards his body instead of the wall, and slipped into the bedroom directly beside us. His lips peppered kisses down the curve of my neck as he lowered me to the mattress. The weight of my languid legs caused them to fall open. Julian gripped the collar of his shirt and pulled it off, and my eyes scanned down his sculpted torso, stopping as his hands undid his jeans and pushed them to the floor. The sight of his naked body would never get old to me. My tongue dragged across my bottom lip as I took in every chiseled curve and plane of his body until my eyes locked with his. His heavy lids made his sandy brown eyes seem even darker. His knee pushed into the mattress on the outside of my leg as he placed his hands on my thighs and slowly smoothed them up my skin, stopping at the waist of my panties; gripping the material, he pulled them off of my legs. My body was humming with desperate need as Julian took his sweet time discarding my panties on the floor. I gripped the hem of his shirt that I was wearing, leaned forward, and pulled it off over my head. His eyes dropped from mine to my bare breasts and a groan erupted from his throat. The deep rumbling sound had my insides begging for him to help me find that euphoric feeling that only he gave me once again.

"You're unbelievably breathtaking." Julian's eyes dragged up my body, from my toes to my face as he repositioned his knee between my legs, followed by his other knee, and he pushed them wider apart so that I was fully open and exposed to him.

My labored breaths picked up a bit as moisture pooled where I needed him the most. "You're killing me," I groaned as I bit down on my bottom lip. My body was on fire, burning heavily for him to take what was his, and he knew it.

"All in due time, Kenzie." His voice was husky as the seductive sounding words rolled off his tongue. My eyes closed as his body covered mine, his erection pressing at my entrance, begging for the chance to enter me which I was more than willing to grant.

Julian leaned over, bracing his left arm into the mattress so that his right hand could massage my heavy breast closest his hand. He rolled my pebbling nipple between his fingers before dropping his mouth onto it, sucking to the point of pulling a guttural moan from my lungs. My voice was raspy as I choked out my plea. "Julian...I need you...*Please*."

His head lowered until his forehead was resting against mine. "I need you too, baby, so damn much." As soon as the words passed his lips he sucked my bottom lip into his mouth as he pushed into me with one swift motion.

Julian's movements were steady and languid as he rolled his hips into me and pulled back. He repeated his evil motions over and over, driving me nuts as I craved a faster pace. With each thrust and pull, my body cried out for more. I closed my eyes and took in the feeling of us being one. There were no boundaries holding us back. Love and desires had been confessed, making everything that we had been through in the short amount of time, worth it.

His arm wrapped around my lower back as he pulled me up flush against his chest. My legs latched tightly around his waist as he continued to rock in and out of me. My body ached as I teetered on the borderline of being pleasurable and painful just before my mouth went slack as a moan ripped from my chest from the intensity of my release pulsing through my body. "Let it out, baby," Julian grunted as his own release pumped through him.

Our bodies collapsed together on the bed before Julian lifted his upper body off of me as my legs fell openly to the sides. Exhaustion from our escapade washed over both of us as a lazy smile spread widely across his lips. I huffed a laugh as he smoothed his fingertips across the damp hair plastered to my forehead.

"I love you," he whispered just before his lips touched mine.

"I love you, too," I breathed out.

Love was a word that didn't really touch how deeply I felt for Julian. My soul was molded to his, and it was crazy to think that could have happened in the short time that we'd been together. But like they proclaimed, when you find your soulmate you just know.

Chapter Twenty Four

    My eyes fluttered open as the light peeked through the curtains shielding the outside world from our oasis in Julian's bedroom. I stretched my arms high above my head, releasing a long growl from the feeling of my muscles stretching and waking. It was my favorite thing to do first thing in the morning. Bringing my arms back down to rest on top of the comforter that was covering my body, I turned my head to take in Julian's sleeping form. His face was aimed towards me with his lips just slightly parted and one arm shoved up under the pillow as the other wrapped around the top of it. He looked so peacefully beautiful.

    We had spent the night tangled in the sheets, experiencing one another in every way possible. Julian brought something out of me that I hadn't felt in quite some time, confidence. As I rolled my body towards him my fingertips made a trail up his bare arm to his shoulder and across his back. I scooted closer so that our naked bodies were flush with one another and placed a lingering kiss against the top of his shoulder before resting my face on his arm. His legs moved just slightly as his back arched in a stretch and his eyelids fluttered open slowly.

"Good morning," A large smile spread across my lips as I spoke softly.

Julian smiled widely back, turned on his side, and pulled me into his chest. His lips pressed against my forehead as I wrapped my arms around his midriff. Inhaling deeply, I closed my eyes and snuggled deeper into him. His natural scent filled my nose, pulling a small, contented sigh from me. Everything felt right in the world, waking up in bed together with absolutely no boundaries between us. A girl could get used to that.

"Have you been awake long?" Julian's face was buried in my hair, but his raspy voice still affected me.

My head angled up towards his, forcing him to remove his face from my hair and tip his chin down to focus on mine. "Only a few minutes." I stretched my neck enough to press my lips against his. Morning breath was not an issue for me, and even if it was I wanted to feel his plump lips against mine. "Mmm," I groaned before pulling back.

Julian's eyes darkened, "You start with noises like that and we won't be leaving this room today." The words alone had chills creeping across my skin as one of his hands skimmed south down my body. His fingers were teasing as they caressed my skin on his path to the curve of my breast before dipping low at my waist and swooping across the apex of my thighs. A gasp passed my lips as he gently massaged where my thigh met my waist. I hadn't realized just how much tension was there until then, and I moaned as my breathing picked up.

"Julian...that feels amazing, but you're driving me crazy already."

A wicked smile played on his lips as he brought his hand back above the covers and slid it into my hair just above my ear. "You're even more beautiful first thing in the morning when you're all hot and bothered."

My eyes shut as I took a deep breath before opening them again. "Saying things like that is just making it worse," I groaned as my legs rubbed against one another, searching for relief.

Julian pushed me onto my back, "I'll take care of you, baby." He slipped his head beneath the covers, leaving a trial of kisses down my body until his mouth was on me. My head fell back against the pillow as I relaxed and enjoyed every little bit of pleasure he was giving me.

Yep, a girl could definitely get used to mornings like that.

Julian leaned a hip against the kitchen counter as he sipped his coffee. I was seated at the breakfast bar sipping my own cup of orange juice as we sat in silence, enjoying the warmth and feel of the morning. The clock on the microwave read ten 'til eleven. The smile that spread across my face couldn't be hidden by the mug as the images of the morning flooded my thoughts.

"What has you smiling like that?" Julian raised an eyebrow as he took another sip.

"Just thinking about this morning."

Julian's own smile mimicked mine. "It's been a *great* morning, huh?"

"Most definitely." I bit the left side of my bottom lip to try and suppress my smile a little. Sipping the last drop of orange juice from my mug I took it over to the sink and rinsed it out.

As I wiped my hands on the dish towel the concerned look that had replaced Julian's flirty one caught my attention. "Something wrong?" I inquired.

He sat his mug down on the counter and waved for me to follow him over to the breakfast bar where I had previously been sitting. Taking my hands in his as we sat he focused his eyes on mine. "We need to talk about what happened at your house between you and Thomas." He paused for a moment before continuing. "What did he say?" His voice was gentle as he questioned me.

My lungs expanded as I took in a deep breath and exhaled it slowly. I knew we needed to talk about what had transpired, about what I knew after coming face-to-face with Thomas; it was a subject I dreaded touching. "Where do you want me to start?" I dragged a hand through my messy hair before focusing my eyes back on Julian's.

"From the beginning. With everything that has been unraveled. I need to hear it all so we can make sure things are as they seem and not lies." Julian was right. I didn't know Thomas anymore; everything I had thought I knew had been turned upside down.

"Okay." I squeezed his hand before letting go and sitting back in the chair. "Once I lowered my gun, after I realized it was really Thomas, we stayed in our same positions in the kitchen; I was near the door and he was by the kitchen counter with the top drawer opened..."

"How are you here? How are you alive?" My voice was like a whisper as I shot off questions I never thought I would ask. Tears ran relentlessly down my face, but I didn't bother to wipe any away because it was the last thing on my mind.

Thomas took a couple steps towards me before I motioned for him to stop by raising the gun again. His hands went palms out into the air, "I'm not going to hurt you, MacKenzie. I never would." His words were like they had always been, soothing and sweet; packed full of the love I thought he had for me.

"You're a liar," I spat. "What about Sara?" Her name fell from my lips like venom as I threw her name at him, proving that he was indeed a liar. If he never intended to hurt me he sure as hell had a funny way of doing things. Infidelity was one of the top things that would destroy any normal person who thought their marriage was perfect, or damn near close to it.

Thomas stepped back like I had slapped him hard across the face. His face morphed from shock to pure sadness. "MacKenzie..." The pain is his voice made it hard to breathe. He wasn't expecting me to hit him with that.

"Don't!" I yelled with anger, shaking the gun towards him. "Don't you stand there and lie to me about any of it, Thomas Cole! I can't handle the lies anymore…I've been living for months upon months with the choices you made…the heartache from finding out that my husband had been cheating on me for a long motherfucking time and fathered a son! A child with someone other than me…" A hiccup from my sobs interrupted my rant, giving Thomas the opportunity to speak.

"Please put the gun down," he begged with caution. "I'll tell you everything if you put the gun down, Mack." Thomas used the nickname only he called me. My heart fluttered from the sound of it rolling off of his tongue and I knew I was in trouble. Feelings for him were making an appearance even after all of the bullshit he had put me through. Seeing him standing before me made it hard as hell to grasp onto the hurt, and not any of the love I had for him.

A heavy sigh left me as I lowered the gun, flipped the safety on, and laid it on the kitchen table chair beside where I was standing. "Talk," I growled. "I want to hear every ounce of what has happened, start to finish. Don't hold anything back from me, either, Thomas. Even if you think it would crush my very soul, I want to hear it." He nodded in understanding.

"Before the explosion in the house I was knocked in the head pretty hard from behind and dragged away by some men who had been on our radar for quite some time. They removed my dog tags in the process. I wasn't sure what they were going to do with them or where they were taking me. A black bag was placed over my head and I knew right then and there that I most likely wouldn't survive. Begging for mercy and my life was not an option. We learned while monitoring these men that begging would only make the torture they would inflict on you worse. They got off on hurting others; creating havoc whenever they could." He walked over to the kitchen table and took a seat in the chair that was facing towards me at the door.

"I spent months with little water and barely any food. They never once videotaped me or forced me to do anything that would hurt my unit, which was odd. As the days progressed I knew I had to find a way to get the hell out of there. The longer they kept me locked away in some run down home, chained to block walls, the more they lessened the amount of security they had on me. I knew it was only a matter of time before they slipped up, so I kept my eyes on their every move, even when they thought I was close to passing out from hunger." Thomas ran a hand through his still-short hair.

One day they left me in the care of two younger boys. It was easy to antagonize them by saying one had told me something the other one didn't agree with. I can't remember exactly what it was but I kept trying to escalate it until they ended up yelling and storming off to find someone to see who was right about what needed to be done. As soon as they left the doorway of the room I immediately started putting all of my weight onto the one chair cuff that was hooked into the block wall behind me. Every so often they would unhook one or the other of my hands, giving me a day without it, and that day just so happened to be it. Lifting my legs into the air repeatedly, I would jerk down with all of my weight until the ring finally snapped off of the wall. I slid around the *doorframe and into the hallway. Apparently the boys were the only two in the entire house and when they left I was there alone. The room where they housed weapons was directly beside where I had been so I grabbed a rifle, which was military issued, along with some other items, and took off towards the front of the residence. Everything was clear, almost too clear, but I chanced it anyway. I ran as fast as my hunger stricken body would allow me, I popped up over the hills and ended up tumbling down them."*

"It took me almost a day to get to a part of Afghanistan where I knew people would help me. Within that day I used the rifle to kill a small fox and cook him on a fire I had managed to build with some of the matches I had stolen from my captive home. Many times I thought I was going to die before I reached safety, but I kept telling myself that I needed to push on, that the Marines had taught me to fight for not only my life but others. I couldn't give up that easily. A family took me in, fed me, and gave me clothes to wear, then put me in contact with someone that could get me out of there, someone that could slowly get me home. The rest is a blur, but here I am..." He outstretched his arms. *"I'm home."*

His story wasn't fully fitting together to me. "How did you get back to the United States?"

"There was a group of refugees that were being smuggled into the United States and I managed to get in the group. I bribed them with my knowledge of how to get around some of the military as long as they would take me with them."

"Thomas, this makes no sense! Why wouldn't you just find the military and tell them who you were? Why would you allow everyone to think you were still dead when you were alive?" I slipped down into the chair beside me from the confusion of his story.

Thomas cleared his throat and stood from the table. "I had a lot of time to think about everything while I was being held captive. Certain details about the raid didn't make sense to me, MacKenzie. I was the only one in that part of the house we were raiding. That never happens. It also happened to be the main part of the place that exploded. What I'm trying to say is...I think someone set me up. Someone wanted me to die in that explosion, I'm not sure who or why, but I feel it in my gut that it was a setup."

The pace of my racing heart was insanely fast as I realized what Thomas was truly saying. Someone had planned for him to die in that raid, he was never meant to come home from that mission and neither of us knew it. My gut was telling me that it had to do with that duffle bag of cash I had found in the locker at the gym. "Do you know anything about a duffle bag full of money?" I closely gauged his reaction to my question but his face never wavered.

"What do you mean?"

"I found a bag full of cash in a gym locker that was yours."

"MacKenzie, I have no idea what that is. I never had any duffle bag full of cash, hell, you knew all of the money I brought in or had. What did you do with the money? I don't want you in any danger." His reply made me realize that he hadn't brought up Sara. He had lied to me about her, so it wouldn't have been too farfetched if he had money elsewhere and was lying to me about that too.

"It's at Julian's in the basement safe. That's not important though. If you'd lie to me about being faithful, wouldn't you lie about money?" My choice of question had him cradling his head in his hands.

Thomas dropped his hands and brought his piercing blue eyes back to mine. "I'm sorry. I'm a giant fuck up, Mack! You deserve better than me, you always have. Sara was fun, that's all she was until I found out about her pregnancy." He gripped what little hair he could on his head and pulled. "I knew I had fucked up when she dropped that bomb on me. Don't think my actions were because of you, they weren't. My mind was all fucked up from being overseas and I thought I could get it all out of my system by being with her. As shitty as it sounds, it worked. When I was with her she got the shittier side of me, you didn't. I've always loved you, more than life itself. She held a different form of my love. Nothing even remotely close to what you held." His words were like tiny knives, carving away at my heart. I knew he was lying about how much he cared for Sara simply because of the note I found at the Bed and Breakfast that day, not to mention how Sara spoke of Thomas. She thought the sun rose and set because of him, if he truly was an asshole most of the time to her she wouldn't have portrayed him in the light she had, would she? But in reality, Thomas had no idea I had met with her. If he wanted to try and smooth things over between us, the best way would be to try and paint their relationship in a way that wasn't true. Thankfully I wasn't the same girl he had left all that time ago when he set off on his tour of duty. I was stronger than before, and I sure as hell wasn't going to allow him to walk on me. MacKenzie Cole deserved better, and that's what she wanted out of life; better than Thomas' heartache and lies.

"Thomas, you don't have to make it seem like something less than it was. If you loved her, admit it. Don't tarnish who she is to you...that doesn't, and won't, change how I feel about what you did. You cheated on me, Thomas! You broke the vows we swore before God. You ripped my heart from my chest and stomped on it repeatedly but weren't man enough to let me go, so you continued to do it behind my back, knowing I had no idea. Knowing my heart only belonged to you. But not anymore. I can't be with you anymore. You being home doesn't change it one bit. I've moved on."

Thomas took a deep breath and closed the distance between us. My breath hitched from his unexpected close proximity as he cupped my cheek, and my eyes shut from the amount of tears swimming within them. "You deserve to be happy. And I'm so fucking sorry for all of the shit I put you through. I'm sorry for being the bastard that couldn't admit to his wrong doings and let you move on with your life if you didn't want me afterwards. I've always been selfish when it came to you. I moved you out here and away from your friends, and I didn't think twice about it. I'm an asshole, MacKenzie. I just hope whoever the guy is, that he is worthy of the person you are." He pressed his lips against mine before stepping back and heading over to the counter and drawer where I had initially found him. After putting everything back in the drawer he closed it.

"What were you looking for?" Thomas looked confused by my question. "In the drawer, what were you looking for when I found you in here?"

Realization washed over him and he laughed a humorless laugh. "I was looking for a key that went to an old memory box that's up in the study. I wanted to take a few things with me."

"With you?"

"Yeah, I was going to leave this town and never come back."

"Were you ever going to tell me that you were alive?"

"No." His admission wasn't surprising to me. If he was going to tell me he was alive he wouldn't have broken into our home to try and take whatever he needed.

"Oh." I cleared my throat and rose from the chair. "You can stay here for a few days. I'm going to grab a few things and head over to a friend's."

"You don't have to do that."

"I know I don't, but you don't have anything and this is just as much your home as it is mine."

Thomas' eyes softened to that look he used to give me when I actually felt his love and didn't only see it through his actions. "I know saying sorry doesn't fix what I've done to you, but I hope you let it go and move on with your life. You deserve the best, MacKenzie. Sorry I couldn't be that for you." I nodded and quickly left the room to gather my things.

So many decisions ran through my head as I grabbed only as many things as I could shove in my purse and left. As I pulled out of the driveway I looked one last time in my rearview mirror at the house that held so many good and bad memories. The home that was housing the man I married, the man I thought died, and the man who shattered my heart. Pushing the gas pedal down I drove as fast as I could to Julian's. The alone time before he would come home was exactly what I needed to figure out all of the craziness that I called my life.

Julian sat there in silence for a few moments as my heart raced, waiting for him to speak. I knew that he was taking in everything I had told him, but it still had me on a nervous edge. "I need to talk to him, Kenzie." Julian rubbed his hand across his chin as he thought. His eyes were distant and full of questions, ones that were most likely for Thomas. Something wasn't sitting right with me, but I didn't want to poke the bear and ask. Julian would tell me if I needed to know, and if he didn't, I would find out myself. I always did.

"I can go with you if you want." My hand linked with his and gave it a squeeze.

"I need to do this alone."

As badly as I wanted to tell Julian no, that I was going with him, I didn't. I knew he and Thomas had things they needed to talk about and if the subject of Julian and me came up it would only make it harder with me in the room. I nodded in understanding of Julian's need to speak with Thomas alone and smiled gently at him.

"He should be at the house. Going there is the only way I know to get a hold of him."

Julian leaned forward and smoothed his hands across my cheeks and into my hairline. "I can see how nervous you are in your beautiful eyes, Kenzie. Don't be. It'll be fine. I just need to be the person to tell Thomas about us. And I need to hear what happened. Some of the stuff you said makes no sense to me, but if he wouldn't tell you the full truth, I don't know that he would tell me." His reassurance calmed me enough to shake away most of the nerves that were buzzing through my body.

"Okay." My lips pressed against his. "I just hate that any of this has to happen."

"I know you do, baby." He rested his forehead against mine. "So do I."

Chapter Twenty Five
Julian

The house was dark as I shut the front door behind me. My right hand was resting on the gun that was tucked into the back of my pants at the waist. I knew Thomas, or at least a previous version of him, but someone can change so easily after being kept captive for periods of time. It was better to be safe than sorry.

"Thomas," I called out sternly, alerting him that I was there. "It's Julian. If you're here we need to talk." My statement bellowed through the house and was replied to with silence.

I scanned the entire place and found that it was empty. Thomas wasn't anywhere to be found so I took a seat at the kitchen table, placing the gun on the placemat before me. The only thing I could do was sit and wait for him to return. *If* he returned.

It was almost ten at night when I checked my watch. I had been sitting in that chair for almost four hours. One thing the Marines taught me was to have patience; otherwise my happy ass wouldn't have been perched in the chair waiting for Thomas to show up. The darkness of the night was thick outside, and almost as thick within the house, but one light above the sink gave me just enough to see throughout the kitchen. The sound of the back door clicking open and shut almost silently caught my attention. I was facing towards the stove, my back towards the large double windows behind me with each entrance to the house on either side of where I sat. My hand was positioned on the gun for precaution as none other than Thomas Cole stepped into the kitchen, with his own Glock pointed in my direction.

"I should've known that she would tell you that I was here." Thomas smiled widely as he lowered his gun.

"She tells me everything," I admitted.

Thomas nodded, acknowledging the underlying message I was portraying by saying that. "So you two, huh?" He made his way over to the table and took a seat directly across from me.

"We make each other happy," I replied simply.

"You're the better guy for her, Cooper." Thomas sat his gun down to mimic the way mine was still sitting on the table. "I won't do anything to get in the way, you're good for her and I'm not."

Thomas reassuring me that he wouldn't do anything to jeopardize what MacKenzie and I had was a lot easier than I had initially thought it would be. He was taking responsibility for his actions, but something still felt off. "I appreciate that." He nodded. "So tell me why you came back. Why are you here if you didn't plan on letting everyone know that you survived the raid and explosion? Kenzie filled me in on everything the two of you had talked about, but I'm still a little at a loss of why you even came back in the first place."

Thomas smiled widely and laughed a short laugh as he shook his head back and forth. "You call her Kenzie? Just like her old friends back home." He was dancing around my question by bringing my nickname for her into the mix. Red flags were waving like a motherfucker.

"Answer the question, Cole."

He cleared his throat and sat fully back against the back of the chair, making himself comfortable. "You wouldn't understand if I told you." Thomas was hiding something. My gut was right, finding out what that something was would be a hard task, but it was officially my mission to get to the bottom of it. Not only for me, but for Kenzie.

"Try me."

Thomas heavily sighed. "Not a good idea, Cooper. I've done things that you wouldn't understand. I'm not the proudest person anymore, that's why I'm leaving. Coming back won't be an option either."

"You're running from something, aren't you?"

He laughed a humorless laugh. "I'm running from a lot of things, Julian." The use of my first name caught me off guard. "Escaping from captivity gave me a new outlook on life. With MacKenzie finding out about my affair, and moving on, there is nothing for me here now."

"What about your son?" My question hit him hard as he sucked in a deep breath and his eyes glassed over. "And Sara? Are you not going to tell her that you're alive? Don't they both deserve to at least know that?" What Thomas was doing made absolutely no sense. He sounded like a man that was giving up on life, not a man who had been given a second chance.

"I can't talk about them." His voice was thick from the emotions of mentioning Sara and his son. "Why did you come here, Julian?"

Avoiding yet another question.

"I came here because you were my brother, Thomas. We spent *years* side-by-side, fighting the same fucking war to keep the people we love, along with our country, safe. I thought you died! Do you realize how badly I had been blaming myself for not being in that room with you? For not being able to save you?" I stood from the chair and slipped my gun in the back of the waistband of my jeans. "I needed to see you for myself, to know that you were truly alive. Even if I don't understand just why in the hell you thought living a double life would help you get through the shitty parts of being a Marine instead of talking to me, I still care about you, man. MacKenzie still cares about you, and I'm absolutely positive Sara cares a helluva lot about you, too. You really need to think about what you're doing before making an irrational decision." I paused. "How did you get into the United States without using your name?"

"You know how."

His answer was very evasive, but it was all I needed to know that someone had set him up with a new identity. Thomas wasn't working alone, he had at least one person who was helping him along. His phone blared to life as he stood from the kitchen table and slid his hand into his front pocket to retrieve the phone.

"Excuse me." He motioned towards his phone before answering it. After a few seconds of mumbling he slid the phone back into his pocket. "I have to go."

He was running, and most likely the person on the other end of that call was helping him. "Answer me one more thing before you go."

"Shoot."

"Where did the duffle bag of cash really come from? The bandings on the cash have the same imprint from those ops you used to do with that group of guys, the ones I wasn't involved with."

Thomas rubbed his hands down his face. "Someone must have stashed it there because I didn't." My eyes narrowed as I watched him. I was pretty good at reading people, but Thomas was just as good at putting up a façade that someone couldn't read. It was why he was involved in that special ops team in the first place. Needless to say, the way he answered my question didn't go unnoticed. He never truly dismissed the possibility of him being part of how that cash got to the States instead of being in military lockup somewhere.

I rounded the table. "It was good to see you again, Julian." Thomas extended his arms for a hug. Without hesitation I hugged him hard, clasping him on the back a couple times. Even after all of the bullshit that had been unraveled about who Thomas truly was, I still wanted only the best for him. He saved my ass on numerous occasions, and I did the same for him. Knowing that he was still breathing and not buried six feet under was more than a relief.

"Take care of yourself, Thomas." I clasped my hand on his back once more before stepping out of the embrace.

"Will do. I'd ask you to take care of MacKenzie, but I already know that you will."

"With my life," I replied instantly as I watched my brother-in-arms walk out the back door and disappear into the night.

Three nights had passed since I had spoken with Thomas. After gathering some of Kenzie's things, including her cell phone, I had gone back to my place and into her awaiting arms. I'd spent the night in a haze though, trying to figure out what the hell was going on with Thomas. He danced around most of my important questions, while being careful not to divulge too much information. Something was badly off, that was obvious, but my hands were tied if he wouldn't fill me in on anything.

So I took matters into my own hands, even after Kenzie had told me it was best to leave it alone.

I killed the engine to my car three houses past the Cole's residence. I'd been observing Thomas ever since that night. So far it was a bust. Thomas came and went, only at night for the most part, and usually by himself. If my gut wasn't telling me that something was off, I probably would've given up watching him after the second night.

Movement to the left of the house just at the fence line caught my attention. A moment later Thomas came walking through the opened gate wearing dark clothing and a ball cap pulled low on his head. A backpack was hanging on his right shoulder as he quickly slipped into the black sedan that he had left parked on the street. As soon as his vehicle was far enough away so he couldn't see mine spring to life, I pushed the ignition button and slowly followed behind him, leaving just enough space to seem inconspicuous.

Thomas had no clue that someone was following him or he would have made the route to his destination more covert. But instead I had been following slowly behind him for twenty minutes when he turned into the parking lot for what used to be an old thrift shop. From the looks of things, it had been abandoned for years. A row of trees separated the two, making it easy for me not to be seen. I pulled into the parking lot and backed up against the trees before slipping from my car with my camera. If something was going down, it was going to be captured in photographs.

I crouched down between two thick trees as Thomas got out of the dark sedan around the back of the building, making it easier for me to see what was happening. A few minutes later a black SUV pulled around from the other side of the building and stopped a few feet away from the front of Thomas' sedan. My heart was pounding in my chest as the driver's side door opened on the SUV. A wild herd of horses galloped to the rhythm that my heart was producing as I waited for the person to step out, and when he did parts of what had been going on started to fall into place.

Gabe Tully.

Gabe had been lying low for a couple weeks. We hadn't heard from him or seen him since three Fridays prior when he had shown up at Kenzie's house while I was there. He had been doing that a lot, saying it was simply a friendly dropping by, which was fine since Loren was usually showing up not long behind him. I wasn't sure if MacKenzie had something to do with that since Loren was freshly divorced and women liked to try and hook one another up with someone they knew. Even though MacKenzie didn't honestly *know* Gabe.

With the camera positioned so that my eye was aligned with it, I snapped numerous photos of the two of them interacting. At least ten minutes had passed by as I watched them talk and even argue about who knows what. I was too far away to hear anything. The passenger's door on the SUV opened and yet another surprise stepped out of that vehicle, none other than the infamous Sara, the woman Thomas had been cheating on MacKenzie with.

She quickly shut the door behind her before taking off in the direction of where Thomas was standing. Once his eyes fell onto her he opened his arms widely and she leaped into them, wrapping her arms around his neck and her legs around his waist. Their lips instantly molded together and the feeling of pure rage seeped through my veins. Something was far from right with the situation before me. The shaking from my anger rippled through my body as I did my best to refrain from crossing through the trees and beating the shit out of not only Thomas, but Gabe as well. My finger pushed the button on the camera to snap pictures of the three of them interacting so I had proof that they were all tied together. There was more to the story than what either MacKenzie or myself had been told. Gabe being in town, Thomas mysteriously being alive, and Sara being at the meeting between them, was not a coincidence, it was planned.

Chapter Twenty Six
MacKenzie

As I pushed through the double glass doors of the attorney's office the sun made my eyes squint. I pulled my sunglasses down from their resting spot on my head and aimed my face up at the sun, allowing it to cascade down on me. The warmth felt nice and the closed-lip smile on my face felt good. What I had filed in the attorney's office was long overdue, but the timing before hadn't seemed right. Not until Julian had informed me about everything he had seen the night he followed Thomas to his meeting with Gabe and Sara.

To say that I was pissed was an understatement. Thomas was back to his antics that I hadn't known about until he had 'died.' But I would have never guessed that Gabe was involved somehow. We had yet to connect the dots, but it was only a matter of time.

As I slid into the driver's seat of my car I twisted my hair up into a bun and quickly secured it with a hair tie that had been wrapped around the gear shifter. My finger pushed the buttons to lower all of the windows and then opened the sunroof. With one more glance at the file folder that was slightly sticking out of my giant grey purse, I smiled widely and pulled out of the parking spot I had been sitting in. The change was coming that needed to happen, and I couldn't have been happier about it.

The wind was blowing through the car, carrying the smell of the ocean with it. I hadn't had a beach day since the getaway Julian had planned for the both of us, and I needed one STAT. The ocean had a way of soothing even the biggest aches that my soul endured. I wasn't sure why, it just did.

The familiar sounds of my favorite upbeat Journey song caught my attention as it faintly played on the radio. My hand quickly pushed the volume button on the steering wheel upwards to a decently loud volume. We were belting out about a small town girl and a city boy in unison; obviously Steve Perry sounded better than I did, but it didn't stop me from singing right along at the top of my lungs.

Loren and I were having our weekly lunch date at Grant's Deli. I kept the music on blast as I pulled into the parking lot and instantly spotted her in our usual spot on the deck. She waved as a wide smile spread across her face, pushing her sunglass up just slightly. I waved back as I closed all the windows in my car and killed the ignition.

"What's the big ass smile on your face for?" she teasingly questioned.

"I'll tell ya in a minute." I pushed open the door to the deli and walked inside.

As always, the place was buzzing with people. Grayson waved from behind the counter and I waved back as I turned and pushed through the door to the deck. Numerous patrons were seated all over the deck. A few friendly hello's were shared as I made it to our designated table and took a seat.

"Tell me the story," Loren automatically demanded before my butt could fully hit the chair.

A closed-lipped chuckle escaped me as I pulled the file folder from my purse and laid it on the table before her. "This," I tapped the folder, "is why I'm smiling like a fool." Lifting my hand, I sat back in the chair and waited for her to open it.

Loren eyed the folder before looking up at me again. "Please tell me it's a marriage license or a pregnancy test results. Something juicy…" Her eyes sparkled at the thoughts of what could be in the folder, and I laughed one of those belly-aching laughs.

"You are a nut, you know that?" My laughter died down as she shrugged her shoulders before flipping the file folder open.

"Holy shit," she gasped. "I definitely wasn't expecting this." Her eyes ran over the document in the file folder a couple times before she looked back up at me. "Are you sure about this?" Her sincerity made me appreciate her being my friend even more.

"I'm positive." My reply was quick and easy. She didn't know everything that had been going on, or had previously gone on. She just knew that Thomas was killed and Julian was the person to help me move on with my life, to learn to live again.

"Well-" Loren closed the file folder and tapped the end against the table a couple times to align the paperwork inside. "If it makes you happy, then I'm happy!" Her reply was just another reason why I enjoyed being around her. She was easy going, never asked too many questions, and understood that some things help a person heal even if others didn't understand. She might not have had all the pieces to the puzzle that I called my crazy life, but she didn't demand them either. Loren took what information I gave her and never second-guessed me.

Effortless chit chat bounced between us as we enjoyed our lunch. Thick laugher echoed through the salty air as she told me about a horrific date she had gone on the weekend before. My stomach ached from the overuse of the muscles that the laughter pulled and stretched. Happiness felt good, even if there were still instances of sorrow lurking around. With Thomas being back and not knowing just exactly what he was up to, the uneasy feeling was still settled deep in my bones. Maybe it sounded strange to say, but I felt like a storm was coming. Not the actual rain, wind, and thunder either.

Pushing the thoughts away I decided to change the subject. "So how are things going with you? Do you feel that the divorce was the right decision? I know you were struggling about it there for a while."

Loren let out a long breath as she sat back in her chair. "I honestly do feel that it was the right decision. We still talk here and there, but I wasn't happy being left alone for months and months while he was gone. I know it's selfish because he is over there fighting for our country, it's not like he was gone partying for long periods of time…I just—I don't know." A frown tugged the corners of her lips down as her eyebrows furrowed deeply in the center. She turned her face towards the street and sighed. "Being lonely is awful. Even though I'm lonely now, after the divorce, it's different than the type of loneliness I felt being married. Does that make sense?"

I nodded in agreement. "It makes perfect sense to me. You were alone more than you weren't, but the feeling of knowing you were tied to another person by marriage made the loneliness seem worse because of the thought of having him at home instead of gone for months upon months."

Loren brought her eyes back to mine and smiled sadly. "That's exactly what I was trying to say."

I reached across the table and covered one of her hands with my own. "You're a strong woman. You'll be just fine. I know it." The tears that were welling in her eyes started to fade as she smiled widely at me.

"Thank you," I smiled and nodded. "I'm so glad we have become closer, I needed someone in my life like you, MacKenzie."

"You and me both." She had no idea just how much I had needed someone like her in my own life. All of the crazy shit that had been going on was a little more bearable after having an outing or conversation with Loren. She was a breath of fresh air in a toxic world. Maybe one day I would be able to confide in her about everything that had transpired, instead of dancing around the full truth.

Staying at Julian's house was nice, but I was missing some of the things I had at my own. It was a subject Thomas and I were going to have to talk about, so I jumped right in and drove there after my lunch date with Loren.

My keys clanged as they dropped on the kitchen counter. "Thomas, are you here?" I called out as I walked through the kitchen and into the living room. He didn't respond so I called out one more time as I headed for the bedroom. "Thomas, I just wanted to let you know it's MacKenzie. Didn't want to startle you if you're here."

Silence again.

As I passed through the bedroom door my eyes instantly fell on a piece of paper and cell phone lying on top of the comforter of our made bed. Instead of packing more clothes like I had planned, I went directly for the note. The cell phone was easy to recognize as the one of Thomas' I had fixed before I knew that he was still alive. I grasped the sheet of paper in my hands and read it.

MacKenzie,

I can't really think of the words to start out this letter, but I wanted to tell you that I'm leaving and I won't be back. This town, the military, all of it isn't for me anymore. Since the raid and being held captive, I've become a different person, one that isn't good for you or the life you deserve. I know that you've moved on with

Julian, please don't feel that you've hurt what we had, because that was me. I'm the one who ruined our marriage by cheating. Julian's a good man, one that wouldn't hurt you, I hope the two of you have a life full of happiness. Sara and our son are unaware of me still being alive, as are the military. The only thing I ask of you is to keep this our secret. Thomas Cole is buried six feet under, much like this secret needs to be. I know it's a lot to ask and that I have no right to do so, but if some part of you still loves the man you used to know…Please, I beg of you, do this for me. If not, I understand.

Sincerely,

Thomas

So many emotions ran through me in a matter of seconds while reading the letter he had left me; sorrow, anger, love, fury, and even understanding. Thomas wanted a clean slate, to move on from all that used to be his life, but what I didn't understand was why he would lie to me by saying Sara and their son had no idea that he was still alive. Julian had seen her get out of the vehicle with Gabe and run into Thomas' arms. She knew one hundred percent that he was alive.

He was asking me to lie for him, to be another pawn in his game. Deep down I wanted to help him, but then again I didn't. Pieces of the Thomas I knew were still there, but they were mixed with a deceitful man that apparently couldn't tell the truth if his life depended on it. Did I want to be in the middle of everything he was doing? No. So right then I decided, if someone were to ask me if Thomas was alive, I wasn't going to lie. Talk about being stuck between a rock and a hard place.

Turning my body, I sat on the edge of the bed and retrieved the cell phone lying beside where I was sitting. My finger held the button down to power it to life and within a couple seconds it was doing just that. Colors danced across the screen as the name of the provider flashed a couple times before disappearing. But it wasn't the colorful display that kept my attention as I shockingly stared at the screen, it was the fact that the message before me read to insert SIM card.

It my frantic state of finding out that Thomas was alive and getting the hell out of the house that night I had not only left my cell phone behind, but also Thomas' old one with all the incriminating information on it. Not that what was on there was federal crime worthy; it was more along the lines of being morally wrong. My body flopped back against the mattress with my arms outstretched in defeat as I cursed at myself for being not only gullible, but half-ass as well. If my emotions weren't fueling me that night I wouldn't have forgotten to grab that phone. Thomas had covered the only piece of evidence I had of his cheating without requiring a DNA test on Sara and his child, and I couldn't even legally do that.

"You stupid, stupid girl." I smacked myself in the forehead a couple times as I laid there thinking about how reckless I had been.

I pushed up from the bed and went into the closet to retrieve a large suitcase. Unzipping it, I flipped the top open and began packing clothes, along with the necessities that I had been wanting with me, when the thought hit me about the note he had left. Thomas had asked me to do him a colossal favor but left the cell phone beside the note so he knew that I would see what he had done to it. He had some balls. I scoffed angrily as I slammed another arm full of clothes into the suitcase and zipped it shut.

Lifting the suitcase up on its wheeled end, I pulled the handle up and wheeled it into the bedroom from the closet. The more I thought about what he had done, the more furious I became. He had made it most likely impossible for me to be able to contact Sara again in the process of deleting everything else. There was no way I could ask around about who she was or anything because I didn't even know her last name. I was quickly batting zero, with no upside in sight.

I took a deep breath and pushed the thoughts from my head. The day had started out with a smile and dammit if I wasn't going to keep one plastered on my face for the remainder of it. I swiped my finger across the screen of my phone and shot Julian a text telling him that I was headed his way within the next ten minutes or so and took one more look around the room that held so many memories of Thomas and me. But the feeling I got when I thought back on those memories wasn't the same as it was right after I thought he had died. I didn't feel sorrow or longing for that time of my life, I felt okay…like it was *just* the past and I was eager to move on from it.

The sound of my phone dinging had an instant smile spreading widely across my face, and somehow it grew even bigger as I read Julian's reply that told me to drive safely because he couldn't wait to press his lips against mine. It was refreshing to have someone that wrote you a simple message that had a smile a mile wide spreading across your face. My only hope was that the crazy part of our lives would be over so that we could build a life together without wondering what ball was about to drop next.

Chapter Twenty Seven

Julian

It had been four days since Thomas had left that note for Kenzie to find. Everything seemed to have died down, with no word from Gabe or Thomas. Loren had been asking Kenzie if she had heard from Gabe, but she couldn't be honest and tell her what was going on, so Kenzie settled on telling her simply that she hadn't heard from him. Which wasn't completely a lie, as neither of us had heard a peep out of him since before I had seen his meeting with Thomas and Sara.

The past few nights we had spent at Kenzie's house, changing all of the locks and having a security system installed to not only cover the doors, but the windows and garage as well. After all of the unknown shit that was going on with Thomas, I didn't want her stepping a foot into that house without it. A couple times I let it slide, mainly because she was a stubborn ass and wouldn't budge on the argument, but once I got my way it was the first thing I demanded to be done to her home. She needed to be safe no matter the cost.

    The night air was cooler than it had been in months, and I had my windows down and my Carolina ball cap turned backwards as I rode down the street that took me directly from Kenzie's house to mine. It was a straight shot that took less than ten minutes to make without traffic. We were crashing at her place for the night so I had to head home for a bit and make sure everything was taken care of; I had run out earlier without setting my own alarm and with the duffle bag of cash stored in my safe it was a priority to set that damn thing.

    Instead of parking outside the garage like I usually did, I pulled completely inside of it and pushed the button that was built into my rearview mirror to shut the door. Waiting until it was fully shut I closed the car door behind me and went inside. I hung my keys on the hook that lined the inside wall of the mud room so that I didn't lose them. They were the only thing I seemed to misplace, and it was my biggest problem. If I didn't hang them up I would end up searching for them for hours. My feet slipped from each of my shoes, and I padded through the kitchen and into the hallway that led to my bedroom.

    The clothes that I had hastily stripped off when I ran in quickly to change were still on the bedroom floor so I picked them up and tossed them in the hamper before I grabbed some clothes for the next day. Kenzie and I were going to have to figure out our living arrangements because running back and forth between the two houses was becoming a pain in the ass, but a pain I would endure for as long as she wanted nonetheless.

The top drawer slid open as I pulled the handle with my hand. Quickly picking out a pair of cargo shorts and a simple navy tank top, my hand reached to the right to place my cell phone on the dresser but I completely missed it, causing my phone to tumble to the carpeted floor beneath my feet. The sound of it hitting was muffled by the carpet but another loud shattering sound rang out. I whipped my head towards the bedroom door as I slowly reached down, picked up my cell phone and slid it into one of the back pockets of the shorts I was wearing. My feet quickly, yet quietly, carried me across the room to the drawer beside the bed where I kept one of my handguns. The sound of it clicking as I took it off safety spiked my heart rate even more than the shattering sound had. I let out a steady breath and switched myself into Marine mode. Whoever, or whatever, had caused that noise was going to come face-to-face with yours truly.

With my left hand secured on the gun, my pointer finger was wrapped around the trigger, ready to fire at any given moment. My right hand was steadying my left as I turned the corner into the hallway and slowly made my way down it towards the living room. Quickly turning the corner I scanned the room and came up empty; that's when their voices caught my attention.

"You sure no one's here?" Gabe asked, looking for reassurance.

"I'm sure! How many times do I have to tell you?" Thomas' anger was growing as he half whispered and half yelled his response to Gabe.

It didn't take me long to realize just what those two fuckers were doing in my home. I crouched down behind the couch as their footsteps echoed against the hardwood floors, alerting me that they were coming my way. All the lights in the house were off, except the one I had flipped on within the bathroom adjoining the master bedroom. But from the looks of things they weren't going towards the master bedroom, they were going towards the safe in the basement. The same safe that housed the duffle bag of money that not only MacKenzie had mentioned to Thomas, but I had as well.

  Numerous curse words silently passed my lips as I waited for them to walk through the living room and to the stairs on the opposite side of the room. Thomas wasn't the man any of us knew, and the fact that he had broken into my home to retrieve the duffle bag of cash that was stolen from a mission he had been on proved it. As my mind raced in millions of directions it hit me, Gabe was on that same mission with Thomas. They were supposed to be using cash as bait to lure one of their targets to purchase weapons of war, but the money never returned. They claimed they were jumped at the drop; numerous people on both sides were killed while the military truck that was housing the cash was blown up, supposedly destroying it in the process. Not only had Thomas and Gabe betrayed their duties as soldiers, but they had also betrayed their country. What they had been doing was not going to go unnoticed, not if I had something to do about it.

  Their voices grew faint as they made their way down the stairs and into the room where I housed my gun safe and my regular safe, along with other important documents and such that I needed to keep. I stood from my crouched position behind the couch and slowly made my way towards the stairs. The feeling of unease was settling deep within my gut, and I knew that no matter what was about to happen, it most likely wouldn't end well. Why the hell Thomas had turned into a person you couldn't trust, one that filled the people around him with lies and deceit, I wasn't sure. I just hated to see him evolve into a criminal when he was once someone that lived and breathed honor. Gabe had always been one that I didn't trust. His over the top opinions and suggestions when we were overseas had a lot of people looking at him in a different light than most. Something was off about him, that much was obvious from the actions that he and Thomas had been doing since showing their faces back in Shallotte.

As I rounded the corner to the staircase I let out a deep breath. With my gun positioned directly in front of me, aimed and ready to fire, I began descending the steps one at a time. Midway to the bottom, just before they would be able to see my feet, the step creaked and I stood frozen in place, hoping they didn't hear it.

"What was that?" Gabe nervously asked Thomas.

Son of a bitch.

My teeth ground together as I waited for someone to come into the doorway. But surprisingly no one did.

"I didn't hear anything," Thomas informed Gabe. "Now get your ass over here and help me crack this safe open." Hearing Thomas say those words pissed me off. At one time he was the closest friend I had ever had, but that seemed like a lifetime ago compared to the man he had become.

Once I reached the step before the final one I took another deep breath. My heart was beating wildly within my chest as I turned the corner into the room. "Put your hands up or I'll shoot." The sternness of my voice had both Thomas and Gabe freezing in their attempt to try to break into the safe.

"You weren't supposed to be here, Julian," Thomas informed me.

"I can't believe the two of you would try to steal from me." The words seeped from my mouth like venom. Fury was flowing through my veins as Thomas turned towards me, still crouched down before the safe.

"Technically you stole from *us*." Gabe quickly stood from his crouched position beside Thomas and pulled a gun on me. "Looks like one of us isn't going to walk out of here, Julian." His eyes were narrowed on me as he all but announced that I wasn't going to be able to walk out of my own home. He was one cocky son of a bitch, because if I remembered correctly I was a better shot than he was.

Thomas rose to his feet. "Julian, put your gun down," he asked sternly.

"Hell no," I growled.

"I was hoping you wouldn't say that," Thomas sighed as he pulled his own gun from the waistband of his black jeans.

The three of us stood in the center of the room, my gun pointed at Gabe while his and Thomas' were pointed at me. I was highly outnumbered, but I was damn sure not backing down. If the Marines had taught me one thing, it was to stand my ground even in the toughest situations, and defend what I believed in; I was going to do just that.

"Here's how this is going to go." Thomas nodded towards Gabe as he lowered his gun. "You're going to give me the combination to this safe." Thomas patted his hand on the front of the safe that stretched almost to the ceiling. "So that I can retrieve the bag of cash that you put in here. We're going to ransack your house, followed by Gabe shooting you in the leg and you're going to claim you didn't see who the robbers were. And if you ever make a peep about what really went down here, you and MacKenzie will be in our crosshairs." Thomas smiled wickedly as he slipped his gun back into the waistband of his pants.

The fact that he was not only threatening me but MacKenzie as well had me seeing red. He claimed to have loved her and would do anything to keep her safe, but the choice he was making was to put her in danger. I wasn't fucking having that. She was my main priority. "You're awfully ballsy for a man who is supposed to be dead," I countered.

"Keep running that mouth of yours and this is going to end differently than Thomas just informed you," Gabe challenged.

"Now, now, fellas. Lower your gun, Julian, and give me the combination before this gets out of hand." Thomas took a step closer to where I was standing and motioned for me to lower my gun.

If Thomas thought I was going to cower down to them and turn my gun over, they needed to think again because it wasn't fucking happening.

"You'll have to pry this gun from my hands."

Gabe grinned, "That can be arranged."

Thomas ran his hands through his disheveled hair. "My patience is wearing thin! Give me the fucking code or Gabe's going to put a bullet in your head."

"It's not fucking happening," I growled. As soon as the words passed my lips everything seemed to move in slow motion. Gabe positioned his legs as I watched his finger pull back on the trigger of his gun. The bang echoed as sharp pain radiated through my shoulder and my body tumbled to the floor behind me. I landed on my side and got a shot off towards Gabe that hit him dead center of his forehead. His body twitched as his eyes glassed over and his last breath passed his lips as life seeped out of him.

"Fuck!" Thomas gasped as he pulled his gun on me again. "I never wanted it to come to this, Julian." He became frantic as he turned towards the safe, running his hands through his hair before turning towards Gabe and placing a hand on his chest. As he took a minute with Gabe I slipped my hand into my back pocket, quickly pulled my phone out, and dialed 911 before positioning it on the floor behind me so he wouldn't notice it.

Laying on the floor in pain as I gripped my shoulder, I held my good arm out with my gun aimed directly at Thomas. I had survived years and years in the Marines, I sure as hell wasn't going out by a fellow Marine's bullet. "You fucking coward!" I spat at Thomas as he stood up and stalked closer to me.

A menacing laugh left him as he stopped a few feet from where I was lying. "A coward doesn't come out on top, Julian." He laughed again.

"You don't have to do this." I tried to keep him talking and frantic instead of ready to put a bullet in my head.

"Oh but I do." His dark eyes narrowed as he stood there with his gun still aimed at my head. "This has been planned for a long, long time. Gabe was actually the one who got the ball rolling by pitching the idea of taking the cash and high tailing it out of the country once we both made it back home, but the raid threw the plan off. We had the perfect plan of staging the ambush that destroyed the money in the explosion of the truck that was carrying it, when in reality Gabe arranged a plan for the money to be moved off of the truck beforehand and stored away. But once the commander told me our unit was going to be involved in the raid on that house of supposed terrorist suspects, Gabe and I had to improvise. The explosion was the perfect decoy to make it seem that I had died during the raid, so all we needed was a body that could be burned beyond recognition which would give me the chance to get new identification from a guy Gabe knew in Iraq so that I could come back to the US as a ghost."

"So Thomas Cole wouldn't be accused of the shit that had and was happening?" I questioned so that the dispatch people would hear his name.

"Exactly. I no longer could be Thomas Cole, I had to become someone new, someone that wouldn't be recognized crossing the border. But once we were gone, Gabe, Sara, Thomas Junior and myself, I wouldn't have to worry about it anymore."

"You have planned to take Sara and your son all along, haven't you?"

"I sure as hell wouldn't leave them behind. That's why I cleared the phone MacKenzie had been getting her information from, and made it a point to make it seem that I didn't want anything to do with either of them, that they were better off not knowing that I was alive because of the life I was living. But now that Gabe has been killed, this puts a cramp in the plan. Sara's not going to be happy that you killed her brother unless I rectify the situation by putting a bullet in you, Julian." His eyes turned sympathetic for a brief moment before he continued as the newly found information about Sara being Gabe's sister sunk in. "I never wanted to have to put a bullet in you, Julian. You were a good friend, a tough Marine, and I cared a lot about you. But once you put yourself in the mix of things I have no choice but to end your life. It's the only way I make it out of here in one piece and still unknown."

"You're not going to get away with any of this, Thomas." I sat up enough to get a better aim at him with my gun still grasped in my left hand.

Thomas shook his head back and forth before cocking his gun. "It seems that I already have."

My finger made quick movement as I pulled the trigger. A split second later a loud bang rang out as Thomas fell to the floor. Sirens were wailing outside the house as I jumped to my feet, still grasping my hurt shoulder and kicked Thomas' gun clear across the room.

"I can't believe you shot me." Thomas clutched his wounded hand with his other one as I kept my gun pointed directly at his head in case he tried something.

"Believe it."

"Why didn't you take the kill shot like you did with Gabe?" Thomas questioned.

"Because I want you to rot in prison," I admitted as the police barreled down the stairs yelling for me to put the gun down and get on the floor.

I held my arms up in the air with my gun dangling from my finger, and pain shot through my shoulder from the movement. "I'm not putting the gun down, but you can take it. I don't want him having the chance to get his hands on it," I countered with the officers who were standing directly behind me.

"Don't move," one of the officers demanded as he stepped forward, retrieved the gun from my hand, and pushed me flat against the floor before cuffing me as one of the other officers flipped Thomas over and cuffed him as well.

"I need EMS downstairs as soon as possible," an officer called out as he took in Gabe's lifeless body a few feet from where we were.

"I need someone to look at my shoulder, I've been shot," I alerted the officer who was pulling me to my feet.

We were taken outside, Thomas to a police cruiser while an EMT checked out where Gabe had shot me. The bullet had gone straight through the fleshy part of my shoulder, making me one lucky son of a bitch since it didn't cause any nerve damage. Another officer put me in the back of his cruiser as he read me my rights and slammed the door shut. I knew it was protocol to arrest all suspects in a situation like ours, but I hated the feeling of the cuffs wrapped tightly around my wrists, and the thought of MacKenzie finding out what had gone down.

Once he slid into the driver's seat I scooted forward and asked for the time.

"It's almost midnight," he sternly replied. MacKenzie was probably already flipping out from the fact that I hadn't showed up at her house like I had promised. Thankfully she hadn't shown up in the middle of all the shit that had gone down or things could have ended up even worse.

Just before we pulled out onto the street, I watched as the EMT's wheeled a black body bag out of the house and towards the ambulance. Thomas might have been back from the dead, but Gabe wasn't coming back…that was for sure.

Four hours after being taken into the police station, I was being released. The detectives took my statement regarding what had happened and why Gabe had been killed. Thankfully the dispatcher that answered my 911 call had been able to hear everything that was happening. It was the only thing that saved me from having charges brought against myself from what the detective had stated.

I rubbed my hand around my sore wrist, still red and raw from the handcuffs as I made my way through the security gate that led out into the lobby of the police station. "Someone will bring your belongings around in just a moment," the secretary informed me as I stretched my sore-as-hell shoulder.

"Thank you," I smiled back at her.

"Julian!!!!!" Kenzie's familiar voice echoed down the hall to my left.

My head instinctively turned towards where her voice was coming from as I took in her frantic form running towards me. The closer she got, the easier it was to tell that her eyes were swollen and red from crying while her bottom lip quivered. She looked like someone had hurt her. I opened my arms widely as she ran directly into them, causing me to wince from the volt of pain that shot from the patched wound, and I wrapped them tightly around her body. Her hold was stronger than ever before as she broke down into soft sobs with her face buried in the crook of my neck.

"I thought—I thought something happened to you!" She continued to cry. "I'm so sorry…it's all my fault." Her words hit me like a ton of bricks. Kenzie was placing the blame on herself when it sure as hell wasn't the case.

"Shhh…" I smoothed my hand down the back of her head. "If you think this is in any way your fault, you better wipe that shit from this pretty little head of yours because it's not." My voice was low as I spoke at her ear. "Everything's over and we're going to be just fine." Her damp lips pressed firmly against the side of my neck as the secretary cleared her throat.

"Here are your things, Sir."

MacKenzie unwrapped herself from me and smiled shyly at the secretary who was holding a basket that held everything I had on me when I was arrested. "Thanks again," I nodded at the lady and took my things.

"Let's get out of this place." I draped an arm around MacKenzie's shoulders as I walked us towards the front door of the police department.

Her arms wrapped around my waist as we continued to walk. The front entrance had steps that led down to the exit doors, but before we reached them Kenzie pulled me to a stop. "What happens with Thomas now?" Her eyes were full of worry as she awaited my response.

The pad of my thumb on my free hand smoothed beneath her swollen eyelids, trying to wipe away the sorrow she had written on her face before I placed my lips gently against hers. "He's going away for a really long time. The charges they are bringing against him are related to the stolen money, faking his death, breaking into both of our homes, not to mention all of the other crimes that were involved. He's getting the book thrown at him, MacKenzie. We won't ever have to worry about Thomas Cole ever again, sweetheart." My hands cupped her face as she took in everything I had told her.

Her eyes closed as a slow breath passed her lips. "I can't believe the monster he truly was." When her eyes fluttered open the beautiful green was even more vibrant from the layer of unshed tears that had filled them. "What about Gabe?" her question was barely audible.

"He's dead."

Her shaky hand covered her mouth as she quietly gasped, "Oh my gosh…"

"I had no choice but to shoot him." I wasn't sure why I had admitted that, but I felt she needed to know more. The last thing I wanted was for MacKenzie to paint me as a murderer. "He was going to kill me if I—"

"It's okay," she cut me off, placing a hand against my face. "There comes a point in life where we all have to do something we don't truly want to do in order to save ourselves or those around us. You did what you had to do, Julian. There is no other explanation needed. I still love you the same."

My face turned into her hand still cupping my face as I placed a hand above her heart. "You have a heart of gold. It's one reason why I love you so damn much." Her wide smile melted my own heart as I lowered my lips to hers. Since we were still in the police station I made it a simple, yet loving kiss before pulling back.

A ruckus at the bottom of the staircase where the entrance of the police department was broke our moment as officers called to someone in their custody to calm down. We both turned towards where the noise was coming from and came face-to-face with Sara as they climbed the stairs. Her hands were cuffed behind her back as two officers escorted her up the stairs. Another officer was cradling a wailing Thomas Junior. I felt bad for what was happening to the little boy, he had no choice in the matter, but hopefully he would end up with a better life.

"You son of a bitch!" Sara seethed. "You killed my brother!" she continued to yell as she thrashed and lunged in the officers' grasps.

MacKenzie's body went stiff, and I knew she was on the brink of letting Sara have a piece of her mind, so I slid a hand down her back and moved us way off to the side. "Don't let her get to you. She's getting what she deserves," I spoke only loud enough for Kenzie to hear me, and she nodded in agreement as her eyes locked with mine.

"Let's go home." She wrapped her arms around my waist and squeezed.

"Sounds good, sweetheart." Once the officers had Sara headed down the hall towards booking, we made our way out of the police station and to my vehicle. The craziness of the day had started to settle on my body, the feelings of exhaustion and soreness were washing over me as we made our way to my beach house just outside of Wilmington because neither of us felt that going back to one of our places was the right thing to do after everything that had transpired within them.

After Kenzie had fallen asleep I slipped from the bed and made my way out onto the back deck of the beach house. There was a gentle breeze blowing as I stood against the railing and listened to the ocean waves crashing against the bank. The salty air and sounds put me at ease after the day we'd had. I never wanted things to unfold in the manner that they had, but everything happens in the way it's meant to, right? That's what I kept telling myself at least.

The door creaked open and a few beats later small arms wrapped around me from behind. Her warm cheek laid against my bare back as her breath danced across my skin. "What are you doing out here?" Kenzie's sleep filled voice brought a mega-watt smile on my face.

"Couldn't sleep," I admitted as I turned in her arms and pulled her against my chest.

Her lips placed loving kisses in a path from my sternum up between my pecs. With each press of her lips it ignited every ounce of love I had for her. The tiny shirt that was barely covering her naked self rode up as she stood on tiptoes to reach my neck; once she was unable to move any further north I gripped her hips and pulled her up so that her mouth was flush with mine. Her legs wrapped instantly around my waist as one of my hands held her bare ass and the other fisted deep into her hair. Our tongues moved in sync as we poured every ounce of what tainted our pasts into our kisses, like we were cleansing our souls so that we could start fresh and new.

A long moan erupted from her as the hand I had cupping her ass moved just enough so that my fingers reached her entrance and teased her. I grinned in satisfaction against her mouth as I swooped my tongue into hers and pulled a handful of her thick hair back so that her sexy lean neck was exposed.

I nipped and sucked down the column of her neck as she panted my name, "Julian…" Her husky voice had my dick stirring in the black boxer briefs I had slipped on before walking outside to enjoy the fresh air. I couldn't get enough of her, every single inch of her body. MacKenzie had every nerve ending in my body hyper aware of her. Our bodies were meant to be connected, molded to fit one another, and that was exactly what was going to happen.

Her hips rocked against my fingertips as they teased her some more. Dropping my other hand from her hair I carried her over to the lounge chair not far from where we had initially been standing. With one hand I slipped my boxer briefs down my legs and kicked them off before taking a seat on the lounger and resting my back all the way against it. My cock was positioned in just the right spot as she pulled the shirt from her body, exposing every bit of her skin to me under the moonlight of the night. The glow it was casting on her body was breathtaking. She looked like a goddess. "You're so beautiful," I whispered as my palm smoothed up her taut stomach until I wrapped it around her neck to lower her mouth to mine.

She slowly moved her core against me, causing a growl to rumble deep within my chest from the desire that was building inside of me. "I need you," she whispered against my lips just before her hand snaked between her legs, gripped my shaft, and positioned it at her entrance. The feel of MacKenzie slowly lowering herself onto me had me grinding my teeth, trying not to lose myself the second she was fully settled.

The angle of the seat made the feeling of her being on top of me feel different than any of the other times before. As she rocked her hips I dropped my head against the cushion behind it and watched with my eyelids at half-mast. With each movement her breasts swayed and bounced. My hands instinctively reached forward and began massaging each of them as she groaned out in pleasure.

Kenzie's head was thrown back, exposing her throat again as her mouth hung slack and she braced her arms deep into my thighs, gripping with her fingernails. She had full reign as she worked her way towards the orgasm she was craving as I watched. There was nothing sexier than the sight before me. My hands moved from her breasts to her waist as she continued to rock her hips against me. I gripped the globes of her ass, pushing her forward until she collapsed onto my chest.

"My turn," I groaned as I picked her up and flipped us both over. One knee was positioned on the lounger while my other foot was braced on the wood of the deck. MacKenzie clawed at my back with each thrust I gave her. The languid moans that passed her lips had me pushing into her even harder. I felt her clench around my shaft as I pushed into her once more, the sound that erupted from her was deep and sexy as she came crashing down around me. "There you go, baby, let go," my voice was strained and deep as I spoke against the shell of her ear.

Her head rolled towards me as her lips frantically found mine. With one hand gripping her hips, I snaked the other around her neck to gently lift her towards me. "I love you with all of my heart, MacKenzie. Every fucking piece of it belongs to you." Our eyes were locked on one another's as I spoke. The words were affecting her just as much as they were me as tears pooled in her gorgeous green eyes, and my throat tightened from the amount of emotions swimming through my veins.

"I love you, too." Her bottom lip quivered as the words passed her mouth. My hips pushed forward once more as my own release crashed down on me. I called out her name as she wiggled her hips back and forth, making the intensity of my orgasm even greater than it initially was.

"Wrap your arms around my neck." She did just that and I scooped her naked body into my arms and padded into the beach house, making a beeline for the shower.

Positioning the handle on a warm setting, I waited until it heated up before I stepped under the fall of the water, holding my hand out for her to take so that she could join me. Her small hand slid into mine as she stepped over the edge of the tub and into the warmth of the stream with me. "This," she placed a kiss against one of the scars on my side, "is how I want to spend the rest of my life. By your side, in your arms, and beneath you, Julian. I can't picture being with anyone else…only you." Her fingertips gently traced up the long, angry scar above the small, scattered ones she had been kissing.

My hands cupped her face once she stood tall again, and I tilted her head up gently so that our eyes were locked. "You're it for me, MacKenzie. I cross my fucking heart." Lowering my mouth I devoured hers once more; I just couldn't get enough.

"It's crazy how life can be so hectic and insane, but in the midst of the storm you find a rainbow that eases the ache. You're my rainbow, Julian. I know that now."

I tapped my index finger against the tip of her nose and smiled. "I'll be whatever in the hell you want me to be as long as I'm yours," I admitted, pulling a beautiful smile from her that brightened her whole face. "Now let me wash you." I rubbed the soap and washcloth in my hands together to lather the cloth.

"Yes, sir." Her words were teasing as I ran the washcloth over her sensitive nipples and down to her core. "Oh," she gasped huskily.

"Oh is right."

Epilogue – Six Months Later
MacKenzie

"Don't you dare!" I shrieked as Julian threw me over his shoulder and took off towards the ocean. His laughter filled the air as he smacked my backside playfully. "I swear…if you drop me in that water, Julian Cooper, I'm going to hurt you!" I warned as my own laughter erupted from my lungs as he picked up his pace of hauling me towards the lightly crashing waves.

"You know you love me," he countered as I saw the water lap around his ankles and slowly become deeper.

He wasn't going to heed my warning. As soon as I felt him pull my body forward I quickly held my breath waiting for the water to envelop me, but it never happened. I slowly peeled my eyes open to find my face directly before Julian's as he smiled widely back at me. "You sneaky ass!" My laughter picked up once more as I smacked his shoulder.

My legs wrapped around his waist to secure me against him as his lips brushed against mine. "Did you really think I would throw you into the ocean if you didn't want me to?" his words danced across my moist lips.

"I honestly didn't know." A smile spread widely across my mouth, reaching my eyes as I slid down his body, planting my feet in the ocean.

With each slow step backwards Julian followed me, like I was his prey. There was no doubt in my mind that he had ulterior motives to his actions, I was just unsure about what they were. Once the water was lapping around my chest, I splashed at Julian. My playful screams pulled some of the fellow beach-goers' attention as I tried to swim away, but I wasn't fast enough. Julian grabbed hold of my waist and easily dragged me back towards him.

"That was a little unfair, don't ya think?" he sputtered out as he ran a hand down his face, trying to clear the salty ocean water away.

"I never said I played by the rules," I joked.

A wicked grin formed across his beautiful mouth as he snaked his hands around me, pulling me into his chest. His lips peppered kisses across my jawline as my head instinctively tilted away, exposing my neck for him to guide down like he usually did. I loved the feeling of his sensual kisses trailing down the column of my throat along with my body. Getting lost in the feeling of his touch, his lips, and his skin against mine was very easy to do, much like what had happened out in the ocean. Before I realized what Julian was up to my bikini top was pulled away from my body, leaving my naked breasts exposed. I sank further down in the water than I already was so that no one could see me. My arms wrapped around my breasts, securing them against me. "Julian!!!" I called out after him in shock as he quickly made his way to the bank, slipping my bikini top into one of the pockets of his swimming trunks. "Get back here!!!" I tried yelling at him once again, but instead of him coming back and giving me my damn top, he turned towards me and smiled a victorious smile.

"You'll have to come to me, sweetheart." His voice was full of amusement as he thought he had won the battle between us. But little did he know I wasn't about to give in.

"You can do this, Kenzie." I gave myself a low pep talk as I latched my hands tighter against my breasts. I was about to brave the storm and prove to Julian that he couldn't pull one over on me like he had tried to do. My feet started moving me forward as the level of the water began shrinking around me. I watched as Julian's facial expression morphed from victorious to disbelief.

"MacKenzie…" Julian's warning tone had me smiling my own victorious smile in return.

"What?" I asked innocently as the water dripped down my naked chest and hands that were still clamped down on my breasts.

A couple guys were standing off to the side with shocked expressions as they talked about what was transpiring before their eyes, but I kept my own directed solely at Julian as I pushed forward, leaving the water behind. As soon as my feet hit the dry sand I took off running towards Julian, still standing about seven feet away. His strong arms wrapped around me as his heavy breaths tickled the shell of my ear. "You're bad…" The desire in his voice sent chills across my damp skin.

"You started it," I chuckled as we made our way up to our beach towels. Julian had me tucked into his side, trying to shield my naked upper half from the world to see, even though my hands still had a death grip on my chest.

"You do know you could have been arrested for indecent exposure," Julian stated seriously. The thought hadn't even crossed my mind. I froze as he quickly bent down and picked up our things, handing me a towel to wrap around myself in the process.

His eyes met mine when I didn't answer, so I quickly shook away the thought of being arrested so that he couldn't declare himself the winner yet again. "But I didn't, now did I?" I smiled as I tucked the towel around my chest and linked my hand with his on the way to our house just a few hundred feet away.

Our flip flops slapped against the damp wood of the walking path as we walked silently towards our sixteen hundred square foot navy blue home. Large white shutters decorated the windows that stretched across the back, facing the ocean. The decision to leave Shallotte wasn't a hard one. After everything that had happened Julian broke the lease on his rental home at the same time that I put my house up for sale. Surprisingly the home I had shared with Thomas sold within a few weeks, and we were off to Julian's beach house to live until we found something.

When we ran across our new home, it only took one tour of the place to know that we wanted it. It was a little higher than the budget we had mapped out, but it couldn't have been more worth the money. The siding and shutters had been freshly painted, along with the inside being completely remodeled.

Olivia Jones apparently had started her own talk show from all of the bullshit rumors she had been spreading around regarding me, Thomas, Julian, Gabe, Sara, and baby Thomas. It was unbelievably ridiculous. Thankfully the few times she had attempted to contact me about it were cut off by Julian. He made it a point to let her know that she wasn't welcome anywhere near either of us. But it still didn't stop her from running that horrible mouth of hers.

I'd learned to let things roll off of me, to move away from the negative and live for the positive. Julian was my positive. It might have happened a helluva lot faster than I would have ever anticipated; and the whirlwind that came barreling into town at the same time he had might have been almost too much to bear, but none of that mattered. My heart was dead set on having him, and there was no reason to fight it…even though I tried like hell.

The last we had been informed of Thomas' matter was that the federal court had set out to prosecute him to the fullest of their powers. He had stolen money from the military, faked his death, committed murder, and attempted to murder Julian. There was no chance in hell of him seeing the light of day outside of a prison within his lifetime. Even if I didn't feel bad for him, I felt sad that he had thrown away his life like he had. You only had one to live, but yet he felt that he could connive and lie his way to a life no one would have known. That didn't work in his favor.

    Sara also had charges brought against her. We couldn't find out much regarding her, just that she was charged with being a co-conspirator in Thomas faking his death, coming back to the U.S., and trying to relocate under a new alias with the money she claimed to know nothing about. I found that *very* hard to believe. She was good at making others feel like she had nothing to do with certain situations; she sure as hell had me fooled regarding her and Thomas. I was hoping she wouldn't pull the wool over the court's eyes when it came her time to face justice.

    What broke my heart about the entire situation was Thomas Junior. That little boy had no say so in the life he was born into, and once he got to an age of truly being able to understand he would learn about his parents; the crimes his father committed and how his mother was complicit in them. I wanted so badly to get custody of him so that maybe, just maybe, he would have a life that didn't require him moving from foster home to foster home, but Julian made me realize that it wasn't the best choice for me. Not because we didn't want a child around, but because the reminder of what had transpired would constantly be there. If Sara was released we would have to deal with her wanting to be in his life. As much as I fought and argued with him regarding the matter I decided he was right when the woman who handled Thomas Junior's case informed us that Sara's grandmother was trying for custody. She had kept the boy for periods of time and seemed to be a wonderful lady; nothing like Sara had been. Allowing him to go to someone he was familiar with, who wanted to love him unconditionally without any reminder of what had once been, was the best choice. I knew both Julian and myself could love him if we took him, but life would have ended up being even more complicated than it had been, so he was better off with his great grandmother.

Julian's laughter echoed through the foyer of the house. "I cannot believe you walked up on the beach topless, even if you had a death grip on those beautiful things to keep others from seeing. I thought I knew for certain you wouldn't do that." His hands gripped my hips as he pulled me into him, my towel dropping from my chest in the process.

"I had a feeling you thought I wouldn't; I had to prove you wrong." My cheeks were hurting from smiling so much.

His lips brushed against mine. "Those guys watching you made me want to pummel them." Julian's admission wasn't one I expected.

"Jealous, are we?" I teased.

One of his hands ran up the front of my body and cupped one of my breasts. "This skin is for my eyes only." His voice had dropped an octave as he kneaded my breast before gently pinching my erect nipple.

"My body is only yours…" My breathy words barely passed my lips before my mouth latched onto his and my tongue plunged deep into his. His tongue stroked against mine, creating a rhythm that was drowning out everything we needed to do, including the lunch date he had set up without telling me exactly what it was.

"Mmm…" Julian groaned as he pulled away, leaving me desire-filled and needy; his eyes roamed down my body and back up again as he let out a low sigh. "As much as I want to throw you over my shoulder and take you into our bedroom for the next few hours, we have to get ready for the lunch date." His annoyance of the fact that he had planned the lunch date, but so desperately wanted me was shining through in his tone of voice.

"Ugh… do we have to?" I whined as I stood on tiptoes to try and reach his lips once more. Julian moved back just enough to make it so that I couldn't reach him and grinned.

"Yes, we absolutely have to." He smacked my backside and gripped it before letting go. "Now go get ready. I'll take a shower in the spare bathroom so it doesn't take as long." With a major pout resting on my face I followed Julian's request and padded into our bedroom to get ready, but not before I dropped my bikini bottoms to show him just exactly what he was putting off having.

As soon as I turned the corner into the living room I spotted Julian standing out on the front porch. His strong back was covered in a short sleeved pale blue button-up that was tucked into the waist of a pair of khaki shorts. He told me to keep it dressy but casual, much like he had. I glanced down at my own attire and smiled. We had matched our colors without even trying. A pale blue sleeveless open scallop pleated dress covered my body, stopping about mid-thigh. I had chosen a pair of white decorative sandals with minimal jewelry and makeup. My hair was in loose beach waves that were pulled around to one side and resting against my shoulder. I stood there watching him through the window for quite a few moments before he turned to face me, almost like he could feel my presence. His own smile spread widely across his beautiful tanned face, showcasing his straight, perfectly white teeth as he motioned for me to join him outside.

Holding my index finger up to tell him I'd be out in one minute, I collected my sunglasses and my wristlet that housed my lip gloss, cash, and license from the kitchen bar before making my way outside to him. "You look nice," I told him as I ran a hand down the collar of his shirt and he leaned down to press his lips gently against mine.

Julian's hand held the side of my neck as his sandy brown eyes bored into mine. "You look absolutely stunning." The sincerity that wrapped around his words made my knees want to give out. My heart was fluttering in my chest as I bit down shyly on my bottom lip. The feeling of my cheeks flushing surprised me, but when Julian had some term of endearment for me, it caught me off guard every single time.

"You're blushing." Julian's grin spread to a full blown smile.

I linked my hand with his and gently tugged him forward. "Let's go, lover boy."

One good thing about living right off the beach was being able to walk around the boardwalk and surrounding areas easily. No vehicle was needed to get there, just your legs, unless you wanted to bike it, of course.

We walked hand-in-hand down the boardwalk towards wherever Julian was taking me. I had no idea what he had planned for us, but I was used to going along with his adventures without him telling me what was going to transpire. His surprises had always been good ones, so I was sure whatever he had up his sleeve was going to be enjoyable.

The sun tucked away behind a couple of massive fluffy white clouds as we reached part of the boardwalk that was roped off as private. "What's this?" I gasped as I spotted a black metal table with a white tablecloth and two chairs, one on each side of it.

My head whipped around towards Julian, but all that I got in return was another breathtaking smile of his. A man stepped out of a small diner-style shack and greeted us, giving Julian a firm hug before escorting us past the roped-off private area and over to the table. Beautiful glassware sat perfectly on each side as Julian held my chair out for me to take a seat. I watched as he spoke to the man before shaking his hand and taking the seat on the other side of the table from me.

The man returned a few moments later with a bottle of wine. As he filled our glasses I couldn't help the giddiness building within me. Julian was a romantic, one that loved lavish dinners and surprises to make me feel loved during every day instead of only special occasions. He was truly one of a kind.

"Thank you, Burgs," Julian praised the man as he filled his glass. "This is the beautiful MacKenzie I have been telling you about." Burgs nodded his head in my direction.

"It's truly a pleasure to meet you, MacKenzie." His accent was a thick Italian one, which surprised me. "You are definitely the sunshine in a storm." A shy laugh bubbled up my chest as I took in his compliment.

"Well, thank you." My cheeks were hot from not only the sun but his words as well.

"I'll give you two some time to enjoy the Veneto." With a wink in my direction he went back into the shack, leaving us to ourselves.

Julian scooted his chair around closer to me before pulling mine around as well, giving us the perfect view of the ocean and a few sailboats way out in the calm waters. "I'll never get tired of this place. The ocean is beautiful and the feel is unbelievably peaceful."

When he didn't respond I turned my face towards him to see why. Julian was watching me with the most loving look on his face that I had ever borne witness to before. Emotions shot through my veins as my heart thumped wildly with love for the man looking at me. He was everything I had been searching for without even knowing that I was searching. It's like my heart was calling out for its other half until it found it within Julian.

I watched as his eyes morphed from loving to unsure as he scooted his chair even closer to me and took my hand in his. "I never thought I would find someone to love as deeply as I do you, MacKenzie Co—"

I placed a finger over the center of his plumps lips to stop him. "Before you continue I have a surprise for you. I quickly unzipped my wristlet and pulled a folded piece of paper from it. Smoothing out the lines I extended it for him to take. As his eyes roamed over the page I waited nervously for his reaction. "It's MacKenzie Lawson, not Cole anymore." Julian's eyes lifted from the paper in his hand to mine as he let out a full-blown chuckle. My eyebrows pulled down deep in the center of my eyes. "What's so funny?" I asked in confusion.

Julian placed the paper on the table and took my hand once more. "Let me try this again." He kissed the back side of my hand and looked back up at me. "I never thought I would find someone to love as deeply as I do you, MacKenzie Lawson, but I have. Through the short period of time we have known one another we have faced more ups and downs than most would ever face in a lifetime. I knew the first moment my heart went wild in my chest for you that I had to have you. Now that our lives have begun to fall into place as one, I want to make sure that you know just how much I adore every little thing about you." One of his hands slipped from mine and covered my heart. "Our hearts beat as one. I've known it for quite some time, just as you have. But now I want us to be one...completely." My eyes widened as Julian removed his hand from my chest and slipped it into the front pocket of his khaki shorts. A small black box fit perfectly in his palm as he flipped the lid open to expose a ring with a single, large heart-shaped diamond with one smaller round diamond on each side of it. My free hand shot to my mouth as I gasped, realizing just what Julian was doing. Tears flooded my eyes and raced down my cheeks as he continued. "Kenzie, baby, please make me the happiest man in this world by becoming my wife."

"Oh, Julian!" I cried as I wrapped my arms tightly around his neck, almost sitting in his lap in the process.

"Is that a yes?" He questioned, rubbing his hands up and down my shaking back as I cried continuously against his shoulder.

I leaned back enough to see his eyes and frantically shook my head up and down. "Of course it's a yes!" The biggest smile that had ever adorned my face spread widely as I laughed with happiness before crashing my lips to his. A few moments passed before he pulled back and took my left hand, fingers out, and slid the breathtaking ring onto my ring finger. "It's perfect," the words left me on a breathless whisper.

"So are you," Julian countered.

My life had been full of highs and lows, worse than your average roller coaster at any amusement park. But no matter how much it tried to throw me off, Julian was there to help me gain my strength to hold on and ride it out. In such a short period of time my world had been morphed from its previous state to something completely different. Something that shined brightly with happiness.

I had never known true happiness until Julian Cooper came into my life, and from that point on I realized that I couldn't live without it…without *him*.

I held my glass up in the air and Julian followed suit. "To a life full of love and happiness." Our glasses clinked together before we both took a large swig of the wine.

"To love and happiness."

In that moment I realized the love that Julian and I had shared from the moment we met was not dishonorable, it was something beautiful that couldn't have been denied no matter what tried to get in its way, simply because the beauty of true love was beyond any other.

THE END

Acknowledgements

First and foremost I want to thank God for giving me the opportunity to write stories for you to read. I've always had a passion for writing, but I never thought I would have the chance to put my work out there for readers to take in. This journey has been beyond anything I could have dreamed of! So secondly I want to thank YOU for reading this. Without you taking a chance on my crazy stories I would've never gotten to this point with my writing career. I still can't believe this is my sixth book!

Clifton Greenwell, you are the most understanding man I have ever met. Pushing me to fight to achieve my dreams without allowing me to throw in the towel when I feel like everything is against me…I love you so much.

Amber Nation, the past year has been remarkable! I'm so thankful that our paths crossed in this book world. I seriously couldn't imagine being in the Indie Community without you as my partner in crime. Thank you for being the person that you are and allowing me to bounce so many wack-ass ideas off of you. I'm sure they can get annoying. Lol! Love ya, girl.

Nacole Stayton, and Kristen Cecil, thank you ladies so much for taking time out to read my rough draft of this bad boy! You ladies kick major ass! Love y'all!

Kay Manis, you are seriously a life saver! Thanks for listening to me complain about so much crapola. You've helped me grow as a writer since coming into my life, and I want to thank you so much for being there. Much love to you, lady!

Beth Maddox, my twinsie! Thank you yet again for being the person that stands behind me and makes sure that I get shit done. You're the best!

Jen Akers, I truly appreciate the hours you spend picking through the madness I call my manuscripts. I am beyond grateful for your hard work and friendship. I couldn't have done any of this without you.

Silla Webb, girl you are a proof reading machine! Thank you, thank you, and thank YOU for proofing my book at the last minute. I could seriously squeeze you to death for it!

Lastly, I want to thank those in the Armed Forces. I wrote the opening of the story after watching a news cast regarding a wife who had lost her husband overseas. It touched my very soul to see that woman breakdown at her husband's funeral. No, the entire book isn't based off of that, it is indeed fiction. But I felt that I needed to put that part of life out there, the heartache from losing someone who went off to War to fight for our freedom. God Bless our soldiers and their families! We couldn't live the lives we do without their dedication and heart.

'Til next time you fabulous people! XOXO

Made in the USA
San Bernardino, CA
08 March 2016